A BOLD P

"Have you thoug[ht] [...] to do next, contessa?" David asked, staring up at her. Her china-blue eyes were wide with surprise, and her pink, pouting lips, though slightly open, were quiet for a change. "No?" He placed his hands on her waist and pulled her closer. "Too bad. Because I have," he murmured an instant before his mouth found hers.

Tessa felt the heat of his body penetrating her green dress, but it was nothing compared to the heat of his mouth. She tasted him, tightening her grip on his wide shoulders, then trailed her fingers up the column of his neck and buried them in the thick black silk of his hair. . . .

Harvest Moon

REBECCA HAGAN LEE

DIAMOND BOOKS, NEW YORK

This book is a Diamond original edition,
and has never been previously published.

HARVEST MOON

A Diamond Book/published by arrangement with
the author

PRINTING HISTORY
Diamond edition/July 1993

ISBN: 1-55773-914-5

Diamond Books are published by The Berkley Publishing Group,
200 Madison Avenue, New York, NY 10016.
The name "DIAMOND" and its logo
are trademarks belonging to Charter Communications, Inc.

PRINTED IN THE UNITED STATES OF AMERICA

10 9 8 7 6 5 4 3 2 1

For my agent, Cynthia Richey, who wanted David's story. For my editor, Carrie Feron, and her assistant, Beth DiPentima, who worked so hard to make it possible. Thanks.

For all those who listened to my ravings and waited patiently, especially: my mother, Alice Smith; Latrell Lewis; Teresa Medeiros; Pamela Morsi; Teresa Beck; Betty Rosenthal; and Jill Metcalf.

And for Steve, who listened most of all.

ACKNOWLEDGMENTS

Once again I'm indebted to Ann Nelson and the staff of the Wyoming State Archives, Museums and Historical Department in Cheyenne, Wyoming, and the staff of the Ohoopee Regional Library in Vidalia, Georgia. Thank you.

PROLOGUE

Chicago & Northern Railroad
Late September 1872

"Tessa, do you think anyone saw us get on?" the small tow-headed boy asked as he scooted closer to the young woman's side.

Tessa Roarke peered out her dirty train window into the darkness before turning back to look at nine-year-old Coalie. "I don't think so, but we'll have to be very careful." She patted her lap, motioning for Coalie to stretch out on the hard bench and place his head there. "I think we're safe." She wasn't at all sure, but she kept her doubts to herself.

Coalie made himself as comfortable as possible, stretching out full length on the bench, using Tessa's lap as a pillow. His boots scraped against the hard wood, adding to the noise surrounding them—the loud clacking of the train as it swayed along the tracks, the belching sound of the smoke from the stack, the periodic whistles, and the snores of the male passengers. Tessa looked down at Coalie's blond hair.

His breathing deepened. She thought he must have fallen asleep, then the sound of his whisper startled her. "Maybe we should go to one of those lawyers." Coalie opened his big green eyes and looked up at her.

"Oh, no," Tessa protested immediately. "No lawyers. I can't abide lawyers. They've no loyalty. They make promises they can't keep and charge people for it. No, Coalie. It's important that we stay away from the likes of them. This has to be our secret. We can't tell anyone."

"I won't tell, Tessa." Coalie sat up and hugged her. "I promise. And I won't go to any lawyers neither."

Tessa kissed his forehead and smoothed back the hair falling across his brow. "I know you won't."

Coalie settled back down, lying across Tessa's lap once again. Tessa sighed, closed her eyes, and tried to rest. Her past was behind her. Her future, and Coalie's, was in the far-off territory of Wyoming. Surely they'd be safe in Wyoming. After living in Chicago and surviving the great fire, how much danger could there be in a town called Peaceable?

At the back of the railroad car a big blond man watched the woman lean over the child. He'd followed them from her apartment and through the dark and dangerous streets of Chicago to the train station. He hadn't expected her to be traveling with a young boy. He hadn't expected her to leave Chicago at all. Tessa Roarke was heading for Peaceable, Wyoming, and there was no way for him to stop her.

*   *   *

Miles down the track, in the tiny town of Peaceable, attorney David Alexander slept soundly, a battered-looking orange tomcat curled up beside him, both of them blissfully unaware that their lives were about to be turned upside down.

CHAPTER 1

Peaceable, Wyoming Territory
November 1872

"Help!"

David Alexander sat bolt upright in bed, instantly awake. He thought he'd heard cries for help in his sleep.

But when he sat silently for a moment, he heard nothing more.

"Was that one of your friends, Greeley?" he asked the battle-scarred cat curled up next to him. "I could've sworn I heard someone." The orange tabby arched his back, yawned, then settled back down in the warmth of the bed.

Though the cat seemed undisturbed David listened intently. It must have been a dream. He didn't hear anything except the tinny sound of an out-of-tune piano from the saloon four doors away. Horace Greeley yawned again. David felt like doing the same. He slipped down under the sheets, pulled the quilts up over his ears, rolled over, and went back to sleep.

The pounding on the back door roused him the second time. "What does a man have to do to get a good night's sleep around here?" he muttered, flipping back the covers. David grabbed his pants and stumbled out of bed. He hopped from one foot to the other as he pulled on his trousers, then stepped into his boots. He stamped his feet, forcing the cold leather over his woolen socks. Pausing a moment, David took time to scratch the soft fur on Greeley's head. "Another fight, no doubt," David muttered to the cat. "In one of the saloons."

The pounding persisted, louder this time. "All right, all right, I'm coming," David yelled.

Raking his fingers through his hair, he stuck his arms into a shirt before he yanked the front door open.

A skinny boy of perhaps eight or nine stood bundled up against the cold in an assortment of dirty rags. "You gotta come quick, Mr. Alexander!"

"Why? Who are you?" David asked, surprised to see a child at this time of night. Usually his midnight visitors were disreputable characters.

"I'm Coalie." The boy stepped forward and tugged on the tail of David's shirt, gesturing toward the commotion down the street. A group of townspeople, bundled up in quilts and heavy winter coats, stood outside the largest saloon in town.

"You gotta come. They're takin' her away." Coalie tugged again, harder.

"Who?"

"Tessa."

David took a step back. He didn't know anyone named Tessa.

Coalie shook his head, gripping David's shirt with surprising force. "Hurry!"

"Just let me get my coat." David reached back through the open door and grabbed his sheepskin jacket from the peg. "Who's . . ." He turned. Coalie was running down the street toward the saloon. "Who's Tessa?" David shrugged into his jacket. He slammed the door of the office behind him. There was only one way to find out. He sprinted after the little boy.

"What's going on?" David asked, pushing his way toward the front of the crowd a few minutes later. He could see Coalie edging closer and closer to the entrance of the Satin Slipper.

"There's been a murder," someone answered. "A stabbing or some such. In one of the girls' rooms. Caught her red-handed."

"Look!" someone else called. "They're bringing her out."

The doors of the Satin Slipper Saloon swung wide. Several men stepped outside onto the sidewalk. In the center of the group stood Deputy Harris, a young woman held close to his side. Dressed in the gaudy costume of a Satin Slipper girl, she stood out: the only woman in a group of men, her bright blue dress eerie in the distorted light of pre-dawn morning.

A knot of anger tightened David's stomach as he watched the faces of the men and women in the crowd. The townspeople milled about, circling the front entrance of the saloon, surrounding the woman like vultures over a carcass. David frowned, lines of concern etching his face. The lawmen had brought her out of the warmth of the saloon into the bitter cold without so much as a blanket around her. The flimsy sleeveless dress she wore was no protection against the frigid Wyoming weather. It left her neck and arms uncovered, exposed to the leers of the men, the wide-eyed stares of curiosity seekers, the cold. David gritted his teeth. The deputy must have arrested her and dragged her from her room before she even had time to find her shoes. Her stocking feet were bare against the frozen wooden planks. David's disgust mounted. She faced exposure and the danger of frostbite in addition to the gossip and speculation of the townspeople while Peaceable's deputies, in thick coats and sheepskin jackets, huddled together on the sidewalk, talking.

Although she was possibly a criminal, David admired her quiet dignity. She didn't shiver or cry or beg for mercy. She simply waited, the center of attention but apart from it. Facing the curious onlookers, she searched the crowd.

Coalie slipped from his hiding place behind a post and rushed toward her. "Tessa!" He moved past her guards and flung his arms around her waist, pressing his head against her skirts. Lifting her bound wrists, Tessa looped them over Coalie's head, hugging him close. She pressed a kiss on the top of his blond head.

"Tessa," Coalie panted, "I brung help." He let go of her long enough to point to David Alexander.

Tessa looked up and found David, meeting his gaze.

Her eyes were blue, David realized, as blue as the dress she wore. She stared at him with an intensity that surprised him. Yet her face revealed nothing except a glimmer of her intense relief at finding Coalie.

As David watched her, witnessing the joy and satisfaction on her face as she held the boy in her arms, he doubted Tessa was capable of committing a crime. She didn't look like a criminal.

And she certainly didn't look like a murderess.

In that moment he decided to take the case.

Deputy Harris obviously didn't like his prisoner holding on to the boy. He raised her arms while one of the other deputies motioned for Coalie to move. Looking up at Tessa, Coalie hesitated for a moment, then stepped away from her. Tears sparkled in his big green eyes. He brushed at them with the back of one hand before he darted into the street. Head down, apparently embarrassed by his display of emotion, Coalie tripped over his feet and fell on his stomach in the street.

"Coalie!" Tessa tugged against the deputy's greater weight, trying to break free.

David jerked in reaction. Without stopping to think, he elbowed his way through the people blocking his path. He reached Coalie's side only moments after another man pulled the boy to his feet.

David looked at the other man, surprise mirrored on his face as he recognized a friend he hadn't seen in years. The morning's events had taken another dreamlike turn. "Kincaid?"

"Ssh." With an almost imperceptible nod of his head, the man met David's gaze. David understood the warning. It was universal. Any man who'd ever been a spy knew that look meant back off. Reaching out, David took Coalie's hand and pulled the boy to his side.

Kincaid faded into the crush of people.

David bent down and brushed the dirt and slush from Coalie's clothes. "Are you okay?"

"You gotta help Tessa." Coalie leaned toward the saloon girl, pulling against David's hand as he called her name. "Tessa!"

She turned, managing a half-smile, apparently for Coalie's benefit. "I'm all right. Everything will be fine."

"Wait!" David shouted to the deputy. "You can't take her to jail."

Deputy Harris stopped. " 'Course I can."

Peaceable's newest attorney sprinted across the street. "What's the charge?" David demanded. He'd heard the accusation from someone in the crowd, but he wanted legal confirmation.

"Murder. She killed a man."

"This woman?" David asked. It seemed so unlikely.

"Yeah." The deputy shuddered. "She slit his throat while he lay in her bed."

"Who is she supposed to have killed?"

"One of Myra's regulars. A man by the name of Arnie Mason."

David looked Deputy Harris straight in the eye. "I'm coming with you." He shrugged out of his coat and draped it around the shivering woman's shoulders.

She glanced up at him, surprised.

David couldn't explain the impulse that had made him leap to the woman's rescue. But then, he couldn't explain anything that had happened so far. The whole thing felt unreal. David smiled. Perhaps he was still in his bed. Maybe he'd wake up in the morning and find this was all a dream.

"Suit yourself," Harris told him. "She can use a good lawyer. But leave the boy out here. Kids ain't allowed in the jail."

David looked down intending to tell the boy where to wait. But Coalie was gone.

David looked back up. The woman's gaze was on the small figure running down the street, but David knew she'd been staring at him. He'd felt the impact of her sky-blue eyes.

Several minutes later, David faced her across the width of a jail cell.

"Did you kill him?" He leaned back against the door to the cell. He felt the cold metal bars on either side of his spine through the layers of clothing—the finely woven fabric of his linen dress shirt and his cotton undershirt. Controlling the urge to shiver, he waited for a response, shifting his wide shoulders into a more comfortable position.

The silence lengthened. David tried again. This time his voice was softer. "I asked you a question. Did you kill Arnie Mason?"

She stared up at him, her large blue eyes wary. "No," Tessa said. "I didn't kill anyone. I wouldn't do anything to risk—" She stopped abruptly. "No."

David studied his client. She sat on the bare mattress of the cot, away from the bars, next to the wall. His coat, draped across her shoulders, gaped open, exposing her dress and a fair amount of flesh. She made no move to close it. She held herself in a rigid pose, her bloodstained hands clenched into fists, her knuckles whitened under the strain. She was shaking, but whether from anger, fear, or cold, David didn't know. He reached for the dirty saddle blanket folded on the foot of the cot and shook it out, nearly gagging in reaction. The blanket was rank. David let it fall to the floor, then kicked it through the narrow space between the bars. David had seen many criminals jailed during his career, but seeing Tessa locked in a cell with a bucket, a bare mattress, and a filthy blanket bothered him. She didn't belong in these surroundings.

"Can we get another blanket?" David shouted to the deputy.

"One blanket's the rule, Mr. Alexander," the deputy shouted back. "There's one on the bed."

"Not anymore. Your last occupant used it for an outhouse." David wiped his hands down the legs of his trousers. "Do we get a blanket or are you planning to let her freeze?"

"One blanket per prisoner."

"Who's responsible for that little gem of a rule?" Sarcasm bit the edge of David's deep voice.

"City council."

David crossed the width of the cell, pulled his coat tighter around her shoulders, and tucked the wool collar securely beneath her chin. He could smell the odors of the Satin Slipper on her. The yeasty smell of beer, the combination of cigar smoke and whiskey, and the tangy, metallic smell of blood. She didn't move, nor did she speak. She simply continued to look at him.

His fingers brushed the fabric of her dress. It was slick and cool to the touch. Satin, he realized. Light blue satin cut low in the front and high at the hem, barely covering her knees. A saloon girl's dress, now splattered with blood. He allowed his gaze to wander. Black net stockings covered her shapely calves and knees and feet. No protection against the harsh Wyoming winter, against the cold seeping through the walls of the wooden jail. "How about a cup of coffee?" He raised his voice enough for the deputy to hear.

"Prisoners get two meals," came the reply. "Breakfast and supper."

"I'm not suggesting a meal," David told him. "I'm talking about a cup of coffee. It's cold back here."

"Sure thing, Mr. Alexander. I'll pour you a cup soon as you come outta there."

"What about her?" David asked.

"Prisoners get two—"

"I know." David muttered an obscenity beneath his breath. Damn bureaucracy. The deputy followed the rules to the letter. David exhaled slowly and pulled out his pocket watch, counting the seconds in an effort to control his mounting frustration. The sun hadn't even risen. Didn't these people realize that with a little cooperation they could all go back to bed until it did? He looked at his client. Though her features were delicate her jaw was set stubbornly. Her deliberate silence puzzled him, yet something about her made him want to help. To take her small hand in his protective grasp. Something he couldn't quite identify. And then, there was the boy . . .

"Are you Tessa O'Roarke?" David asked, using the surname he'd gleaned from the deputy. Her name sounded Irish and so did her brogue.

Tessa raised her head. "It's Roarke. Not O'Roarke. Tessa Roarke." Tessa looked him over. Tall, broad-shouldered, and well muscled, he dwarfed the cell. He was handsome; there was no doubt about that. But his type of good looks differed from the rugged handsomeness of her brother. His skin was copper-tinted, smooth-shaven. His eyes were dark, his features more refined. Tessa took a deep breath. The scent of him filled her nostrils, surrounding her senses. Clean.

Unlike Arnie Mason. So unlike the sour metallic scent surrounding Arnie Mason. Tessa turned her gaze back to his face. He blinked. Arnie hadn't blinked. His blue eyes stared sightlessly while the dark blood ran in rivulets from his throat onto her dingy white sheets and her dress. Her blue dress.

Tessa glanced down. "Sweet Mary!" His blood stained her dress. Shocked anew, she bolted up from her seat. David's sheepskin jacket slid to the floor.

He stepped forward.

"Look at me." She tugged at the fastening of her costume. "Sweet Mary, look at me." Her gaze darted from her dress to David's face. "No, don't! Turn your back!"

Standing there, facing her, David refused to obey. He watched as she reached behind her and began to yank at the opening of her gown.

Tessa Roarke unbuttoned as far as she could reach, then turned and presented her back to him. "Please, help me. I can't stand to—"

"Bring a blanket," David shouted to Deputy Harris.

"Only one bla—"

"Forget the damned rules, Harris. Just bring another blanket!" David barked out the words before turning his attention to the small cloth buttons on Tessa's dress. He moved a couple of steps closer.

She moved with him, the top of her head bumping his chin. David backed away.

"The deputy is bringing another blanket." He raised his voice loud enough for the words to carry back to the deputy. "A clean one. And some warm water."

Tessa nodded.

David stared at the locks of heavy red hair that had escaped her bun and hung down her back. His fingers itched to touch it.

He forced himself to return to the task at hand.

David moved aside the thick mass of hair to undo the tiny satin-covered buttons on her gaudy costume. It was a first for David. He'd never undressed a client before. But he'd never represented a woman before, or rushed to a jail to save one. He had her dress half unbuttoned before he realized she wasn't wearing a corset. The dress was cut too low and too close to her body to accommodate one. He felt the chill of her skin as he opened her dress, smelled the cheap flowery perfume used by the women at the Satin Slipper. But it didn't smell cheap on Tessa. It was light, floral, intoxicating. David shook his head as if to clear it as Deputy Harris arrived with a fresh blanket. He could feel himself going through the motions, knew he was awake, yet everything still seemed unreal. Like a dream.

He finished unbuttoning her gown, then handed her the blanket as she slipped it off, along with her stockings. "Comfortable?" David asked.

"Not very." She sat huddled on the cot, the blanket wrapped around her. Beneath it her underclothes clung to her skin, but Tessa kept them on. Removing her dress with him there had probably been bad enough; removing her undergarments would surely be unthinkable. She hoped the night wouldn't hold too many more humiliations. "But I'd rather wear this"— she lifted a corner of the blanket—"than those." She nodded toward the blue dress and the black net stockings.

David shoved the discarded clothes through the

bars, and Deputy Harris quickly removed them. Minutes later the deputy brought two mugs of steaming hot coffee along with the water without being asked a second time. He even threw a few more scuttles of coal into the stove, but the heat barely penetrated the cold of the hallway and the cell.

David grinned as he watched Tessa Roarke sipping her coffee. It was remarkable how quickly rules, even city council rules, could be broken, to soothe a distraught woman. He studied her as he sat across from her in a straight-backed wooden chair. She appeared calm. David cradled his own cup of coffee in an effort to warm his hands. "Can you tell me what happened?"

Tessa fixed her gaze on him. "I could."

"Well?" David waited.

She answered him with a question of her own. "What about Coalie?"

"What about him?" David took a sip of coffee.

"Is he all right? Was he hurt?"

"He's fine."

"Are you sure?"

"Yes. Now it's your turn," David reminded her. "I answered your question. You're supposed to answer mine."

"Who are you?" she asked. "Why are you here?"

"That's two more questions." David shifted his weight on the uncomfortable chair, then stood up. "My name is David Alexander. I'm an attorney. I've come to offer my services."

Tessa snorted in disbelief. It was a tiny, elegant snort, but a snort all the same. "Out of the goodness of your heart?"

"Maybe," David answered.

"No, thank you. I'll keep my own counsel," Tessa replied, not wanting to admit she didn't have the money to pay him. She didn't want to admit the pittance she earned at the Satin Slipper barely covered room and board.

"That wouldn't be wise." David looked at her closely. She obviously didn't want him as an attorney. And he certainly didn't need the aggravation. He studied the dark bluish rings under her eyes and the way her teeth bit at her bottom lip. She might not want him, but she *needed* him. And for some reason he wanted to help. "You're going to need a good attorney, Miss Roarke."

"Are you a good attorney?" The musical lilt in her voice was very pronounced.

"My clients think so."

Tessa stood up and took a couple of steps toward him. "What about you, Mr. Alexander? Do you think you're the *best?*"

"Not the best," David answered. "But good."

"Good enough for a saloon girl accused of murder?"

"Yes," David told her.

"At least you're honest." She turned on her heel and walked back to the cot, carefully stepping around David's coat. "I hope you're right."

Deputy Harris spoke from just outside the cell. "I'm gonna have to cut this short, Mr. Alexander."

"I'm conferring with my client."

"Well, you're gonna have to come back later," the deputy said. "I gotta make my morning rounds through town, checkin' the windows and doors. I can't leave you in the jail by yourself."

David turned to face the lawman. "Afraid she'll escape?"

"Maybe. Maybe not. I ain't takin' no chances. I've seen her kind before," Harris commented. "Cold-hearted murderess." He motioned for David to step forward as he turned the key in the lock and swung the heavy iron door open. "You can come back during business hours. A few hours in a jail cell will probably do her good. Help reform her."

Narrowing his dark gaze at the deputy in a scathing look, David stepped through the opening.

"You're leavin' your coat," Harris pointed out.

David glanced to where his coat lay on the floor next to her cot. "She can keep it."

"But it's cold out there. The wind is biting."

"I don't have far to go," David reminded him. "I'll manage without it for now." Even as he said the words, David planned to return. His jacket gave him an excuse. It was foolish, and he knew it, but despite his experience with duplicitous women, David felt drawn to the jail and the exasperating woman locked inside it. The look she'd given him just wasn't that of a murderess. He was convinced of it. And he knew what it was like to be misjudged.

He paused outside the cell, glancing back at Tessa. She remained seated on the cot, the line of her back impossibly rigid. "Will she be all right?"

"Sure. She's got the place to herself. For today."

David suddenly realized the jail was empty except for Tessa Roarke. "Where is everyone?"

Harris chuckled. "We let all the drunks go home before breakfast. Saves the citizens the cost of feedin' 'em. She won't have to worry about company until the saloons fill up again. Then I don't know what we'll do." He stared at David. "Can't put anybody in with her, and we do lots of business on Friday nights." There were only three cells in the entire jail.

"I'll find someplace for her to stay," David promised.

"How you gonna manage that? She's a damn murderess."

"She's an *alleged* murderess," David snapped at the deputy. "And I don't know how I'll manage, but I'll find a place for her to stay."

The lawman looked skeptical.

David couldn't blame him. He found it hard to believe his own words. Nothing made sense. He had plenty of cases to keep him busy. Business cases. Deeds, wills, contracts, and land plats were stacked on his desk awaiting attention. They were all clean, uncomplicated, predictable cases. But this . . .

"Mr. Alexander?" Her soft voice reached him as he opened the door.

"Yes?"

"Can you get me out?" She paused. "Coalie needs me."

David inhaled deeply. He was crazy to take her on as a client. This whole night had been crazy. David hoped he was still sleeping. If he was lucky, he'd wake up soon and realize this had all been a fascinating dream.

CHAPTER 2

Returning to his office after lunch, still somewhat distracted by his thoughts on the case he was hoping to build, David nearly stumbled over something lodged in the doorway.

"Ouch!" The grunt of pain came from the dirty bundle curled up on the threshold. A wooden box full of soiled rags, brushes, and boot black sat beside it.

"What the devil . . . ?" David looked down.

A face appeared. It belonged to Coalie.

"What are you doing out here?" David said, bending down to help the child to his feet. Unlocking the door, David ushered Coalie inside the room, just as Greeley, too long confined, scrambled through the open door in a blur of orange stripes. "I'll have the stove going in a minute. You need something hot to drink." David turned his attention to the stove. Coalie hovered near the door, wooden box in hand.

David stoked the embers, then added more coal.

"Come on in and get warm. You can tell me what you were doing on my doorstep." David shrugged off the new coat he'd purchased at the mercantile after leaving the jail.

"I was waitin' for ya." Coalie inched forward, closer to the stove and set his shoeshine box down. "I seen ya goin' in and outta the saloons all mornin'."

David filled the coffee pot and set it on the stove. A few drops of water trailed down the side and sizzled on the iron surface. "I thought I caught a glimpse of you trailing me." David pulled his leather desk chair closer to the warmth, then shoved the straight-backed visitor's chair in Coalie's direction. "I lost you at the funeral home."

"Ya didn't lose me, exactly. I came back here to wait for ya." Coalie paused. "Don't like dead bodies. They give me the willies."

David nodded in complete understanding. His first clue. David scratched the boy off his mental list of suspects. Coalie couldn't have murdered Arnie by himself, and with his fear of the dead, it was unlikely that he'd helped someone else.

"Can't say that I blame you," David agreed. He didn't care for funeral parlors much himself. He hadn't liked questioning the undertaker or inspecting the gaping slash across Arnie Mason's throat.

"Did ya get Tessa outta the jail yet?" Coalie sat down.

"Not yet."

"Then what'd ya do in the saloon?" Coalie got up and sniffed the air around David's chair. "Ya don't smell like old Clayburn. Ya don't smell drunk." He said the words warily.

"I asked questions," David admitted.

"Anybody can do that," Coalie told him. "It's gettin' the answers that matters."

Greeley meowed loudly outside the door. David got up and let him in. The cat padded around the floor, weaving his way around David's legs. David bent to pick him up. "You don't seem to have a high opinion of my abilities," he commented, petting the ugly orange cat. "Why did you come to my office to get me last night?"

"Heard it was yer job, gettin' people outta jail," the boy replied matter-of-factly. "When I saw who it was on Tessa's bed, I come runnin'. I figured she'd need help." David eyed Coalie with new awareness. He was wise beyond his years. Too wise.

"I think you're absolutely right." David set the orange tom on the floor. Greeley brushed against his ankles, then headed back to his favorite spot on the windowsill in the spare bedroom.

"Then we got us a deal?" Coalie stared up at the tall man. "Ya gonna help her?"

"First I want to know what Tessa Roarke is to you. Is she your sister? Is your last name Roarke, too?"

Coalie thought for a moment. "Nah. My name's Donegal. Coalie Donegal."

"Is Tessa your mother?"

He shrugged his shoulders. "She takes care of me," he answered vaguely. "Are you gonna help her?"

"I'll try." David nodded in affirmation, then walked back to stand in front of Coalie's chair.

Coalie stood to face him. "There's just one thing."
"What's that?"
"We ain't got the money to pay ya."
"Don't worry about it." David shrugged.

"Tessa and me don't take charity." Coalie straightened to his full height. "But I'll work for ya. To pay for Tessa."

David thought for a moment. The little boy looked at him so proudly, David had to take him seriously. "I could use a helping hand to run errands, do a few chores, keep an eye on the place . . . that sort of thing."

Coalie looked around the office, taking in the stacks of books and papers scattered across the desk and table.

"I'll give you a key to the back door and a bed of your own," David said, "but there will be rules to follow. I expect you to go to school like the other children in town. And you'll do your chores in the mornings and after school." David had learned that Coalie lived with Tessa Roarke, and with Tessa in jail, Coalie had no place to stay.

David stretched his tired muscles and ran his long, lean fingers through the silky strands of his ink-black hair. He was a fool—and probably would be served right when Coalie and Tessa skipped out in the middle of the night. But he was willing to take a chance. And in the meantime Coalie was a vital link to Tessa Roarke. Maybe his only link. David stuck out his hand. "Do we have a deal?"

Coalie stared at the large outstretched hand, then at the face of the man offering it. "What about my shoeshine business?"

"You can continue in your free time if you want to," David told him, "but only after your schoolwork and chores are done. And only if you agree to stay away from the saloons."

Coalie nodded, having apparently decided to trust him. He placed his hand in David's. "You sure do have a lot of rules, but it's a deal."

David studied the small hand. It was caked with dirt, red from cold, and roughened from hard work. Black half-moons marked his fingernails. If he had his way, no child would have to work for a living. But David recognized pride when he saw it. He took the boy's hand and gripped it firmly. "I'm pleased to meet you, Coalie."

Coalie shook his hand in reply.

"Come on," David prompted. "I'll show you your new room."

By David's standards the room was tiny. It was smaller than his sleeping quarters at the office and much smaller than his room in the bachelors' wing at the ranch. The room was barely large enough to hold a narrow bed, a dresser, and a washstand, but Coalie's big green eyes lit up in wonder at the size of the room and the furnishings. He walked around, reverently touching the down coverlet and the quilt folded at the foot of the bed. Walking over to the window looking out on the back alley, he fingered the checked fabric of the curtains.

Coalie glanced at the windowsill and grinned at the orange tomcat, showing David an uneven smile where permanent teeth were filling the gaps left by baby teeth.

"I hope you like cats," David said. "Horace Greeley has the run of the place." David affectionately scratched Greeley's head. The cat bumped at his hand, rumbling his pleasure.

"I don't mind 'em at all," Coalie replied.

David placed his hand on Coalie's shoulder. "Good. Follow me. I'll get your key." David led the way back down the hallway, walked to his desk, and removed a key from the top drawer. "This is for you," he told Coalie. "It unlocks the back door."

Coalie carefully pocketed the key.

"That's settled, then," David said. "Now I need to find Tessa a place to stay."

"She always stays with me," Coalie said. "We stay together."

"Not this time," David replied. "I'm a bachelor. Tessa can't stay here with me. She'll have to have a room of her own, someplace other than the Satin Slipper."

He looked down at Coalie. "I guess you know Myra Brennan at the Satin Slipper has already given Tessa's room to someone else?"

"Yep."

"Then we need to check the hotel and the boarding-houses about a room, and we should stop in at the mercantile." It occurred to David that he'd begun to think of her as Tessa rather than Miss Roarke. He'd have to remember to call her Miss Roarke in public.

"Why? The mercantile don't have rooms to let."

"I know. But it has clothes—dresses. Tessa's going to need something to wear home from the jail. Her saloon dress is ruined, so I thought we'd buy her another dress. A different type of dress."

"Can we get a green one?"

David grinned at Coalie. "Maybe. Is green your favorite color?"

"Nah." Coalie waited while David pulled on his new coat. "I like red. Tessa likes green."

Horace Greeley ambled from the spare bedroom and trotted along at David's heels. Coalie followed both of them out the front door, where Greeley began an exploration of the alley. Coalie picked up his pace until he was walking abreast of David Alexander down Main Street toward the mercantile.

David ruffled the boy's hair. "So you think a green dress will please her?"

"No doubt about it," Coalie answered. "But I don't think any of the people in town'll be willing to let Tessa stay with them. She's gonna have to stay with us." He looked up at David. "And I ain't at all sure what she'll say about yer cat."

An hour later they entered the jail. Coalie sat quietly while David discussed Tessa's situation with the sheriff.

"You *can't* release her into my custody. She's an unmarried female. What about her reputation?" David fought to keep his voice at a conversational level as he shoved the legal document back across the sheriff's scarred oak desk.

"I don't have a choice, Mr. Alexander, and neither do you." Sheriff Bradley was perhaps forty-five, but his white hair, his weathered face, and the determined glint in his eyes made him look like an ancient warrior. "The hotel won't take her, and the boardinghouse won't neither. You said so yourself. Do you have any better ideas? I can't take her home with me. My wife wouldn't stand for it if I brought a soiled dove into the house. What do you want me to do with her? Send her to Fort Laramie? Or Cheyenne? She's charged with killin' a man. I can't let her go, and I can't keep her here with a bunch of rowdies. That'd be askin' for trouble." The sheriff fixed his gaze on David. "You're the only one who can put her up."

David glared at the man. "You know how people talk. If she stays with me, her reputation will be shredded overnight."

"She's a saloon girl," the sheriff stated bluntly. "If she ever had a reputation, it's shot to hell by now. Besides, you're representing her. I don't think staying with you until this mess is resolved will do her any more harm. Might even help."

David raised an eyebrow. He was from a prominent family, but he was also one-half Cherokee Indian. He seriously doubted that living, even briefly, with a man of mixed blood would help Tessa Roarke's reputation.

"Well," Sheriff Bradley repeated, "it can't do her any more damage. Besides, there's the boy. You said he'd be staying with you. He can chaperon."

David glanced to where Coalie sat next to the potbellied stove, holding the brown-wrapped packages and balancing a hatbox on his knees. "An eight- or nine-year-old boy is not a suitable chaperon."

The sheriff smiled. "You'd be surprised. Well, I guess you're just gonna have to chance it. 'Cause I don't have a choice." He took the ring of keys from the drawer of his desk. "Do you want her or not?"

David knew when to admit defeat. "I'll take her."

"Well, then, she's yours. Temporarily, anyhow." The sheriff grinned. "Let's go get her."

Tessa looked up as the sheriff turned the key in the lock and swung the iron door open.

"I'm releasing you to Mr. Alexander's custody, Miss Roarke. He's your lawyer. He'll take good care of you."

David's large frame hovered behind the sheriff.

Tessa took one look at him. "Over my dead body."

"Don't you think one dead body a day is enough, Miss Roarke?" David asked.

"I'd rather stay here." She glanced at the sheriff, then the lawyer. She couldn't go back to Chicago even if she wanted to. She couldn't risk taking Coalie back there. And there was no place else—except the Satin Slipper.

"You can't stay here," David told her. "By tonight this jail will be full of rowdy men. The sheriff needs this cell."

"Is that true?" She directed her question at the lawman.

"Yes." Sheriff Bradley explained, "I'd have to put men in there with you, and that's against regulations."

She inched back closer to the wall and planted her feet on the bare mattress. "I have no place to go except the Satin Slipper, and I doubt I'd be welcome."

David moved to stand in the doorway of the cell. "I'm not taking you back there, Tessa."

She liked the way he said her name. His voice sent shivers up her spine and made the hair on her arms stand on end. It seemed to rumble from deep within his chest, like the purr of a big tomcat. It was a wonderful voice. It seemed to surround her with warmth and understanding. It made her want to trust him, to run into his arms and lay all her troubles at his feet, and that confused and frightened her. She couldn't allow herself to feel that way. She couldn't afford to trust him. Not yet.

Tessa tilted her chin up a notch higher and faced him regally, as a queen would face a subject. "Where else can I go?"

"With me," he said. "You'll be going with me."

Tessa's blue eyes widened in surprise, then narrowed dangerously. Holding her blanket tightly against her, she bounded off the bed and crossed the narrow confines of the cell to stand a few steps away from the handsome attorney. "I don't know what you've been told, Mr. Alexander, but I *don't go with men.*" Having said her piece, Tessa returned to the cot and sat down with her back to David Alexander and the sheriff.

Momentarily perplexed by her reaction to his statement, David quizzically looked at Sheriff Bradley.

The older man shrugged.

David was just about to wash his hands of the whole affair when understanding dawned. He allowed himself a tiny smile before he spoke. She'd misunderstood his intentions right from the beginning, and it was time to set her straight. "I'm not asking you to go with me, Miss Roarke, in the way you obviously think. I'm offering you a place to stay. I don't require a bedmate at the moment. Especially not an unwilling one. You're not expected to fulfill that role."

Tessa whirled around, facing him once again. The blanket twisted, caught between the curve of her hip and the mattress, exposing her slim ankle and the shape of her leg to just above the knee. "Why not? Everyone else seems to think it's part of my job."

"Not as far as I'm concerned." Even as he said the words, David remembered the tempting look of that leg, the softness of her flesh as she removed her garter and slid the net stockings down her legs. He remembered the scent of her perfume, and that underneath the rough wool blanket and his sheepskin coat, Tessa

Roarke wore only the briefest of undergarments.

Tessa watched him. She saw the tightening of his full mouth and the spark that flared in his dark eyes. She'd seen that look before. It aroused her anger and her sharp tongue. "Maybe you think that because I work in a saloon, there's something wrong with me."

"On the contrary, Miss Roarke." David's voice rumbled deep in his chest, his awareness of her evident in every word. "I don't see a thing wrong with you." He stared at her lovely face, into the deep blue of her eyes until Sheriff Bradley cleared his throat. It took a moment, but David regained control. "Except that you're in a great deal of trouble. I simply meant I don't impose my . . . uh . . . carnal needs . . . on my female houseguests."

"I'm not one of your female houseguests."

"You will be."

"What will your fine lady wife say about that? Will she like having a . . . murderess in her house?"

Even though she practically spat the words at him, her question was so . . . normal, so typically female, David almost smiled. "There's no need to fish for information, Miss Roarke," he said to satisfy her curiosity.

"I don't have a fine lady wife or any other kind of wife. There's only me. And the boy in there."

"Coalie?" Tessa's blue eyes brightened.

David looked at Tessa. The expression on her face reminded him of his mother when she spoke of her children. "Yes, Coalie. A little kid about eight or nine. Big green eyes. He's smart. Smart and tough. Maybe too tough."

"He's had to be." Tessa spoke quietly. "Just to survive."

"That may be true," David said. "But there's more to life than just surviving."

"Meaning?"

"He's a child taking on a grown woman's problems." David stared at her. "He's the one who came to get me this morning."

Tessa flinched. "Where is he now?"

David glanced at the sheriff. "Waiting in the front office in a chair next to Sheriff Bradley's desk."

"You brought him to this jail?" Tessa's voice rose in anger. "You exposed him to this . . . this . . ." She sputtered, so angry she forgot her words.

"What have *you* exposed him to?" David countered.

"Love," Tessa answered.

"The Satin Slipper's brand of love?"

"No," Tessa said. "My brand." She met David's penetrating gaze without flinching.

David couldn't think of a retort. Suddenly he couldn't think of anything except Tessa Roarke and her brand of love. He wondered how it would feel. Standing there, staring down at her, he wanted to know.

Sheriff Bradley cleared his throat. "Why don't I go get the boy?" He turned and started toward the hall door.

"Fine," David agreed.

"No," Tessa objected.

Sheriff Bradley paused. "She's your client," he said to David. "You make the decision."

"Go get him."

"No. I don't want him to see me in here," Tessa insisted, raising her voice. "I won't allow it. Take him home. At once."

David didn't much care for her tone. She could be as prickly as a porcupine. Her mood changes, as varying as the Wyoming weather. He liked her softness when she spoke of Coalie. He hated her imperious manner, though. She sounded like the queen of England ordering him around. He'd tried to be patient and understanding, but he'd be hanged if he'd continue to put up with her superior tone. She was much too arrogant for a saloon girl accused of murder. "Where do you suggest I take him, contessa?" He flung the noble title at her. "He doesn't seem to have a home at the moment."

That stopped her. "But I paid my rent."

"Really? Well, they forgot that apparently when you were arrested this morning," David reminded her, "for the murder of the man you'd 'gone with' last evening, Arnie Mason." He felt the knot tighten in his gut as he spoke the words, felt it tighten as he waited for her to protest, to call him a liar, to swear she hadn't "gone with Arnie Mason." And David felt the bile rise in his throat when she didn't declare her innocence. "You don't have a room at the Satin Slipper, and that boy no longer has a home, because you no longer have a job." David turned back to the sheriff who stood waiting patiently. "Sheriff Bradley, please go get the boy. He wants to see her."

"The rent is paid through the month," Tessa told him. "Myra Brennan might not want me back, but she can't throw Coalie out."

"She already did," David told her. "She gave your room to someone else and all your belongings along with it."

"What?" Tessa thought of her mother's silver and black onyx rosary lying on the washstand and the envelope of precious photographs hidden away in her room. "She can have the room, but not my things. She's not going to get away with that."

"Come with me." David used her anger to his advantage. "And we'll see that she doesn't."

Tessa stared down at the wool blanket draped over David's coat. The blanket ended at mid-calf, exposing a fair amount of bare flesh and a pair of trim ankles. "It's bad enough that everyone in this town thinks I'm a murderess." She brushed her hand over the rough wool blanket. "Do you intend to prove to them that I'm a loose woman as well?"

"You work in a saloon," David pointed out. "What are the townspeople supposed to think?"

"That maybe I like to eat," Tessa retorted.

David hid the smile that threatened to tip the corners of his mouth upward. Though she resembled a porcelain doll, she was quick and tough, tougher than most of the lawyers who were his opponents in the courtroom. He turned to the sheriff one last time. "Go get the boy."

The sheriff nodded, then ambled up the hall to his office.

"I don't want Coalie to see me like this," Tessa told him.

"He has a present for you," David said.

She met his gaze, her blue eyes showing surprise. "A present? For me?"

"Yes." David smiled. Her childlike pleasure in a surprise made her forget her hostility. David had a sudden urge to touch her, to caress the tiny freckles that dotted the bridge of her nose.

"What is it?"

"I'll let Coalie show you. They're his gifts."

Her eyes widened. "You mean there's more than one present?" She could barely contain her curiosity.

"Lots more," David told her as he stepped away from the bars. "Here's Coalie. I'll leave you two alone for a while." He smiled at her. "And, Tessa . . ."

"Yes?"

"Enjoy them."

Tessa met his knowing brown-eyed gaze. The expression on his face and the way he spoke to her, in that deep purr, told her that David Alexander had had more to do with choosing the gifts than Coalie.

She shivered at the thought and a warm feeling settled deep inside her.

"Mr. Alexander!" Coalie's call echoed up the hall a few minutes later as David sat in the office at the jail. "Tessa wants you to come here."

"I'll be right there," David answered. He looked at the sheriff. They'd heard Tessa's spontaneous oohs and aahs of delight through the thick door separating the cells from the office.

"She sounds right pleased with all them female frills you bought her," the sheriff commented, pouring himself a cup of steaming hot coffee. "Probably wants to thank you."

David shrugged. "She had to have a decent dress to wear."

"You coulda borrowed some of your sister's," the sheriff reminded the younger man. "Hell, I was going to suggest you borrow some of my wife's. That Harris is a good deputy, but he don't know beans about how to treat a woman prisoner. He left her sitting back there wrapped in a blanket all day. He coulda got something from some of the women in town."

"I doubt if she'd have accepted anything," David admitted, "or if the women would have loaned any clothes to a woman accused of murder. This way she has something of her own. She's not beholden to anyone."

"Except to you," the Sheriff pointed out.

David's fulminating glare spoke volumes.

A different man might have retreated from that look, but Sheriff Bradley scratched his head and changed the subject. "Wonder what Myra's got against that little girl in there? Renting her room to someone else is one thing. Giving away her personal belongings is something else. Makes you wonder, though, doesn't it?"

David didn't get a chance to answer. Coalie's shout interrupted once again. "Mr. Alexander, Tessa says to hurry. It's cold back here."

"Take these." Sheriff Bradley tossed the ring of keys at David. "In case you need 'em. I want to finish my coffee while it's hot."

David caught the keys, then opened the thick door and followed the hallway back to the holding area.

"What is it?" he asked.

Tessa stood near the cot holding a green calico dress and several small white garments clutched against her chest. "I need help with these," Tessa told him, blushing as she held out the underclothes.

"Coalie can help you." David held up the ring of keys, selected the one with her cell number, and unlocked the door.

"Coalie's a little boy."

"I'm a grown man," David reminded her.

"I know," Tessa agreed. "You know about these things. Coalie doesn't." She paused a moment, then shifted the clothing against her so David could see the white laces of the corset.

"He lived in a saloon," David said. He couldn't believe it. She actually thought Coalie had never seen women in underclothes and corsets while living in the Satin Slipper?

"I kept him away from the other women as much as possible," Tessa said. "And I made sure he didn't see . . ." She blushed even redder and tightened her hold on the clothing.

"Tessa never let me see her unmentionables," Coalie told David. "Just dresses and nightgowns. And I only saw her when she was all covered up."

"Coalie said you bought these clothes," Tessa explained to David. "He said you asked for a bonnet, a pair of shoes, a green dress and for all the foundation garments. Including ladies' unmentionables."

"I did."

"He knows all about unmentionables," Coalie piped up, extolling David's virtues, fascinated with the forbidden topic.

"Then you should understand why I can't get dressed without help," Tessa said to David. "Not if you expect me to wear this." She nodded toward the dress. "I have to wear a . . . you know . . . or the top won't fit properly." She lowered the garments and the blanket a fraction so he could see her problem. "Please."

She was tall and slender but well endowed. David realized the dress's narrow high-necked bodice required a corset. Without the support and the constriction of the foundation garment, he doubted she could get the top fastened all the way. And if she managed to do so, the cotton fabric would cling to her, revealing more than it concealed.

"Oh." David managed the one word. She needed him to help her dress. She needed him to act as lady's maid, lacing her corset, tying her petticoats, buttoning the back of her dress. Coalie had selected the green calico because he thought Tessa would like the color. And David had never given it a thought, and his thoughtlessness had come back to haunt him.

"I'll see if I can find somebody to help you," David said.

"Who?" Tessa asked. "Deputy Harris? Sheriff Bradley?"

"One of the women in town. Mrs. Bradley, maybe."

Tessa looked skeptical. She'd heard part of his conversation with the sheriff, and Coalie had told her the rest. "Please," she repeated. "I want to leave here."

Her wanting to leave the jail was only part of the reason she'd asked for his help, David realized. She understood about the women in town, and somehow she knew they'd judged her and found her guilty. He admired her courage and her stubborn pride.

"All right. I'll do it," David said suddenly, knowing there was never really any doubt. He'd managed to undress her. He ought to be able to dress her, despite the strain on his nerves. "Coalie," he said to the boy, "go up front and wait in the sheriff's office. We'll be there in a few minutes."

Coalie looked to Tessa.

"Do as he says," she reassured Coalie. "I'll be there in a minute. And, Coalie, don't worry. Everything will be all right."

David wasn't as confident. He had the feeling his life was changing beyond recognition. Taking a deep breath, he opened the door to the cell and stepped inside.

Tessa waited until Coalie closed the door leading to the sheriff's office behind him. Dropping the blanket and the clothes on the cot, she turned her back to David and reached for a long white chemise.

A gentleman would have looked away, but David forgot about being a gentleman. He forgot the niceties. She was a beautiful woman dressed in the heavy black silk stockings he'd bought her, pantalets, and her new shoes. He studied her legs that seemed to go on forever—right up to the soft white skin of her back and the delicate outline of her spine. As he stared at the graceful curve of her back for the second time in one day, David wondered what the hell was he going to do with Tessa Roarke?

CHAPTER 3

"Stay close to me. We have to pass by the Satin Slipper. My office is a few doors beyond it." David Alexander moved a step closer to Tessa, inclined his head and spoke near her ear. "I worked hard to build my practice and my reputation here in Peaceable, and I'd like to avoid trouble." Silently he added, And the possibility of a nice juicy scandal.

Tessa shivered. She could feel his warm breath caressing her, feel his hand comforting her as it rested lightly against the small of her back, holding her within reach as they walked down the sidewalk.

He'd just warned her that he didn't want trouble. Well, neither did she, and there wouldn't be any as long as Myra Brennan agreed to return Tessa's things. But if Myra didn't cooperate, all hell was liable to break loose. Biting her lip to keep from speaking her mind, Tessa marched on, dressed in her new green calico dress and matching bonnet, ignoring the censorious looks in the eyes of the curious spectators.

She felt the stares of the people burning into her back as she passed, heard the growing rumble of voices gossiping about her, judging her. But Tessa didn't falter. She wouldn't allow the people of Peaceable to see her nervousness. She kept her head up, her eyes forward, and her back rigid as she passed through Peaceable's muddy streets. She raised her chin a notch higher as they approached the Satin Slipper Saloon. Several scantily clad saloon girls, former acquaintances, lingered in the doorway, whispering. Three of the upstairs girls had wrapped themselves in blankets and braved the bitter cold wind to stand on the balcony. Tessa wondered which one was the new occupant of her room and the owner of her personal possessions. The thought brought a spurt of anger. Tessa clenched her gloved fists.

Coalie moved closer to Tessa's side, carefully matching his steps to hers before grabbing hold of her hand. She unclenched her fist as Coalie slipped his hand into hers. She gave his smaller hand a tiny squeeze of encouragement.

"Murderess!" Myra Brennan, owner of the Satin Slipper, stood on the boardwalk blocking their path.

Tessa started at the unexpected attack, half turning to face her accuser.

"Don't pay any attention to her," David instructed. "Chin up, eyes forward. Pretend she isn't there."

"Murderess!" The accusation was louder this time and the saloon girls joined in, echoing their employer.

Tessa turned to David. He read the anger burning in the depths of her big blue eyes.

"Don't say anything," he warned. "Just look straight ahead." His fingers tightened on her elbow as he spoke. "Trust me. I'll handle this. I'll take care of you." As soon as he said the words, David knew they were true. He understood that Tessa Roarke could take care of herself, but he wanted, needed, to do it. He wanted to take care of her.

Myra Brennan took a step forward.

Tessa held her ground.

David inhaled, steeling himself for the confrontation, knowing it could get ugly. The mood of the crowd could easily change from curiosity to anger. David released Tessa's elbow and stepped forward. As he did so, David noticed that Coalie had let go of Tessa's hand and moved to stand in front of her.

"Good afternoon, Miss Brennan." David tipped his hat and smiled his most disarming smile.

"What's good about it, lawyer man?" The saloon-keeper's carefully painted face was a mask of outrage and betrayal. "Certainly not you taking the side of trash!"

David continued to smile. "Every man and woman," he said, nodding toward Tessa, "is entitled to the best defense possible."

"And people tell me you're the best," Myra drawled. "At lawyering. At everything. But I wouldn't know."

David looked at Myra Brennan. She had once been a very lovely woman, but the ravages of time, late nights, liquor, and too many men had left their marks on her face, dulled her brown eyes, and coarsened her pale complexion. David softened his gaze, trying not to show his distaste as he looked at her. "Myra, you know a man in my position can't afford to play favorites. I treat everyone equally."

One of the saloon girls gasped at his words. He'd clearly insulted her. David Alexander uttered those words to Myra Brennan each time she approached him. Nearly every person at the Satin Slipper knew of Myra's weakness for the handsome lawyer. The lady saloonkeeper had never made a secret of her desire to have the half-breed attorney in her bed.

Myra didn't give up easily. "She's dirty Irish trash. She killed Arnie!"

David struggled to contain his temper. "She's no dirtier than the rest of us." David turned from Myra to face the people crowding around, who were avidly listening to the confrontation. "And the law says she's innocent until proven guilty." He turned back to Myra, but this time David didn't smile or try to hide his distaste. "Good day, Miss Brennan." He tipped his hat once again in a gesture of dismissal.

"Always fightin' for the helpless, eh, lawyer man?" Myra smiled at David as she moved closer. She caressed him, trailing the tip of a red-painted fingernail along his cheek, the corner of his mouth, and the curve of his full lower lip.

David didn't move. Myra's hand brushed over his lip again. The lace of her cuff touched his chin. Resisting the urge to brush her hand away, David concentrated on the fine bones of her wrist. An angry red welt encircled it, marring the porcelain perfection of her skin. He forced himself not to smile. It wasn't like Myra to reveal imperfections, even slight imperfections.

"Well, I say, the helpless be damned and the trash, too." Myra leaned closer to David until her lips were almost touching his. "What do you say to that, lawyer man?"

David stepped back, away from the predatory female, away from the musky scent of her, which irritated his sensitive nostrils. "I hope you never become one of the helpless, Myra."

Tessa stood rigidly viewing the distasteful scene, her anger mounting with every second. She ached to step between David Alexander and the saloonkeeper and to shove the older woman's hands away. She could feel the tension between them. It was so thick she could almost taste it. Tessa ground her teeth in an attempt to control her temper and avoid trouble.

She waited for long moments until David stepped away from the saloonkeeper. She felt his hand on her arm as he urged her forward. Tessa stared at a point above Myra's head, willing herself to ignore the woman. But she couldn't ignore Myra's triumphant, knowing smile. Tessa knew it meant that Myra had won. And that she wouldn't get her belongings back.

Tessa saw her opportunity and took it. She jerked out of David's grasp, slipped past Myra, and dashed into the Satin Slipper.

"Stop her!" Myra yelled to the bartender once she realized Tessa's intent.

David knew immediately where Tessa was headed. He took off after her, but the barkeep beat him to the stairs. They raced each other to the top with David trailing a step behind the bartender, Liam Kincaid.

On the landing David collided with one of Myra's girls coming down the stairs. He stumbled backward, allowing Liam to gain another step on him.

Tessa grasped the doorknob of her former room, turned it, and flung open the door.

"Oh, no, you don't." Liam gripped her arm above the elbow.

Tessa whirled around. "Take your filthy hands off me, you rogue!" She swung her free arm at Liam's head. He ducked just in time.

"What the hell?" Liam asked, bewildered by Tessa's reaction.

"Let go of me." She spat the words at him. "Don't touch me!"

David rounded the corner and grabbed Tessa about the waist. "I've got her." He turned toward Tessa, his face mirroring his fury. "Calm down."

Liam let go of Tessa, then stepped back out of the way.

Tessa nearly shouted again in frustration. "I want my mother's rosary back! I want my phot . . . things!"

"I know you do," David told her, "and we'll get them, but I shouldn't have let you come here. We'll get your things back a different way."

"They belong to me. She has no right." Tessa squirmed in David's arms.

Myra Brennan stood just below the landing. "I have every right," she said, "to take my share of your earnings."

"I paid my rent." Tessa glared at the older woman.

"You had a man in your room," Myra reminded her. "Last night. I get a share of those earnings, too."

"Running a lewd house, Myra?" David asked. "You know that's illegal."

"I just rent the rooms, lawyer man. Who the girls see and what they do is their business. But it's only fair that I charge for overnight visitors. The hotel does."

Tessa felt David Alexander's body stiffen momentarily in reaction to Myra's words before he moved away from her. He released his hold on Tessa's waist, grasping her arm instead. It was the only place he touched her.

She looked from David to Myra. "I didn't invite anyone into my room."

"He was there," Myra said with finality. "That's all that matters."

"I don't go with the men." Tessa's gaze darted back to David Alexander. "Myra knows that!" She looked from Myra to Liam. "Both of you know it. Please, tell Mr. Alexander!"

David gritted his teeth, a muscle ticking in his jaw as he sought to keep a rein on his rising temper. "It doesn't matter," he said, pulling Tessa toward him, then leading her back down the stairs. They had drawn a crowd. Just what David had hoped to avoid.

"What do you mean, 'it doesn't matter'?" Tessa demanded. "It matters to me."

David's reply was scathing as he stared at her. "I can tell." He indicated the curious spectators avidly eyeing the confrontation. "Satisfied?" he asked. "All you had to do to avoid this was follow my instructions."

Tessa's temper flared under his verbal assault, but she fought back the biting words that were on the tip of her tongue.

"What did I tell you, lawyer man?" Myra called as David led Tessa down the street, Coalie close behind. "Irish trash."

David unlocked the door of his office with undisguised relief. He'd managed to cool his temper during the walk to his office, but it was still simmering beneath his calm surface. David opened the door and ushered his charges inside, closing the door behind them.

Tessa stepped inside and looked around. Compared to the room she and Coalie had occupied for the past five weeks, David's office and living quarters seemed enormous. Tessa gravitated toward the potbellied stove, and Coalie hurried to stoke up the fire. The coal bin was nearly empty. Coalie grabbed the bucket and started toward the door at the back of the office, which opened into the alley.

"I think I'm entitled to some answers," David said, his attention drawn to the stove and to Tessa.

Two pairs of eyes looked up at him. Tessa's blue ones were cautious, guarded, but Coalie's huge emerald-green eyes were shining.

"From you." He pointed at Tessa, taking care to exclude Coalie. David removed the key to the coal box from a nail near the door and handed it to Coalie. "You did well out there in front of the crowd." He patted the boy on the shoulder as Coalie headed outside to get more coal. Then he turned to speak to Tessa. "You should have followed my instructions."

Tessa, busy removing David's oversized coat, froze at his words. "Why should I?" She looked at David as if he'd suddenly sprouted horns.

"Because you need me," David replied. "You need me to defend you."

"That'll be the day." She dropped his coat into the nearest chair, then made a show of wiping her hands on her skirt as if his garment had soiled them.

David frowned, glancing out the window to make sure Coalie was out of earshot before he answered. He thought about lying to reassure her, then decided to tell her the truth. "It *is* the day. The evidence I've gathered so far is damaging, but at least it's mostly circumstantial."

It was Tessa's turn to frown. "Circumstantial? What does that mean, Mr. Alexander?" Her haughty manner was back.

"It means, Miss Roarke," David began, moving to stand in front of her. He halted, losing his train of thought. Her eyes were on a level with his mouth. Funny, he hadn't noticed that in jail. She had seemed smaller and maybe a bit more vulnerable sitting rigidly on the hard cot. But she damn near matched him in height as well as obstinacy. "It means," he repeated, "that on the surface of this investigation, you look guilty as sin."

Tessa faced off with her attorney. "What about below the surface?"

David shrugged, then walked to his desk, sat down in the comfortable leather chair, and rested his elbows on the blotter, his long fingers forming a steeple against his full lower lip. "Why don't you tell me?"

It was tempting. Tessa wavered a moment, torn between self-preservation and an even greater need to protect a defenseless nine-year-old boy. She wanted to tell David Alexander her side of the story and be done with it. But to do so would endanger Coalie. She couldn't take that risk unless she knew she could trust David with the information.

"You might as well tell me now," David said quietly watching the changing expressions on her face as she pondered the situation. "Telling me the truth is the price you're going to have to pay to stay here under my protection."

Tessa turned back to the stove and began to warm her hands. "Nothing changes." Her voice was soft but laced with bitterness. "Everything has a price."

"That's right, Tessa. When you cause a scandal, you pay the price. My price is the truth."

"I didn't kill Arnie Mason," Tessa said. "That's the truth."

"Do you know who did?"

Tessa shook her head. "It happened so fast. And the room was dark. I couldn't see clearly. I only saw the movement. And . . ." She suddenly remembered the feel of warmth on her face. "And something hit me in the face."

"What hit you?"

"I don't know. Something light. Warm." She shuddered, brushing her cheek with the back of her hand. "I thought it was blood."

David began to pace the length of the room. "Did Arnie Mason have any enemies that you were aware of?" He turned to face her.

Tessa let out a harsh, bitter laugh. "I didn't know Arnie Mason. I'd seen him around the Satin Slipper, but I didn't know him." She looked her attorney straight in the eye.

"What was he doing in your room if you didn't know him?"

"He wanted something from me. But I didn't kill him."

"Did you lure him up to your room so someone else could kill him?" David asked the question, though he dreaded the answer.

"What kind of a person do you think I am?"

"Answer the question," he demanded. "Please."

"I woke up and he was there."

David looked skeptical. "You always sleep fully clothed?"

"I'd been on my feet all night. I was tired. I dozed off. There's no law against that."

"But you invited him to your room?"

"No." Tessa's face mirrored her disgust at his question. "I didn't invite him."

"Then how did he get in?" David raked his fingers through his hair in a show of frustration.

"I'm thinking he opened the door and walked in. Just like everybody else."

David ignored her sarcasm. "Why didn't you simply lock the door?"

"Because," Tessa answered bluntly, "the doors on the rooms of the Satin Slipper don't have locks."

That surprised him. He'd never thought about the lives of the women who worked in places like the Satin Slipper. Never wondered if they'd all chosen their profession. Saloon girls were simply there. To serve.

David studied his client for a moment, staring into her beautiful blue eyes. He wondered suddenly if she'd had a choice. "So you couldn't have kept Arnie Mason out of your room, even if you wanted to?" Or anybody else, he added silently.

"No." Tessa met his gaze and David caught a fleeting glimpse of the vulnerability she kept hidden deep inside. "That was the price I had to pay for our shelter," she told him. "A room of my own, but without a lock on the door."

Before David could formulate another question, the back door opened and Coalie stepped inside, the full bucket of coal bouncing against his leg. When David reached for the heavy bucket Coalie heaved a mighty sigh. Then he looked at Tessa, his eyes shining with excitement.

"Coalie, why don't you show Miss Roarke where she'll be staying while I fill the stove and make some fresh coffee?" David didn't have the heart to spoil the boy's pleasure. He set the bucket by the stove, scooped up a shovelful of coal, and added it to the glowing embers.

Coalie grabbed Tessa's hand and led her across the main room to the door on the left side of the short hallway. "This is your room, Tessa," he told her as he turned the porcelain knob. "See, it's got a lock and key and a window and . . ." He opened the door with a flourish.

"Curtains." Tessa breathed the word reverently, hurrying across the tiny bedroom to touch the red-checked material.

"They ain't Irish lace." Coalie's brow wrinkled when he recalled how he and Tessa used to lie in bed at night and talk about living in a grand house with Irish lace curtains at the windows and a silver crucifix on the wall. "And you don't have a silver crucifix, but there's a bed big enough for two and room for a cradle, and there's feather pillows and quilts and everything." He looked up at Tessa, seeking reassurance.

"Oh, Coalie." Tessa turned to the little boy. There were tears in her eyes as she fell to her knees and opened her arms. "It's grand. It's simply grand." She sat on the floor of the room holding Coalie pressed against her body until she heard the tread of David's heavy footsteps in the hallway.

"It's not much." David spoke from behind her, unable to resist seeing her reaction. "But it has a lock and a key." David reached around, removed the key from the outside of the lock, and placed it in Tessa's palm. "Feel free to use it."

She looked up, and her gaze was caught and held by David Alexander's intense dark-eyed stare. Tessa didn't know how long they looked at each other; it could have been minutes or hours, but David finally broke the spell when he turned and retraced his steps into the main room of his office.

Searching for some task to occupy his mind and cover his growing agitation, David lifted the coffee pot from the stove, his long strides quickly covering the distance to the sink. He was in trouble. Big trouble. God, she was a beauty! And worse than that, she was a beauty who sent his pulse racing. But it wasn't just her looks. There was something else about her. Something that called out to him, urging him to make her a part of his life. He wanted to protect her, to surround her with warmth and food and security. He wanted to take care of her and Coalie, and that scared the hell out of him. He hadn't been this drawn to a woman in a long time. David recognized the warning signs, but this time he was afraid he might be too late to prevent the damage. He might be too late to save himself. Unless . . .

He could withdraw from the case. He *should* withdraw from the case. David repeated this decision in his head for the hundredth time since he'd met Tessa Roarke. He removed the lid from the pot, threw in a handful of ground coffee beans, then filled it with fresh water from the pump. He paced back to the stove and slammed the coffee pot down on the burner. He should take her back to the sheriff and tell him to find her another attorney. That's what he should do. David stalked to the front door and flipped the sign to Closed.

He sensed trouble hovering just over the horizon. He could see it, feel it, and he knew from bitter experience what to expect. There would be another scandal. A scandal every bit as damaging as the one that had cost him his career in Washington. Representing Tessa Roarke would bring a myriad of problems he'd be better off without. He knew it as certainly as he knew his own name, and yet he couldn't bring himself to withdraw from the case.

Why not? The answer was there in her stubborn refusal to tell her side of the story, in her quiet pride, in her fierce determination to fight for what was hers. David had seen it the moment Deputy Harris escorted Tessa from the Satin Slipper. He'd seen it again there in the bedroom when she met his gaze.

David paced over to the cupboard and removed a cup, then stomped to the stove and filled it with boiling coffee. He realized he was willing to court scandal and disaster and any number of minor catastrophes because she needed someone to believe in her innocence. And he knew how it felt to have a whole town turn against you. Remembering that feeling, David gulped his coffee. The scalding liquid burned his tongue, the roof of his mouth, and all the way down his throat as he forced himself to swallow it. Damn. He had to get out. He needed to get away from Tessa to think before he did something more serious than burn his mouth on a hot cup of coffee. David had to get out of the office before he marched into the guest room, took Tessa Roarke in his arms, and kissed her. Or shook her. He finally admitted he'd been wanting to do both since their first meeting in the jail. Grabbing his coat, he opened the front door and stepped outside. He stood on the wooden sidewalk breathing in gulps of the cold air, squelching the feelings threatening to suffocate him.

Turning to the west to let the setting sun warm his face, David began the long, cold walk down the street.

In the bedroom Tessa heard the front door open and close. She heard the scrape of his boots on the boardwalk seconds later. She and Coalie were alone in a strange place once again.

She got up from the floor, took Coalie by the hand, and together they explored the living quarters.

Tessa quickly discovered there weren't any homey, womanly touches in the apartment except in the room David had given her. The office was crammed with boxes of papers and books, piles of loose papers and big, thick, dusty books. The storeroom was nearly as bad. The shelves contained more boxes and more books. A small cot with a pillow and a couple of wool blankets stood in the far corner; the space underneath was stacked with books.

Coalie could stay there, Tessa decided, rather than in the room with her. That way they could both have their privacy.

She opened the door to the other bedroom and walked inside. A huge bed layered with several patchwork quilts occupied one wall. She opened the armoire across from the bed and peeked inside. It was filled with men's clothes—wool suits and linen shirts. Several pairs of boots and two pairs of dress shoes were lined up across the cedar bottom. A plain square table stood near the headboard on one side of the bed and a gentleman's mirrored shaving stand on the other, a razor, strap, shaving mug, and a comb and brush on top of it. The only other piece of furniture was a straight-backed cowhide chair in the corner near the window. There were no pictures, no personal mementos, no satchets or little bowls of potpourri, nothing to echo the personality of the man except the piles of papers and books and a patch of orange cat hair that clung to the center of the quilt.

Tessa sighed. The place could use some cleaning and a woman's touch. She found a broom in the storeroom.

"Okay, young man," Tessa said to Coalie, once they'd covered the small apartment. "Let's see what we can do with this place."

CHAPTER 4

Tessa stood in front of the stove stirring a pot of beans. David could smell them as soon as he opened the door to the office. He stepped inside, closing the door behind him. "I found Horace Greeley outside."

She jumped at the sound of his voice, dropping the wooden spoon into the simmering beans. She murmured something beneath her breath as she fished for the utensil. "Ouch!" Tessa jerked her hand away from the pot, then immediately licked the tips of her burned fingers, soothing the hurt. "Look what you made me do." She turned to David. He was holding the big orange tomcat she'd chased outside with the broom. "That was the only big spoon I could find." She made an attempt to retrieve the spoon with her other hand, and this time she succeeded.

"I'm surprised you found one at all." David watched as she hurried to the sink on the back wall of the office and pumped water. She rinsed the spoon before returning to the stove. "I don't do much cooking," he admitted. "I usually eat at the restaurants around town. I thought that's what we'd do tonight."

"I don't think you thought about it at all," Tessa snapped. "If you had, you'd have known I won't be going out for all the town to stare at."

She was absolutely right. He hadn't given dinner any thought. He'd been too busy thinking about other, more important things, like how he was going to endure living with her during her case.

After setting Greeley on the floor, David moved toward the stove. "It looks as if you've made yourself at home." He glanced around the room. A pot of coffee boiled alongside the beans, two opened tin cans sat in the dry sink. A wooden-handled kitchen knife lay beside them. Two mismatched china plates, two earthenware mugs, and two spoons were set out on the table that had been in his bedroom. His leather desk chair and two office chairs were arranged around it.

She'd swept the room and rearranged the furniture to her liking. Even his desk was neat, his papers and files carefully stacked on the surface and on the floor and the bookshelf behind it.

"May I?" He lifted a mug off his desk, reached around Tessa for the coffee pot, and poured himself a cup of the brew. Staring at the two place settings, David felt like an intruder in his own home. He knew his feelings were unreasonable. She hadn't known when to expect him back. But still it bothered him to know he'd been excluded from their family supper.

Tessa followed his gaze as she stirred the bubbling beans. "I didn't know when you were coming back," she explained, smoothing her right hand down the front of her skirt, "or *if* you were coming back. We were hungry. Coalie found some food in the store-room next to your boxes of books and papers—two cans of beans and three tins of horse meat."

David glanced at the labels on the cans in the sink. "What did you do with the horsemeat?" He was almost afraid to ask. "It's for my cat."

"I put it in a dish for him."

She watched as the animal jumped from the floor to the table and began nosing around. "Outside." She began to stir the beans even faster. "Two cans of beans. That was all there was." Tessa rushed on, embarrassed and angry. "No flour, no sugar, no potatoes, no tea." She looked at him challengingly.

David stared at the becoming flush of pink high-lighting her cheeks, then at the hollow of her throat revealed by the collar of her green calico dress. He could almost see the rapid beat of her pulse. "I apolo-gize, Miss Roarke. In my rush to get you out of jail before nightfall, find a suitable place for you to stay, and get some decent clothes for you to wear, I gave little thought to the mundane necessities like flour, sugar, potatoes, and tea." He looked her straight in the eyes.

Tessa swiped at a lock of red hair that had fallen from her tidy bun. "Well, you should've. You have food for that cat," she said, pointing to the ugly tomcat missing part of one ear. "Is he any better than we are?" She knew she was being unreasonable, but she hated feeling so awkward.

"He lives here." David set the mug of coffee on the desktop, turned, and started for the door.

"Not if you don't get him off my table." Tessa stood with her hands on her hips, the spoon clutched in her left fist. "Where are you going?"

"Out." David caught Horace Greeley before he stepped on one of the plates, lifted him from the table, then set him on the floor.

"When will you be back?" She knew she didn't have a right to demand answers, but she couldn't help herself. She didn't want him to leave, but she wasn't going to ask him to stay. "I can set another place," she offered, "but I'll need to know how long to hold supper."

"You and Coalie go on with your meal," David told her.

"What about you?"

David smiled his most devastating smile as he opened the front door. "Me, Miss Roarke? Don't worry about me. I'm just needin' a drink of something stronger than coffee," he said in a thick brogue that was a perfect imitation of hers. He tipped an imaginary hat in her direction and stepped back out into the cold night air.

Tessa watched him go, then flung the wooden spoon to the floor in frustration as she suddenly remembered the way Myra Brennan had traced the contours of David Alexander's lips with the tip of her painted fingernail. Tessa wouldn't have been at all surprised to learn he intended to spend the night in the woman's bed.

Bending down, Tessa picked up the spoon and walked back to the storeroom to call Coalie to supper. Returning to the sink, she rinsed off the spoon, then ladled beans onto the two plates she'd set on the table. Well, Myra was in for a big surprise. She wasn't going to have everything her way. She wasn't going to get away with keeping Tessa's belongings. Tessa would go to the Satin Slipper to get what was hers. David

Alexander didn't want trouble, but that was just what the man would get if he dared to stand in her way.

Tessa sat down at the table. She could plan her strategy while she ate.

"Lee, I've got to take another look at Tessa's room." David Alexander sat at the bar of the Satin Slipper Saloon, nursing a shot of whiskey.

"There's no way Myra's gonna let you in there to snoop around," Liam Kincaid replied.

"Have you been in there since the murder?" David asked.

Liam shook his head. "Myra kept me busy all day counting beer kegs and whiskey bottles. Too busy to look around."

David grinned. "Then you are working on a case."

Liam glanced around, studying the other patrons at the bar. Most of the regulars were too drunk to remember overhearing his conversation with the lawyer. "What gave you that idea?" His gray eyes were wide with feigned innocence.

"I think it was when you pretended not to know me," David replied dryly. "We've only been friends for ten years. And colleagues as well."

"Former colleagues," Liam reminded him. "You quit working for our Scottish friend after the war, remember?"

"But you're still with him, aren't you, Lee?" David pinned his buddy with a knowing look. "Or should I say Liam?"

"It's Liam," Liam acknowledged, giving his friend a meaningful glance.

"For now." They spoke simultaneously.

It had been a joke among the three of them—David,

Lee, and David's cousin Reese Jordan—when they worked for the famous detective, Allan Pinkerton. Any name they used for work was always temporary. David had met Lee several times over the years since the war, and each time he'd been using a different name.

"Liam Kincaid is my *real* name," Lee said. "At least, part of it."

"You're really Irish?" David was clearly surprised. In the years he'd known him, David always assumed Lee's Irish brogue was part of his disguise.

"Only on me father's side." The thick brogue was in evidence when Lee spoke. He leaned over the bar closer to David and busied himself by wiping spilled beer off the polished mahogany surface.

"How long have you been here?"

"Just under five weeks." Lee finished wiping the spill and then poured another beer for one of the customers.

David sipped his bourbon. "Why haven't I seen you?"

"This is my third bar in five weeks," Lee told him. "And the other two weren't the kind of place a prominent Peaceable attorney would frequent."

"I don't frequent this one either. I'm only here to investigate."

"That makes two of us." Lee nodded as one of the saloon girls called out an order, then began filling three heavy mugs with foamy beer.

"I need to get into that room." David reemphasized his reason for patronizing the Satin Slipper.

"There might be a way," Lee began, "if you don't mind mingling with the sporting girls. One in particular."

David groaned at the prospect. His head ached from the thick cigar smoke, the clash of strong perfume and unwashed bodies, and the yeasty scent of beer and bourbon. David rubbed his fingers across his eyelids while his thumb massaged the throbbing ache in his temple. Lee slapped another shot of whiskey in front of him. "Which one?" David was wary. He wasn't sure he'd be able to mingle, as Lee phrased it, with one of the numerous overpainted, underwashed, overused women in the Satin Slipper unless she was passably clean and reasonably attractive.

"There she is." The bartender nodded toward one of the saloon girls.

David looked up.

"There. The brunette with the yellow ostrich feathers in her hair. She got Tessa's room."

She was attractive despite the abundance of paint and powder, and from where David sat, she appeared fairly clean. "Is she one of the . . ."

"Uh-huh, and it'll cost you. Two dollars." Liam Kincaid leaned close to David's ear as he wiped at a nonexistent spot on the bar with a white dish towel. "And I'd advise you make your transaction before Myra comes downstairs, or all hell's liable to break loose, especially since Myra made her feelings for you pretty clear to everyone this afternoon. I'd hate to see her snatch the poor girl bald-headed."

"Don't remind me of this afternoon." David shuddered.

"Just tryin' to help out an old friend." Liam raised one dark blond eyebrow at David. "You know the saying, 'Hell hath no fury . . .'"

"All right," David snapped.

Lee grinned as he motioned to the saloon girl wearing the bright yellow ostrich feathers in her dark curls.

The brunette made her way to the bar with a movement that should have dislocated her hips. Several men whooped and hollered at the display of her undulating buttocks. One or two patted her posterior affectionately. She laughed and teased the customers as she squeezed through the crowd around the card tables.

Liam grinned at her. "Her name's Charlotte. Rhymes with 'harlot,' and believe me, the name fits. The things she can do with her mouth . . ." Liam broke off. "Or so I've heard. Here." He slid two shot glasses of whiskey across the bar to David just as Charlotte approached.

David got to his feet, picked up one of the glasses, and handed it to the woman. "May I buy you a drink?"

"A drink and anything else you like." She took David's arm, pressing it against her ample breasts as she murmured in his ear.

"I like what I see." David's voice was a deep, husky rumble as his gaze roamed over her, moving from the top of her brown curls to the tips of her yellow satin slippers, then back up again, lingering on the length of her legs, encased in black fishnet stockings, and the curve of her breasts spilling out above the neckline of the canary satin gown. A silver and black necklace, which looked suspiciously like a rosary, hung around her neck. A silver cross dipped down into the valley between her breasts. David studied the necklace for a moment before settling his gaze on her red-painted lips. The cross was Celtic.

"I don't usually go with a gentleman when I'm working the floor." Charlotte leaned even closer to murmur in David's ear. He wondered idly how the seams of her dress held together under the unusual stress placed upon them.

Behind her back, Lee rolled his eyes in disbelief at Charlotte's blatant lie.

"Is that so?" David pretended an interest he didn't feel.

"That's right, sugar," Charlotte confirmed. "For two dollars, I'll give you whatever your little ole heart desires." She took David by the hand and began to lead him toward the stairs.

Lee slid David's untouched glass of whiskey down the length of the bar. "Don't forget this, Mr. Alexander," Lee said, his voice full of respectful subservience. "You'll need it."

David swallowed the liquor in one gulp, then slid the glass back down the bar to Lee. "Thanks." David grimaced as the fiery liquid burned its way to his stomach.

Lee bit back a smile. "Don't mention it." He turned the shot glass upside down over the cork of an unopened bottle of Scots whisky and shoved the bottle toward David. "Enjoy your evening." He winked meaningfully.

David Alexander nodded in understanding as he grabbed the bottle and headed toward the stairs with Charlotte leading the way.

Lee's gaze followed David and Charlotte the harlot up the staircase. It promised to be one interesting night. He shook his head as he picked up the dish towel and began to polish the bar once again.

Tessa held her breath, trying to control her racing pulse. She wished she'd given a little more thought to her hastily improvised plan. The smells of the Satin

Slipper brought back a rush of memories. It had been hard enough to sneak up the back stairs without being seen, but then . . . She peeked around the corner. From her vantage point beneath the stairs she had seen David Alexander at the bar in deep conversation with Liam Kincaid. Not just a casual conversation but a friendly one. They obviously knew each other—well.

Though she felt a twinge of disappointment, there was a feeling of cynicism as well. She'd been right to suspect David Alexander. He was in league with Liam, a man who'd been her sworn enemy since she'd first seen him. Tessa pressed closer against the wall. For the moment, undetected escape was impossible. She'd just have to wait them out, watch, and see what she could learn.

Placing her hand in her dress pocket, Tessa felt the slick surface of the envelope she'd just slipped out of the lining of the trunk in her old room. She breathed a quick sigh of relief. Her pictures were safe and back in her possession. But her rosary was missing.

Standing hidden in the shadow of the stairwell, Tessa watched as David Alexander, whisky bottle in hand, escorted one of the girls toward the stairs. Tessa bit back a gasp of outrage when she realized the painted hussy was wearing her silver and onyx rosary as a necklace, the silver filigree cross nestled in the crevice between her generous breasts. Tessa had to keep herself from reaching out and snatching her rosary from around the girl's neck. She focused her attention on David instead. What was the man up to?

She waited until she heard their footsteps on the treads above her head, then bolted from her hiding place and followed them up the stairs.

Lee Kincaid looked up from the bar where he was

busy arranging liquor bottles. He caught sight of a flurry of green calico skirts rounding the corner at the top of the stairs reflected in the mirror above the bar. He smiled to himself. The girl had spunk. No doubt about it. Too bad she hated the sight of him. He thought about intervening, then shrugged his shoulders, dismissing the idea. It was better to forget he'd seen her. David would have to handle this on his own.

Lee finished arranging the liquor bottles, humming a cheerful little tune beneath his breath as he worked.

CHAPTER 5

Tessa eased the door of the room open a crack. Praying it wouldn't squeak, she glanced inside. It was just as she thought. He was there in her old room, sitting bold as brass on the bed with his back to the door. Hadn't he learned better than that? Anyone could sneak up from behind. Or was he too busy eyeing the woman's rear end as she bent to pour him a drink to worry about danger?

He was every bit as bad as she expected.

She slipped inside the room, dropped down to her hands and knees, and crawled to the curtained alcove at the foot of the bed. Hidden behind the curtains, Tessa sat on a pile of feminine garments. She studied the assortment of clothing. The frayed lace edge of a nightgown peeked out from beneath a scarlet satin dress. Tessa recognized the nightgown as one of her own. Lifting the hem of her calico dress, she tucked the undergarment into the waistband of her drawers. She worked quickly, barely daring to breathe for fear of discovery and nearly panicking when her foot caught the edge of a hatbox and scraped it along the wooden floor. Tessa leaned forward, shifting her weight on the pile of clothes as she peered through the break in the curtains.

"What's that noise?" Charlotte looked up from her empty glass into David Alexander's dark brown eyes.

Tessa froze.

The rustling sound coming from behind the curtain stopped.

"Must be a mouse." David casually leaned forward on the bed, reaching for the whisky bottle on the floor. Looking under the corner of the bed, he caught sight of a bit of green calico. Damn her. He should have known she couldn't be trusted to stay where he left her. David picked up the liquor bottle, righted himself, and filled Charlotte's glass. "Over there." He gestured toward the dresser. He splashed a drop of whisky into his glass, then set the bottle back on the floor.

Charlotte giggled as she insinuated herself onto his lap. "I could have sworn the sound came from behind the curtain."

Tessa clasped a hand over her mouth, willing her heart to stop pounding.

"There it is again." Charlotte moved even closer to David. "I heard it squeak."

David pushed himself upright and got off the bed. He took Charlotte by the hand and pulled her to her feet. Nudging the whisky bottle closer to the bed with his foot, David grabbed the top of the blanket and flipped it back. "Then we'd better get under the covers," he invited, "I'm afraid of mice."

Charlotte giggled again. It was a sound that grated on Tessa's nerves. "A big, strong, handsome man like you? Afraid of a mouse?"

Afraid of a mouse? Tessa silently mimicked the other woman. He shouldn't be, she thought uncharitably, when rats like him were so much bigger.

"I'm afraid of lots of things." David's throaty laugh was deeply suggestive.

I'll bet, Tessa silently sneered.

"Really?" Charlotte asked.

"Uh-huh." He still held one corner of the blanket. "What do you think I should do about it?"

"Climb in." Charlotte stripped off her yellow dress and shoes and crawled into the bed. "And I'll tell you all the cures I know." She smiled invitingly. "Don't forget the whisky."

David grabbed the neck of the bottle.

"Leave the glasses," Charlotte spoke from beneath the covers. "We won't need them if we agree to share."

Gritting his teeth, David eased into bed beside Charlotte the harlot and pulled the covers over their heads.

"Why, sugar, you've still got your clothes on," Charlotte commented.

"I thought we'd play a game," David said.

"What kind of game?"

"I ask questions and you answer them." David explained the rules.

Charlotte looked suspicious. "You ain't weird or nothing, are you? What happens if I can't answer them?"

"Nothing strange. I'll give you a shot of whisky for each answer."

"What do I get if I can't answer?" She was still suspicious.

"I get the whisky," David assured her.

"Sugar, you do know my weakness," Charlotte teased, giggling again. "Can I ask some questions of my own?"

"I don't see why not," David answered agreeably.

"What are we gonna do after the questions and answers?" Charlotte asked.

"What do you have in mind?" David pretended innocence.

"I'd like to see what's under this nice suit you've got on." Charlotte reached for his shirt buttons.

David held her off. "First the questions and answers, then the other . . ." He hoped Charlotte would earn enough shots of whisky to forget about the other. He hoped he'd be sober enough to fend off her advances if she didn't forget, and he hoped Tessa got an earful.

"Well, let's get going, sugar," Charlotte murmured from beneath the covers. "I'm mighty thirsty. Ask me a question."

"How long have you worked at the Satin Slipper?"

"Going on three years. That one was easy. Sugar, pass me the bottle."

David obliged.

Charlotte took a drink. "My turn," she said, "Now, I've got a question for you. A big, handsome man like you has to have needs: why don't we ever see you upstairs around here?" She ran her hand down his shirt once again.

David grinned. "The Satin Slipper is full of beautiful women. I couldn't possibly choose from among all of you."

He probably wouldn't have to, Tessa thought. The women would simply line up beside the bed and wait their turn. There was a rustling under the sheets, then Tessa heard David ask, "Don't I get a drink?"

Charlotte giggled again. Tessa gritted her teeth at the sound of it. "Nope, 'cause I'm not at all sure you told the truth, sugar." That "sugar" grated on Tessa's nerves along with the giggle.

"Oh, well," David teased, "I guess you'll just have to answer another question. What can you tell me about what happened here last night?"

"I knew it was too good to be true," Charlotte whined. "You're interested in her. Tessa."

"I'm just an attorney," David answered. "Besides, why would I be interested in Tessa Roarke when I have a warm, generous woman like you in my arms?"

That does it! Tessa nearly bolted from her hiding place before she realized she'd give herself away. She settled back down on the pile of clothes and fumed. Generous was right.

"Come on, Charlotte, you can tell me," David cajoled. "What was going on between Tessa and Arnie?"

"I can't answer that." There was an edge to Charlotte's voice.

"Can't you whisper it? Nobody else will hear." David raised his voice to make sure his words would carry through the thick curtain.

"I don't think so." Charlotte hesitated.

"Even for a drink?"

"Well, I don't guess it'll hurt to whisper." She reached for the bottle.

"Answer first. Just whisper in my ear."

She did and David handed her the bottle. "That wasn't so bad, now was it?"

"Sugar," Charlotte answered between gulps of whisky, "the only good thing about this game is you and the whisky. When can we play something else?"

Tessa waited until the whispered conversation, the rustling of sheets, and the giggles subsided into snores before creeping from her hiding place. According to what she'd heard, the barmaid had drunk a lot before she'd passed out. Tessa wasn't sure quite how much David had drunk, but he hadn't seemed to enjoy his game or Charlotte's favors. She tiptoed to the bed. The snores were louder, deeper. Tessa carefully lifted the blanket. Charlotte lay on her back. Her mouth was open and she was snoring. David lay beside her, his breathing deep, his wide chest rising and falling, rhythmically. Tessa eyed him suspiciously, but he appeared to be asleep.

Tessa leaned over him, reaching toward Charlotte and the rosary just inches away.

David moaned in his sleep, moving his head against the pillow. A strand of Charlotte's dark hair tickled his nose. Tessa grasped the lone lock of hair just as David moved to brush it aside. His fingers met hers, closed around her wrist, and moved her hand aside. Tessa cursed in frustration.

"Now, now, Charlotte sugar," David said clearly. "You know ladies shouldn't curse."

Almost as if he were wide awake.

Negotiating the dark stairs leading down the outside of the saloon was hard work. Tessa mumbled to herself as she made her way down them. How dare Myra Brennan give her room and her personal belongings to Charlotte the harlot? And how dare that . . . that . . . lawyer find anything at all attractive about such a woman? Tessa's anger smoldered as she ran through the dark streets back to David Alexander's law office. The nerve of him. The gall to leave her alone in a strange place while he went to the Satin Slipper for a little fun with Charlotte the harlot. And then to confuse her with that . . . prostitute. Unlocking the back door, Tessa lit a lamp and made her way quietly down the hall to check on Coalie. Assured that he still slept soundly on his cot in the storeroom, she tucked a quilt around his thin shoulders and placed a kiss on his cheek. She closed the curtained doorway to the storeroom behind her before entering her own room. She took the envelope out of her pocket, then reached up under her skirt and released the nightgown she'd tucked inside the waistband of her drawers. Clutching the envelope in her hand, Tessa let the flannel nightgown fall to the floor. She opened the envelope and took out the precious photographs.

Holding the first one close to the lamp, Tessa studied the face. Her brother Eamon smiled back at her. She blinked away tears, before pressing a kiss to the sepia-colored surface. On impulse she removed the other photos. One showed a man in profile, his face half-covered by bushy sideburns and a thick mustache. A series of numbers was written in ink across the bottom of the picture. She knew now that this man was Arnie Mason, but she didn't know why Eamon had carried a photograph of him in his coat pocket. Tessa slipped the second picture back into the envelope and looked at the third. This one featured a smiling, fair-haired young man dressed in a plaid shirt and stiff denim trousers. Tessa studied the photograph again, although she didn't need to. She knew what she'd see. She'd examined the picture over and over again since she left Chicago. It was a photograph of Liam Kincaid. A younger Liam, minus the attractive blond mustache he currently sported, but Liam Kincaid all the same. It, too, had been found in her brother's coat pocket the day he died.

Afraid to leave the envelope out where it could be found, Tessa went to the cupboard in the main room of the office. She located a small paring knife in the back of one of the drawers. After taking the knife to her bedroom, Tessa cut a slit in the left side of her mattress, under the sheets beneath her pillow, and placed the envelope inside for safekeeping.

Now she had another reason to stay, she told herself. A reason besides Arnie Mason. David knew Liam Kincaid and that meant he knew more than he was letting on. It appeared that David might be useful in answering the questions that had plagued Tessa since her brother's death. She had to keep close to David Alexander, lull him into a false sense of security, and find out how deep his involvement with Liam Kincaid went. And she had to stay with David Alexander in order to protect Coalie.

Tessa finished her task and remade the bed. Tired, she struggled with the fastening of her dress until she finally opened enough buttons to shimmy out of it. The green calico was pretty and made of durable fabric, but it was not a dress Tessa would've chosen for herself. It wasn't practical. Getting in and out of it without help was nearly impossible. She unhooked the petticoats at her waist, pulled her corset cover and chemise over her head, and tossed them onto the bed. She picked up the nightgown and sniffed it. It was clean. Thankfully, Charlotte hadn't worn it. Tessa carried it with her into the office. Standing in front of the potbellied stove, Tessa worked at the knot in the laces of her stays. Once she had it undone, she took the big wooden spoon out of the cupboard, reached over her shoulder, and shoved the long handle between the corset and the laces, then wiggled the spoon back and forth. Where was the man when she needed him? Her arms aching from the effort, Tessa finally managed to loosen the strings. With a satisfied sigh, she pulled the corset over her head, then donned the comfortable nightgown. Gathering up her stays, Tessa returned to her bedroom and tucked it into the dresser drawer along with her other unmentionables.

She straightened the bedroom, then went into David's office to wait. Tessa stood next to the stove. The coffee pot and the covered plate of beans she'd left for David were still warming on the burners. Everything was as she'd left it. Now all she had to do was wait for him to return.

She closed her eyes. It had been a long, horrible day and a night full of surprises. More than she'd bargained for. Tessa was exhausted, tired to the bone, but she didn't dare fall asleep. Not yet. Opening her eyes, she sighed, then jumped in fright as something soft brushed against her ankle. Her heart pounding, Tessa looked down and recognized Greeley. "Don't sneak up on me like that. I've had enough scares for one night," she admonished the cat, before reaching down and lifting him into her arms. "You'd better watch yourself," she warned. "I don't much care for cats. Or their owners." She pressed her nose against his orange fur for a moment, feeling heartened by his loud purr, then set him on his feet. Greeley trotted off down the hall. Tessa watched him go, then sat down on a chair beside the stove to wait for David Alexander.

* * *

David pulled his collar up around his ears. The night air was just as cold as it had been when he'd left his office hours ago. Though his eyes were bloodshot and his sight bleary, David was able to see his way along the street in the moonlight. His normally long strides were uneven and unsteady, testimony to the long hours he'd worked and the amount of sleep he'd missed. Sleep. He'd left Charlotte snoring, in drunken oblivion on the tiny bed where, earlier in the day, Arnie Mason's lifeblood had soaked the sheets and stained the mattress before trickling down to the hard plank floor.

It still made him shudder. David had paid two dollars to engage a prostitute in conversation, then spent the time asking leading questions and studying the little room in minute detail. She'd drunk half a bottle of whisky before her tongue was loose enough, her senses dulled enough, to relax her guard and talk about the murder and the occupants of the saloon.

He jerked to a sudden halt outside his office door, fumbled in his trouser pocket, and pulled out his key. He had Tessa's silver rosary in his other pocket, but this . . . David knew he'd seen it before—on someone. If he could just remember where and on whom. He studied the length of chain entangled around his key. It was gold and very delicate, part of a necklace or bracelet, with a tiny Celtic cross dangling from one end. A Celtic cross, David thought, sometimes called an Irish cross. He carefully unwound the broken chain, and closed his gloved fist around the tiny links. David slipped it into the safety of his coat pocket. He'd found the piece of chain wedged in a crack in the wooden planking near the washstand as he leaned forward to pick up the bottle of whisky Charlotte had set on the floor by the bed. David knew the value of that gold chain; it could be a vital piece of evidence in his search for Arnie Mason's killer. He just hoped to hell it didn't belong to Tessa Roarke.

David leaned toward the door and attempted to insert the key. It bounced off the keyhole, slipped from his grasp, and fell to the sidewalk with a loud metallic ping. David swore vehemently, first in Cherokee, then in English, and bent to retrieve it.

He groaned in agony, cursing louder as his head struck the polished brass doorknob. He grabbed the key from the wooden planks near his right boot and, holding it firmly, aimed again for the keyhole below the knob.

Suddenly the door opened. Off-balance, David lurched into the office, only to be brought up short by the feminine softness pressed against the front of his coat.

Tessa staggered beneath his weight. Reacting instinctively, she wrapped her arms around his waist to steady him and keep them both from falling to the hard floor.

David grabbed hold of her.

She gasped in shock when the cold metal key touched her shoulder. It burned through the nightgown she wore, just as the bitter cold wind whipped the door back on its hinges and whirled through the office. Tessa stepped back, half-dragging David with her.

"Come inside," she hissed through teeth clenched against the cold. "You're freezing both of us!" She released her grip on him, moving farther back into the room, stamping her bare feet against the wooden floor in an effort to warm them.

David lunged forward.

Tessa stepped around him and slammed the door before hurrying toward the stove. She hugged herself, rubbing her arms, shivering in the chilly air. She turned back to him, opened her mouth to speak, then closed it without uttering a sound.

He stood completely still, just inside the doorway, staring at her.

Tessa sighed heavily, then walked over to him. She took the door key from him and placed it on his desk, then grasped his index finger and jerked his calfskin glove off his hand. The other glove followed. Tessa laid them next to the key. She unwound the scarf from his neck and shook the snow from its folds. After tossing his muffler in the direction of the chairs arranged near the stove, she began unbuttoning his heavy coat and brushing the snowflakes from his shiny black hair.

David watched her as she went about the task of undressing him. She removed his clothing automatically, with complete disregard for the fact that he was a grown man. She undressed him as if he were a slow, backward child, and she was afraid he might catch cold. But David was a man, a man very much aware of her nearness and her own scant clothing. His heart thudded against his chest as she undid the last button on his jacket and pulled it open. He moved then, for the first time since she'd closed the front door, pulling Tessa forward into his arms, wrapping her up inside his coat to warm her against his body.

Tessa absorbed his warmth, pressing closer to him. The heat of him banished the chill throughout her body, leaving only her feet exposed and frozen. She shifted in his embrace, moving closer, rubbing her face against the softness of his linen shirt. She sighed in sheer bliss. He was the embodiment of all that was warm and strong and safe. Tessa inhaled the scent of him, seeking the clean, masculine smells she remembered from the jail. But she got instead the odor of cheap cigars, beer, whisky, and perfume. Too much perfume. A sweet, cloying fragrance she'd smelled too many times to count.

Forgetting her plan to lull him into a sense of security and remembering how he'd looked with that harlot, Tessa shoved at his chest, pushing away with a force that took David by surprise.

"You've been to the Satin Slipper," she stated.

"What?" David was momentarily stunned by the sudden change in her. His warm, willing kitten had turned into a spitting hellcat.

"The Satin Slipper," she repeated, carefully enunciating each word so his drink-sodden brain could comprehend. "You've been to the Satin Slipper."

"And?" David prompted, wondering where the discussion was heading and why.

"And you've been drinking and carousing, no doubt." Her brogue thickened with each word, her breasts heaved against the fabric of her nightgown, her cheeks pinkened, and her blue-eyed gaze shot daggers at him. She gave every appearance of a woman betrayed.

The accusation fascinated David. "You knew I was going to get a drink," he reminded her. "I told you before I left."

"Before you ran out of here, you mean," Tessa retorted. "And I thought you were going to get a drink, not while away the whole night in the bed of some . . . you know . . ." She looked up at him, then turned on her heel and headed for the stove.

"How do you know I was in bed with one of the girls?" David asked, wondering if she'd try to lie.

"You stink of cheap women and drink. Where else could you have been?"

"At the bar," David answered, waiting for her reaction.

"I'll heat some water so you can wash."

"I don't want hot water."

Tessa ignored him, taking the kettle from the stove and carrying it to the pump.

David followed her as far as the stove, then opened the iron door and shoveled a scoop of coal inside.

Tessa finished pumping the water and turned to face him. "Hot or cold, it makes no difference to me. But I'll not have you drunk and stinking of excess while I'm here."

David slammed the door to the stove closed. "I'm not drunk." Tessa's self-righteous act was beginning to wear on his already thin restraint. He had been to the Satin Slipper. She knew damn well he'd been there and what he'd done because she'd been there watching him when she should've stayed where he'd left her in the apartment.

"I suppose you always fumble around trying to unlock doors and making enough noise to wake the dead while you're doing it." She raised her chin a notch higher, looking down the slope of her upturned nose.

"I did have a drink or two," David admitted, wondering all the while why he found it necessary to explain himself to her when she already knew what'd happened. "But I'm not drunk."

Tessa snorted in disbelief. "A drink or two? More like the whole bottle, I'd say. I know Irish whiskey when I smell it." She slammed the kettle down on the stove with enough force to send drops of water up the spout and out onto the hot surface where they sizzled a moment before disappearing.

"Scotch," David corrected. "It was Scots whisky and only a half a bottle." He reached over and grabbed the handle of the coffee pot, shaking it a bit to measure how much remained in the pot.

Tessa marched to the sink once again and returned with a clean cup. She handed it to David without a word.

"Thank you." He reached for the mug. Their fingers touched a second before Tessa snatched her hand away. "I'm not drunk." He moved closer to tilt her chin up with his index finger. "You don't have to worry about that."

"I wasn't worried." Tessa moistened her lips with the tip of her tongue.

David stared, mesmerized by the sight of her pink tongue licking her lips. Suddenly he wanted to do that. He wanted to lick her lips. "Good. Because you never have to be afraid of me."

"I'm not."

David raised one eyebrow, silently questioning her words.

Tessa wet her lips once again.

David almost groaned aloud as his body reacted to the sight. He placed his cup on the table, no longer thirsty for coffee, but for the taste of Tessa's lips. Wanting, needing to reassure her, David forced himself to finish his thought. "Despite what people say about Indians and half-breeds like me, I want you to know that I'm not a mean drunk."

Her blue eyes opened wider at his admission. "You're not?"

"I'm not." David smiled, and Tessa realized once again what a handsome man he was. Extraordinarily handsome. His dark brown eyes, copper-tinted skin, aristocratic nose, and beautifully-shaped lips were almost perfect. "Liquor doesn't make me want to fight or be cruel or slap women around."

"It doesn't?" Tessa was surprised. All the men of her acquaintance, including her father and brother, had gotten ugly when they drank to excess. She couldn't contain her curiosity. "What does it do to you?"

"It makes me want to take a woman in my arms and make love to her all night long." He answered her honestly. This time he didn't smile.

David stared at her face, his dark eyes searching.

"Oh." The simple word was all Tessa could manage. She leaned toward him, the sound of his deep, husky voice and the look in his eyes coaxing her closer to his waiting mouth. She breathed deeply and once more the smell of the Satin Slipper intruded, tainting him. She caught herself just in time, placed her hands against David's inviting chest, pushed him into a chair by the table, and glared down at him. Tessa had seen David work his charms on Charlotte and she wasn't about to fall into the same trap. "From the amount of liquor you drank and from the way you smell, I'd say you enjoyed most of the night with someone. Myra, perhaps?" She wondered if he'd tell the truth, or if he'd try to weasel out with a lie.

David looked up at her and suppressed a smile. The she-cat in Tessa bared her claws once again. She expected him to lie. He surprised her by telling the truth. "No," he told her. "Not Myra. Charlotte the harlot."

Tessa's blue eyes widened at his honest reply.

"She has your old room, you know. And most of your things." As David watched impassively, Tessa took a step backward. He didn't like the way his words seemed to cut into her any more than he'd liked the way her claws felt ripping into him. God, he thought he'd given up spying. He didn't like games. He didn't like the way she tested him, trying to catch him in a lie or the fact that he was forced to uncover her secrets to find the truth. And he'd done nothing but try to help her, yet she still didn't trust him. That stung. And while David knew he was bordering on deliberate cruelty, he couldn't stop the flow of words. "I spent the night drinking with Charlotte, encouraging her to talk to me. I listened to her describing in excruciating detail every sex act known to man. And do you want to know why, contessa?"

She shook her head.

"I did it because I'm trying to find some evidence that will keep your pretty little neck from swinging at the end of a rope. I did it because I need some answers. I needed to search your old room." He dismissed her with a sharp look and a wave of his hand. "If I stink of whisky and the perfume of unsavory women, you only have yourself and your stubborn silence to blame. And since my presence disgusts you, I suggest you take yourself off to bed."

Tessa took a step forward. "Wait, I—"

"Go to bed."

"But—"

"It was nice of you to wait up for me, but it won't be necessary in the future." David's tone was sharper, more cutting, than Tessa had ever heard it.

"You bumble-headed man." Tessa walked to the stove, picked up the plate of beans, and slammed it down on the table in front of him. "I didn't wait up for you to be nice. I did it because I wanted to see what condition you'd be in when you got home. I wanted to know what time you got home and how you'd spent the night—drinking or gambling or . . . or whoring." She banged a spoon down next to his plate. "And I wasn't disappointed."

David wearily rubbed the bump on his head, then at the bridge of his nose where a headache was beginning to form. "Weren't you?" he asked. "Even a little? When you couldn't get your hands on this?" He reached into his trouser pocket, pulled out the silver and onyx rosary, and placed it on the table.

"How . . ." Tessa grabbed the rosary.

"I heard you open the door and sneak behind the curtain," David said. "And I saw your green skirt peeking out when I looked under the bed. You were looking for this, weren't you?"

"You knew? You weren't asleep?" Her voice rose.

"No. I wasn't asleep. I took the rosary off her when we were drinking under the covers. I wasn't very subtle, but then I was afraid you might try to yank it off her neck." David picked up the spoon.

"I thought . . ."

"I know what you thought." He ate a mouthful of beans. "I said a lot of those things to Charlotte because I knew you were listening to every word."

"But—"

"I'd appreciate it if you don't say anything more tonight. I've heard all the talk I can stand. And we've both said enough. So do me a favor and just go to bed. We'll talk later."

Tessa turned on her heel, padded barefoot down the short hallway toward her room, and slammed the door.

"Tessa . . ." David's voice reached her.

"What?" she demanded.

"You needn't bother to lock it. I'm too tired to be interested."

She paused for a moment, listening, then locked it anyway, just to spite him.

David heard the distinctive click of the key turning in her lock. "I haven't had that much whisky." His voice carried down the hall.

In the space of a couple of days, his whole life had been turned upside down. All because some hot-tempered, redheaded Irish girl had been unfortunate enough to have Arnie Mason get killed in her bed. And David had the feeling it would be quite some time before he could return to his quiet, peaceful . . . isolated existence.

He banked the coals in the stove, blew out the oil lamp suspended overhead, and headed toward the storeroom. He paused there long enough to make sure Coalie was sleeping before heading toward his own room. On impulse David paused in front of Tessa's door and reached for the porcelain knob. Checking.

Tessa saw the doorknob move, heard the slight rattle of metal.

"Thanks for supper," David said softly.

"You're welcome," she answered. "Thanks for my rosary."

"You'd have gotten it on your own eventually."

"But I didn't have to," Tessa whispered. "You got it for me." She clutched the rosary close to her heart as she listened to the muffled thud of his footsteps as David tiptoed away from the door.

CHAPTER 6

Tessa entered the office the next morning to find David seated behind his desk, engrossed in a towering stack of legal papers. A wisp of steam floated up from the coffee cup near David's right hand. He didn't speak, nor did he look up at her, but Tessa knew he was well aware of her presence.

The door leading to the alley opened and Coalie, dressed in his assortment of grimy clothes, brought in a full scuttle of coal. "Good mornin'." He spoke to David, but grinned at Tessa. "I finished polishin' all your boots, so I brought some more coal for the stove."

Tessa glanced at the stove. The container next to it already brimmed over with coal.

"Thank you," David said before speaking to Tessa. "I put a fresh pot of coffee on to brew."

Coalie dumped the bucket of coal, then shrugged his thin shoulders.

"I prefer tea," Tessa told him.

"We don't have any." David looked up from his desk.

"Then I'll wait until we do."

"Suit yourself," David replied, taking a sip from his cup of coffee.

Tessa ignored him and spoke to Coalie. "I can see you've been busy this morning. I think it's grand of you to help Mr. Alexander."

"He isn't helping out," David said, correcting her. "He's working for me. We made a deal."

"What?" Tessa shot a look at David. "You're making Coalie work for our room and board? I was put in your custody. He had no say in the matter. I won't let you take advantage of a child." Tessa stalked across the room to stand in front of David's desk.

David ground his teeth in an attempt to control his temper. He took a sip of strong coffee before facing her. "I'm not taking advantage of anyone," he said softly, slowly.

"Oh, really?" Tessa's blue eyes flashed fire, and a loose lock of bright red hair escaped the confining knot on the top of her head to fall across her forehead. She swiped at it in irritation. "I've never known a landlord who didn't."

"Tessa." Coalie jerked at the sleeve of her dress.

"Not now." Tessa tried to shrug him off.

"But, Tessa," Coalie insisted, "he's paying me." He stuck his hand in his pocket and pulled out a silver dollar. He showed it to Tessa.

"He's paying you?" Tessa asked, gaping at the silver dollar in Coalie's palm.

"He is," David answered. "The princely sum of a dollar a day."

Tessa couldn't believe her ears. A dollar? That was

an enormous salary for anyone. Especially a nine-year-old boy. She looked to Coalie for confirmation.

Coalie nodded, smiling proudly.

"Just for carrying coal and heating water?" Tessa had to ask. She knew grown men who didn't earn a dollar a day.

"He does all sorts of things," David told her. "He's my handyman."

"Is this true?" Tessa turned to Coalie.

"Yep," Coalie proudly answered.

"Why didn't you say something?" Tessa blushed hotly, angry at herself for jumping to conclusions and angry with David Alexander for allowing her to.

"I didn't think it was necessary." David met Tessa's gaze. "Coalie and I have a business arrangement. He agreed to work hard, and I agreed to pay him a fair salary. In cash. At the end of each week."

"But that's a lot of money," Tessa protested.

"I can afford it."

She turned to Coalie. "See that the man gets his money's worth," Tessa admonished gently. "I'll not have it said we didn't pay our way."

"Aw, Tessa, I know that." Coalie's ears pinkened around the edges.

David stood up, stepped around Tessa, walked over to Coalie, and ruffled his hair. "I've got no complaints." He looked from Coalie back to Tessa, then down at his feet. "My boots have never been shinier."

Coalie beamed.

"Now," David continued, "why don't you wash up before we go to the mercantile?"

Coalie raced toward the pump at the back of the room.

David interrupted him. "There's a basin and clean linen in my room."

Coalie changed direction in mid-stride, then turned toward the short hallway and David's room.

"And, Coalie . . ."

"Yes, sir?" Coalie halted to listen.

David walked to the stove and removed the kettle. "Use plenty of soap and warm water." David closed the distance between them in three steps and handed Coalie the kettle.

Nodding an affirmative, Coalie grabbed the kettle and hurried to do David's bidding.

Returning to his desk, David picked up his mug and crossed back to the stove to pour himself another cup of coffee. "What's the matter, Miss Roarke? Get up on the wrong side of the bed?"

"What's that?" She stared up at him, not quite sure she'd heard him correctly.

David ignored her question, intent on asking more of his own. "Or just unaccustomed to waking up alone? Is that what has you spoiling for a fight this morning?"

"I didn't sleep alone. Your mangy cat slept with me." She smiled sweetly. "Probably sick of your company."

"Is that so?"

"Yes. And I don't blame him. It's just that . . ."

"What?" David asked.

"In general, I don't care for cats," Tessa replied. "And in particular, I don't care for this one's owner." She dared him to contradict her.

"That's too bad. Because for the moment you're stuck with both of us. If you don't like Horace, keep him out of your room, but don't vent your spleen on the boy."

"I never—" Tessa began.

"It upsets him. He cares a great deal about you."
The tone of David's voice implied that he found that
difficult to understand. "If you want to discuss something with me do it when Coalie isn't around. Understood?"

"Perfectly," she said. "As long as you do the same."

"Fine." Satisfied with the results of his little lec-
ture, David dismissed the topic. "Now take this." He
handed her a pencil and a blank sheet of paper.

Tessa took the pencil and paper.

"And make out a list of things you want from the
store. Coalie and I will pick them up when I finish my
business at the jail."

"You're going to the jail?"

"I need to talk to the sheriff." David took a sip
of his coffee. "Sit down." He waved her toward his
desk. "And make out your list. Coalie'll be finished
any minute."

Tessa sank down in the chair. She carefully placed
the paper in the center of the blotter and awkwardly
took the pencil in her left hand. She wrote out her list
and handed it to David.

David glanced at the scribbles on the piece of paper.
"What the devil is this?"

"My list."

"In what language?"

"The Irish," Tessa told him, bluffing.

"I don't think there's anyone at the mercantile who
can read this." David smiled, a dimple showing in one
cheek, as he saw through her bluff. "You'll have to do
it again." He handed her a clean sheet of paper.

Tessa hesitated.

"Go on," David urged, when she continued to stare
at him. "Put down everything you want—clothes,

soap, tea, whatever." He quirked an eyebrow at her, and a dimple at the corner of his mouth transformed his serious expression into a roguish smile. "I have an account at the mercantile. I can afford it."

"I don't know how to spell English!" The words seemed to burst from her lips as a row of wrinkles creased her forehead. She stared down at the white paper, the pencil clasped awkwardly in her hand. A red flush crept up her cheeks and her eyes sparkled with tears of frustration. "I don't know how to spell anything."

As David watched, two droplets rolled down her face to fall on the blank piece of stationery. She brushed them away with an angry wave of her hand.

"What?"

Tessa raised her head. "I can make out some words here and there, but all I can truly read and write is my name."

The belligerent look on her face cut into David's heart. "Show me."

Gripping the pencil tightly and holding the paper steady with her right hand, Tessa bent her head and laboriously printed her name. Finished, she handed the paper to David. She held her breath, waiting for his reaction.

David set his coffee mug aside and studied the paper. The letters were big, childishly formed, and unevenly spaced, but they were recognizable. "Tessa," he said quietly. "Very good."

Tessa let the pencil drop from her hand and released the breath she was holding with a sigh of relief. She'd done it. She'd remembered.

"Can you write anything else?" David asked. "Your surname?"

"No," Tessa admitted in a tiny voice. "My brother was teaching me."

He frowned at the thought that crossed his mind. "Does anyone else know you can't read and write?"

"Just my brother, Eamon," she told him. "But he's dead. He died right before I left Chicago."

"I'm sorry." David responded to the sadness in her voice. He hadn't known she had a brother or that she'd come to Wyoming from Chicago. But then, he knew next to nothing about Tessa Roarke. That lack of knowledge was something David intended to change. The thought of all the pain and the secrets she kept hidden bothered him more than he liked to admit. "What about Coalie?"

"He thinks I'm so grand," Tessa said. "Do you think I'd be proud to tell him I couldn't read nor write anything except my name?"

"No," David told her. "But you can learn."

"How?" She was almost afraid to ask the question, afraid he wouldn't have an answer or that he'd tell her she was too old to master the skills of reading and writing.

"I can teach you."

"Now?" Tessa straightened her back and picked up the pencil once again.

David was touched by her eagerness. "Not this minute."

Disappointment clouded her fine features.

"I can't this morning, but I'll agree to give you lessons if you tell me everything about Arnie Mason."

Tessa dropped the pencil as if it burned her fingers, sucked in a ragged breath, and stared at David in something akin to horror.

"That's not fair," she accused.

"Life often isn't. And believe me, Tessa, before this is over that's what I'll be fighting for. Your life." David's dark eyes reflected the seriousness of his task. "I know you have secrets and I know you'd like to keep them, but sometimes I don't think you realize how serious this all is. I need to know what I'm up against, and I'll use every weapon in my power to get what I need. How badly do you want to learn to read and write?"

"Real bad," Tessa admitted. But not enough to risk Coalie's security, she thought.

David watched the play of emotions on her face, knew she was weighing her options, and knew he'd lost when she didn't pick up the pencil. "Think about it," he suggested.

"I'm ready," Coalie announced as he ran to stand in front of David. He held up his hands and waited patiently for inspection. "I washed my hands and face, even my neck and ears. With soap. Can we go now?"

David took the boy's hands in his own and studied them, looking for signs of dirt. He gave a nod of approval as he let them go. Then, lifting Coalie's chin with the tip of his finger, he inspected the boy's face and the area behind his ears. "You did a fine job, but I'm afraid our plans have changed a bit." David paused to check his pocket watch. "I have to get to the jail before nine, so I need you to escort Tessa to the mercantile to get what she needs."

Tessa glanced up at him, surprised. "I'm allowed to go to the mercantile?"

"You can go anywhere in town as long as you're with Coalie or me," David cautioned, "except the depot and the stage office. And the Satin Slipper." He stared at

Tessa, then at Coalie. "I'm trusting you, so I expect you to give me your word of honor. Okay?"

"Okay." Coalie stuck out his hand.

David took his hand and gripped it in a firm handshake. "Tessa? Agreed?"

"Agreed." Tessa extended her hand as Coalie had done.

David stared at her hand. It was delicate, with long, slender fingers. Her nails were ragged and bitten down to the quick, but clean. He took her hand. Her palms were rough, and callused. Hardworking hands. He intended to shake her hand and seal their bargain, but he surprised himself and Tessa by raising her hand to his mouth.

Tessa shivered at the rush of warmth flooding her body when David gently pressed his lips against her hand.

A shock of awareness jolted her. She stared up at him. The flicker of deep emotion in his dark eyes pleased her. She held his gaze for what seemed like an eternity, reluctant to let it go.

Coalie tugged on Tessa's hand, breaking the spell. He gently pulled her toward the front door, then took his hat down from the lowest peg and jammed it on his head. "Hurry, Tessa." The expression in his shining green eyes clearly showed his excitement.

David followed Coalie to the door and removed his heavy sheepskin coat from the peg above Coalie's. "Take this," he said as he placed the garment around Tessa's shoulders for the second time in two days, and handed her her bonnet. "I'd hate for you to catch cold." His dark eyes sparkled as he smiled down at her.

She was instantly engulfed in leather and sheepskin.

The remembered scent catapulted her back to the jail. Suddenly the prospect of a trip to the general store with money to spend imbued Tessa with optimism.

"Tell Miss Taylor to put your purchases on my account. I'll meet you in front of the mercantile in an hour or so."

"What if she doesn't believe me?" The terrible thought made her voice higher than normal, and she had to tie the ribbon beneath her chin twice before she got it right.

David took out his wallet, removed several bills, and handed them to Tessa.

Tessa shook her head, refusing the money.

"Take it. If she doesn't believe you, pay in cash." He paused, giving Tessa the chance to reconsider.

She took the money and tucked the crisp bills into the pocket of his coat.

"Don't forget to meet me outside the store in an hour or so," David reminded her as they parted ways on the sidewalk.

CHAPTER 7

On Saturdays the general store did a brisk business, and this Saturday morning was no different. Customers milled about, searching for foodstuffs, supplies, fabrics, notions, and the hundred other items crammed on the tables and shelves. The ladies' corner at Jeffers's Mercantile was particularly popular. The latest shipment of goods from Cheyenne included exotic teas, bath salts, milled soaps, and perfume from faraway London and Paris. The women of Peaceable and the wives and daughters of the surrounding farms and ranches congregated there to ooh and aah and spend their precious savings on the expensive luxuries. Because it was the first shipment in nearly three months, Mrs. Jeffers had covered a table with her finest linen and set out an assortment of tea and cakes to entice the ladies to sample and buy.

Two grizzled old men, Jeffers's Mercantile regulars, sat huddled over a game of checkers at a table near the Franklin stove, grumbling over the ruckus while they helped themselves to the cakes and cookies.

The brass bell over the front door jangled merrily as Tessa and Coalie entered the building. Tessa's eyes widened with surprise at the sight of the enormous amount of merchandise and the variety of goods. She hadn't expected to find a store like this in a small town like Peaceable. Drawn by the warmth, the smell of baked goods, and the low buzz of feminine voices, Tessa took a hesitant step forward.

Coalie, eager to begin the shopping expedition, bumped her from behind.

Tessa took a moment to tuck a stray lock of bright red hair back under her bonnet and to smooth a tiny wrinkle from her green calico skirt. She wet her dry lips with the tip of her tongue and moved toward the front counter.

"May I help you?" A slightly plump middle-aged woman with a friendly smile and beautiful thick gray hair looked up at Tessa.

"I've come for . . ." Tessa cleared her throat, then spoke with more authority. "That is, I need to pick up some supplies."

"Certainly." The woman was brisk and business-like. She stepped around the counter. "May I have your list?"

"I don't have a list." Tessa spoke quickly, her Irish brogue more noticeable with each word. "But I can tell you what I need. I know everything by heart." She looked to the other woman. "That will be all right, won't it?"

The older woman smiled. "That will be fine." She gestured toward the coat tree near the door. "Why don't you take off your coat while I get a pencil and paper?"

Tessa unbuttoned David's coat and hung it on a hook.

She turned to find Coalie had already shed his coat and was standing in front of the jars lining the top of the main counter. Inside the jars were candies of every imaginable color and flavor. Coalie eyed them longingly. Tessa did the same.

"Help yourself," the woman said as she took a pair of spectacles out of her pocket, perched them on her nose, then reached for a pad and pencil. She smiled encouragingly.

Coalie looked to Tessa for confirmation.

Tessa paused, then nodded. "He said we could get whatever we wanted."

Coalie didn't waste any more time. He lifted the lid off the nearest jar and removed two candy sticks, one for himself and one for Tessa, then proceeded to do the same to each of the jars. He paused as he reached the last flavor. "Do ya think we ought to get some for Mr. Alexander, as well?" He popped a licorice stick in his mouth, then handed the rest of the candies to Tessa.

"Mr. David Alexander?" the saleslady asked.

"Yes," Tessa answered.

"You can get him one of each if you like," she confided, "but his favorite flavor is peppermint." She tapped the pencil against the jar full of peppermint sticks, then lifted the lid as Coalie reached in and pulled out a handful of candy.

The older woman introduced herself as she handed Tessa a paper bag. "I'm Lorna Taylor. I'm a friend of Mr. Alexander's. You must be visiting the ranch?"

"No, ma'am." Tessa shook her head. She didn't look up, but busied herself stuffing the candy into the brown sack.

"Oh, well, excuse my prying. I'm pleased to meet you anyway, Miss . . . ?"

"Roarke," Tessa said. "Tessa Roarke. I'm pleased to meet you, too. And this is Coalie." She put her arm around Coalie's shoulders and pulled him forward a bit to greet the nice lady.

"I've seen you before." Lorna peered through her glasses at Coalie. "You were in here yesterday shopping with Mr. Alexander."

"Yes, ma'am," Coalie confirmed, pleased she'd remembered.

Lorna drew in a breath. "Then you must be . . ." She looked at Tessa, then toward the ladies' corner where Mrs. Jeffers gossiped with the women. She took Tessa by the arm and steered her in the opposite direction, away from the conversation. "Never mind." She smiled brightly at Tessa and Coalie as she reached into her apron pocket for the pad and pencil. "Now, my dears, what can I get for you?"

"Flour, sugar, coffee." Tessa reeled off the necessary items.

Lorna wrote it all down. "Ten pounds of flour, ten pounds of sugar, five pounds coffee . . ."

"And canned goods." Tessa glanced at Coalie. "And maybe some bacon and ham."

"Don't forget tea," Coalie reminded her.

"Tea." Tessa moved away from Lorna toward the display of teas in the ladies' corner. "Do you have East India tea? I don't much care for coffee."

"We'll save the tea for last," Lorna said hurriedly. "Now, what else?" she asked, steering Tessa back.

"Horsemeat." Tessa started to explain, but Lorna interrupted.

"I know," she whispered conspiratorially. "For the cat."

"Lorna!" A small, frail-looking woman in a day dress of dark blue wool trimmed in black velvet excused herself from the group of admiring women and called to the saleslady once again. "Lorna, what else did Mr. Alexander buy yesterday for that creature from the Satin Slipper?" She slipped away from the women to get a better view of her employee. "Oh, I'm sorry. I didn't realize you were waiting on a customer." She glanced at Tessa as she apologized for the interruption, but her smile didn't reach her eyes. "I won't keep you, Lorna. I can see you're busy, but I was telling Mrs. Riner about Mr. Alexander's hasty visit yesterday afternoon. I was warning her not to be too shocked when that murderess appears in court wearing one of the dresses she made for the store. But I couldn't remember which dress he bought." Margaret Jeffers glanced back to her group of ladies. "I told them you would know, since you waited on him. He even bought a complete set of unmentionables, didn't he? He took a long time choosing the dress. Awfully picky, if you ask me, when you consider it was for a *saloon woman*. Which dress did he finally buy?"

"I really am busy at the moment, Mrs. Jeffers." Lorna grabbed Tessa's elbow and stepped back. "I'm filling an order. A very large order."

"Wait a minute. It'll come back to me." Margaret Jeffers stared at her employee, then at the customer standing by her side.

"He bought a green calico," Tessa interrupted.

"That's right." Margaret snapped her fingers and turned to look at Amelia Riner. "He bought a calico. A green calico just like the one this young lady is weari—" She gasped. She studied Tessa, taking in her appearance from the top of her bonnet, which had graced the millinery section of her store until yesterday afternoon, to the tips of Tessa's black leather shoes. Shoes that had come to Jeffers Mercantile by way of Chicago.

"Just like the dress I'm wearing?" Tessa said. "It *is* the one I'm wearing."

"Get out!" Mrs. Jeffers spat the words at Tessa. "Get out, you . . . you *saloon* trash! How dare you darken the door of a reputable establishment?"

Tessa stood her ground. She could feel the flush of blood staining her face and it made her fighting mad. She had no reason to feel embarrassed, no reason to hang her head or run and hide from the looks of horror on the faces of the gently bred ladies in the store. She was innocent; she hadn't killed Arnie Mason, and respectable or not, working in a saloon to put food on the table and a roof over her head wasn't a crime. It was honest labor, nothing to be ashamed of. Tessa stayed where she was and looked Margaret Jeffers straight in the eye. "This reputable establishment is open to the public." She handed the bag of candy to Coalie. "I'm a customer. Mr. Alexander asked me to come here and get what I needed. He said to put everything on his account."

"I'll do no such thing." Margaret Jeffers was indignant. "I don't sell my goods to riffraff." She reached for the bag of candy.

Coalie stepped back.

"Riffraff?" Tessa's face grew even redder. She took a step forward, her fists clenched at her sides. "You think an important lawyer like David Alexander is riffraff?"

"He is if he associates with you. Riffraff." Mrs. Jeffers advanced. "The lot of you. Saloon girls, no-good painted hussies, and half-breed Indians." She bared her teeth in a smug, superior smile as Tessa took another step.

"Mr. Alexander said—"

"This store doesn't belong to David Alexander. It belongs to me. And I want you out of it. Immediately."

"You won't put my supplies on his account?"

"No, I will not."

"Then I'll pay with cash money." Tessa walked to where David's jacket hung near the door, removed the bills, and waved them. "I've got plenty." She allowed Mrs. Jeffers to see the denominations of the bills. "And I'm willing to pay for everything I buy. Today."

The store owner hesitated for the barest second, but stiffened her resolve at the sound of the collective gasp coming from the ladies' corner. "Your money isn't good in this store. It's dirty money."

Tessa nodded, then reached for Coalie's hand. "It's your loss." She put the money back in her pocket. "Come on, Coalie. She's not interested in our business." Tessa looked down and met Margaret Jeffers's steely gaze. "We don't want to darken the door of a struggling little mercantile when we can send to Chicago for all the supplies we want." Tessa looked Margaret Jeffers in the eye. "It isn't as if we don't have money."

Coalie thrust the bag of candy sticks into Tessa's hands. "I don't want 'em. They have better candy in Chicago."

Tessa turned her back on Mrs. Jeffers and walked to the coat tree. She removed Coalie's hat and coat and handed them to him, then pulled David's heavy coat from the hook and slipped it on. She glanced back at Lorna Taylor, then walked over and placed the paper bag in Lorna's hands. "Thank you."

Lorna smiled. "You're welcome."

"Not in my store she isn't." Mrs. Jeffers rounded on her employee. "And neither will you be if you continue to associate with the likes of her."

Tessa opened the door. "Don't let her bully you, Miss Taylor," she advised.

"Bully?" Margaret shrieked.

"Yes, bully," Tessa repeated. "That's what you do to Miss Taylor, and that's what you are—a small-minded bully. It's a pleasure not to do business with you."

Lorna Taylor couldn't hide her smile of pleasure at the look on Margaret's face.

Seeing it, Margaret Jeffers pointed a finger at her employee. "If you take her side, you're fired."

Tessa looked at Lorna. "There are other jobs. Better jobs."

"Like the Satin Slipper?" Margaret Jeffers commented.

"Maybe," Tessa said.

"She'll find herself there," Margaret warned. "If she continues to associate with you and David Alexander."

"Well," Tessa said to Margaret, "it can't be any worse than working for a bully like you. The hours are long, and the place is loud, but the class of people there is much better. Saloons don't cater to snobs."

Tessa took a dollar bill from her pocket, then walked over to Margaret Jeffers, opened her hand, and let the bill fall to the floor at Margaret's feet. "Here's a dollar for your time and two candy sticks." With that parting shot, Tessa and Coalie left Jeffers's Mercantile.

Shaking with reaction, Tessa held back her sobs until she was halfway down the street, then burst into angry tears. She wanted to run to the depot and buy tickets for the first train heading out of Peaceable. She wanted to run away again, but she'd given David her word and she'd keep it even if it killed her.

"Thanks, Sheriff." David closed the front door of the sheriff's office and stepped out onto the wooden sidewalk. He took his watch out of his pocket and opened the cover. There was plenty of time to meet the doc at the funeral parlor before he joined Tessa and Coalie at the mercantile. David wanted a last look at Arnie Mason's corpse. Something about it nagged at his brain, tugged at his consciousness, just out of reach. It was a shame Dr. McMurphy was visiting his sister-in-law in Virginia. David trusted Kevin McMurphy's expertise and his sound judgment. David only hoped Doc Turner knew half as much.

Inhaling deeply, David closed the watch, dropped it back into his waistcoat pocket, then raised his arms above his head, stretching the aches out of his large body. He was over six feet tall and he'd spent far too many hours hunched over a desk. He turned to his right and caught a glimpse of green out of the corner of his eye. Tessa and Coalie were sitting quietly on a wooden bench outside the sheriff's office.

Lowering his arms, David approached them. "Finished so soon?" he asked.

Tessa didn't look up, and Coalie merely shrugged in greeting.

"I thought you'd have a dozen or so packages for me to carry," David teased. "Or . . . oh, no, don't tell me. You're having a wagon deliver the supplies."

"Not exactly." Tessa's voice had an edge to it.

A quiver of alarm shot up David's spine. "Tessa? Is something wrong?"

"Not anymore," she answered brightly.

"You did go to Jeffers's Mercantile?"

"We went," Tessa replied, "but we didn't find anything we really needed. Or wanted." Still she didn't look up to meet his gaze.

"At Jeffers's Mercantile? You've got to be kidding. They carry everything that anyone could possibly need."

"Not for me."

"What about flour, sugar, and tea?" David studied Tessa. "You did get that, didn't you? Coalie?" David glanced at the boy squirming on the wooden bench.

"Tell him." Coalie nudged Tessa in the arm.

"What is it?" The quiver of alarm grew into something more. A heavy feeling settled in David's chest.

"The ladies at the mercantile are probably still in shock because Coalie and I dared to darken the door of a reputable establishment." The angry words burst from Tessa's lips. "That woman wouldn't put our purchases on your account, nor would she take our money. It wasn't good enough for her. She says it's dirty, just like us." Tessa's small frame quivered with anger.

"Lorna said that?" David couldn't believe his ears.

"No," Tessa told him. "Not Lorna. The other one. Mrs. Jeffers. She called us riffraff and ordered us to leave her store, as if we weren't good enough to shop there." She raised her chin a notch higher.

David bent down in front of her. He touched Tessa's chin with one finger, lowering the angle a bit so he could see the militant expression masking the vulnerability in her eyes.

"What did you say?" he asked Tessa.

"I told Mrs. Jeffers I didn't want to shop at her mercantile. I had money enough to order my supplies from Chicago . . ."

"Chicago?" David interrupted. "Couldn't you think of someplace closer?"

"I was angry," Tessa told him.

"I can tell." David found it hard to keep a straight face. He'd have paid money to see Tessa angrily facing off with Margaret Jeffers.

"Do you want to know what happened or not?" Tessa demanded.

"I wouldn't miss this retelling for anything."

Tessa eyed him suspiciously. "Then quit interrupting."

"I'm sorry." David almost laughed, but quickly coughed to cover it up. "Please continue."

She repeated the confrontation almost word for word, then ended her recitation with a flourish. "I told her we could order supplies from Chicago, then I told her that the Satin Slipper catered to a better class of people than the ones in her store. And then, I dropped a dollar on the floor in front of her and left." Tessa glared at David, waiting for his reaction.

She didn't have to wait long. One corner of his mouth turned up in a smile before he burst into laughter.

"It wasn't funny," Tessa informed him.

David sat down on the bench and laughed until his ribs ached. "Oh, contessa, I can just see Margaret Jeffers's face when you told her the Satin Slipper had a better class of customers."

A smile broke through the stern set of Tessa's lips. She glanced at David, saw the humor mirrored in his dark eyes and the lines of mirth bracketing his mouth, and started to laugh with him.

David laughed until he couldn't laugh any longer. Then he sat watching Tessa. He was angry at the women in town and ashamed of the way they'd treated her, but he was proud of Tessa. Proud of the way she'd behaved. David knew how it felt to be ostracized. He knew how much it hurt. Reaching out, he took Tessa's hand and gave it a reassuring squeeze. "My mother always says it's better to laugh at your woes than to cry," David explained. "I hope she's right."

Tessa smiled up at him, liking the feel of his strong hand holding hers. "I feel better now."

"Tessa, I'm sorry you had to go through that ordeal," David murmured. "I sent you to the mercantile because I knew Lorna would be there. I thought she'd take care of you. I don't know why she stood by and let Margaret Jeffers throw you out of the store." David let go of Tessa's hand, stood up, and began to pace, his frustration evident in every step.

"It wasn't her fault," Tessa said, feeling a little sad now that David had let go of her hand. "She tried, but Mrs. Jeffers—"

"Come on." David reached down and grabbed Tessa's elbow.

"Where are we going?" Tessa asked, though she was pretty sure she knew.

"Back to the mercantile."

"Not me." Tessa held back. "I said my piece. I've had enough."

David paid no attention. "We're going back to Jeffers's and buy those supplies you wanted."

"No." Tessa pulled against him. She knew she was being cowardly, but she was tired of confrontation. She knew she should march back in there at David Alexander's side and demand that she be treated like any other paying customer, but not today. Not this time. "Please. It doesn't matter."

"It matters," David said, but he stopped tugging on Tessa's arm and looked at her face. She'd laughed, but she was laughing through tears. And right now she looked tired, tired of fighting. David recognized the feeling. He'd been there himself once or twice. She needed time to herself. Time to regroup. David abruptly let go of her arm. "Come on," he urged, his voice soft, gentle. "I'll walk you home."

"Thanks," Tessa said as she walked between them, Coalie on one side, David Alexander on the other.

"Don't thank me," David warned. "I've got to get to the undertaker's in a few minutes, but as soon as I finish there I'm going to Jeffers's Mercantile and have a talk with Margaret Jeffers myself."

"Take your time at the undertaker's. Mrs. Jeffers'll probably need some time to recover before she talks to you." Looking up at David, Tessa giggled. "She was in shock when we left," she warned him. "But, you know, it was almost worth it just to see the look on her face when I compared her store to the Satin Slipper."

CHAPTER 8

The crowd at Jeffers's Mercantile was even thicker than before. Word of Margaret Jeffers's confrontation with the murdering little saloon girl had traveled like wildfire. Nearly half the people in town jammed into the store to listen to the details while they waited for David Alexander's arrival. Everyone knew he was coming. It was simply a matter of time.

Down the street, Lee Kincaid lounged by the entrance of the funeral parlor, his hat pulled low over his eyes, concealing his face. He'd gone on the pretense of paying his respects to Arnie Mason, but he was lying in wait for David. Lee intended to waylay him before David had the chance to make a fool of himself in front of the townspeople, twelve of whom would be jurors at Tessa's trial.

Lee heard about the incident at the store almost as soon as it happened. He'd gone in to pick up a few personal items minutes after Tessa left and heard six or seven versions of the encounter from at least that many women. Women who gossiped in the ladies'

corner. Lee knew they'd drawn the right conclusion.
It wouldn't be long before David Alexander showed
up to defend Tessa's honor. David was nothing if not
straightforward.

Lee waited patiently. He heard the brisk steps of
Doc Turner as they passed him and headed toward
the buggy parked in front of the undertaker's. Lee
raised the brim of his hat a fraction, then peeked
through the window. David was coming down the
stairs. Lee waited until the front door opened.

"What the hell?" David blurted as someone grabbed
hold of his arm.

"Shut up," Lee muttered, pulling David away from
the doorway to the side of the building, away from
prying eyes. "You took long enough," Lee told him.
"I've been waiting nearly half an hour." He let go of
David's coat sleeve and, turning to face him, pushed
his hat back away from his face.

"Lee." David released a breath. "What the devil are
you doing here?"

"I need to talk to you."

"Can it wait? I'm on my way—"

"To Jeffers's Mercantile." Lee smiled at the look of
surprise in David's dark eyes. "I know. So does the
rest of the town. Half of 'em are waiting for you at
the store."

"What?"

"They want to see the show," Lee said bluntly.
"They want to see the big lawyer make a fool of
himself over a bit of saloon fluff."

"That's not . . ." David raked his fingers through his
black hair, realizing suddenly that he'd left his hat at
the office. "I won't—"

"If you go storming in to confront that Jeffers bitch

you will," Lee replied. "David, think. Use that keen lawyer brain of yours. Tessa Roarke is accused of murdering a man."

"She didn't do it."

"How do you know?" Lee asked.

"She told me."

"And I suppose you take everything your clients tell you as the gospel truth?"

"No. But I know Tessa isn't lying. I feel it in my gut."

"In your gut?" Lee stared at his friend, studying him. "Or in your groin?"

David's lips thinned to a tight line. His face hardened, the coppery skin stretched across his cheekbones. "If you weren't my friend, you'd be picking yourself up off the ground." David clenched and unclenched his fists in an effort to control his fury.

"I know," Lee said. "But if I weren't your friend I wouldn't be here. I wouldn't give a damn if you made a fool of yourself in front of half the town. And you can't go storming into Margaret Jeffers's store demanding satisfaction without looking like a fool. You're thinking like a man, not an attorney. This is Wyoming, David." Lee's voice hardened. "Women sit on juries here, or have you forgotten?"

David slumped against the rough boards covering the outside of the funeral parlor. "Damn." He closed his eyes and pinched the bridge of his nose in a gesture of weariness, then raked his hand through his hair once again. "Damn." He opened his eyes and met Lee's penetrating gray-eyed gaze. "You're right."

Lee chuckled, showing straight white teeth. "I know I'm right."

"I got so damn mad," David confided. "Beneath all

the bluster, Tessa was near tears. She didn't even cry when she was jailed."

"You've always been a sucker for a woman's tears," Lee reminded him.

"Yeah," David admitted. "God help me, so I have."

"Are you certain she's innocent?" Lee shuffled from one foot to the other, uncomfortable with the question he'd had to ask. They both knew he wasn't just asking if she was innocent of the crime of murder, but innocent in other ways as well.

"She didn't kill Arnie Mason." David knew he was only answering part of Lee's question, but it was the only answer he could give. He wasn't certain about the rest. And he sure as hell didn't want to talk about it with Lee.

"Can you prove it in court?"

"Not yet."

"What's she told you about that night?"

"Very little, except that she didn't kill him."

"Then how can you be so sure?" When he looked at David, his expression was skeptical.

"Tessa Roarke is left-handed." David moved away from the side of the funeral parlor and began to retrace his steps to the front of the building. "Have you seen the wound in Arnie Mason's throat?" David asked his friend. "I mean, have you really looked at it? Studied it? Tested it?"

"No." Lee shook his head. "Not as carefully as you seem to have."

"Then let's go take a look," David suggested, clapping Lee on the shoulder with the palm of his hand. "I'd like your opinion."

"As long as you don't make me look at him too long." Lee smiled roguishly, his eyes twinkling. "I had to look at the son of a bitch nearly every night at the Satin Slipper. I don't relish the thought of him ruining my sleep now that he's dead."

"Neither do I." David smiled. "But I'm afraid it's too late for me. I haven't had a good night's sleep since the bastard was murdered. And I don't expect to have one until I prove that Tessa is innocent." He opened the front door of the funeral parlor and allowed Lee to precede him.

"Speaking of Tessa . . ." Lee hesitated before stepping inside.

"Yeah?"

"What do you intend to do now about the little incident at the mercantile?"

"That's a hell of a question to ask me," David said. "You just talked me out of storming in there and demanding justice."

"I talked you out of storming in there and acting like a hot-tempered fool. I didn't say I thought you ought to let it pass."

"What do you suggest?" David entered the funeral parlor on Lee's heels.

"I don't know. I'm not a lawyer, but I feel sure you'll think of some punishment suitable to the crime."

"Thanks for your vote of confidence." David's voice was full of sarcasm as he followed Lee into the room where Arnie Mason was stretched out in a yellow pine box.

"Don't mention it." Lee studied the corpse, flinching a bit as he loosened the starched white collar and pulled it aside. "Looks like Myra Brennan outdid herself when she decided to outfit Arnie for all eternity."

"What?" David was puzzled. "Myra Brennan paid for this?"

"Sure," Lee said. "And very well, I might add. See?" He fingered the fabric below the removable collar. "French handkerchief linen. Expensive. Like something you'd wear, not something Arnie would own."

"But why?"

"They were lovers," Lee replied matter-of-factly. "Didn't you know that?"

"I knew he worked for her, and that he was at the Satin Slipper almost every night. But that hulking brute of a man Myra's lover?" David shuddered, staring at the scarred, battered face of the corpse. "No, I didn't know."

"Yeah. It does seem incredible when she has such a *tendresse* for you." Lee stopped his rambling and focused on the expression on David's face. "You do know that, don't you?"

"Yes." David grimaced. "I do know she has a certain fondness for me, despite my 'unfortunate' heritage."

"Or maybe because of it," Lee suggested. "She does profess to hate all inferior beings—Indians, half-breeds, Irish. . . ." He grinned at David. "But she sure has an interesting way of showing it—accosting you on the street in broad daylight, accosting me in the storeroom every chance she gets."

David looked surprised at that admission.

Lee laughed out loud. The sound echoed through the funeral parlor, bringing a sharp disapproving look from the proprietor, who had entered a moment earlier. Lee ignored the undertaker, focusing his attention on his friend instead. "You didn't think you were the only one, did you? Because you aren't. You're her favorite—the best-looking and the richest—but you aren't the only one."

"Interesting," David said.

"Yep," Lee agreed. "I do believe the lady doth protest too much."

"Yep," David echoed. "It makes me wonder why."

"I thought you'd see it my way," Lee told him. "And, David, getting back to Tessa and the mercantile . . ." Lee examined the knife wound a few minutes longer, then closed the collar over the gaping hole.

"I wondered when you'd remind me again."

"Have you decided what to do?"

"Yes."

"Good." Lee looked up and met David's eyes. "Because I think you're absolutely right about the knife wound." He glanced down at Arnie one last time, wincing. "Nasty business, throat-cutting. This is definitely a right-handed slash. I don't think the Roarke girl killed him, either. Trouble is, I don't know who did."

"Neither do I," David answered. "But I intend to get some answers right after I pay a visit to the mercantile."

"I'm glad that's settled." Lee nodded in satisfaction. "Now we can get the hell out of here. This place and this dead son of a bitch give me the creeps."

The citizens of Peaceable who had congregated in Jeffers's Mercantile waited all morning and part of the afternoon before David Alexander made his appearance. The assortment of tea and cakes had been consumed long ago, yet the women continued to browse in the ladies' corner, and the men took turns facing each other over the black and red squares of the checkerboard. People who hadn't been present at the morning confrontation showed up with orders for coffee, sugar, ten-penny nails, and spools of thread. Jeffers's Mercantile was the most popular spot in Peaceable on this particular Saturday.

David was aware of the circus atmosphere the moment he opened the door and crossed the threshold. All movement stopped. Every head turned toward the door. The sound of the brass bell seemed abnormally loud.

David acknowledged the gathering with a nod of his head as he walked across the room to the counter. He smiled a greeting at Lorna Taylor.

"Good afternoon, Miss Taylor. Is Mrs. Jeffers in?"

"David . . ." In her agitation Lorna addressed him by his first name.

"It's all right, Lorna." David's voice was a rough whisper, his assurance meant for Lorna alone. He raised his voice as he continued. "Will you get Mrs. Jeffers? We have some business to discuss."

Lorna stepped away from the counter and, turning her back on David, exited through the curtained doorway that led to Mrs. Jeffers's office.

Moments later Margaret Jeffers stepped through the curtains much like an actress making an entrance onto the stage. She had exchanged her dark blue wool dress trimmed in black velvet for an afternoon gown of crimson silk.

David bit back a smile. He hadn't seen Margaret earlier in the day, but he recognized full military battle dress when he saw it. He knew his opponent had dressed for the engagement.

"Good afternoon, Mr. Alexander." Margaret was polite, courteous. "What might I do for you?"

"I think it's what I can do for *you*," David announced. "I've come to settle my account."

"That's not necessary, Mr. Alexander, until the end

of the month," she answered sweetly. Too sweetly for David's taste.

"But I want to settle up now. I don't like to leave things undone." He was implacable. "I'll be having my household orders shipped from Chicago from now on."

Some of the customers gasped at his statement. Jeffers's Mercantile was the largest, finest store in all of Peaceable. Margaret Jeffers carried everything. It was unthinkable to pay the freight costs on orders from Chicago when you could buy what you needed in Peaceable.

"Oh, now, Mr. Alexander, don't be ridiculous," Margaret began. Lorna, standing off to one side, winced at her employer's choice of words. David Alexander wouldn't appreciate being called ridiculous. "Why, the freight charges alone will be double what you pay right here."

"I appreciate your concern, Mrs. Jeffers, but I assure you that I can afford to pay the cost of shipping. In fact, I prefer to pay it."

"What?" Margaret Jeffers responded, shocked at the idea.

"I prefer to deal with merchants"—David paused for effect—"who appreciate my business."

Margaret smiled at him, gritting her teeth. He was a formidable adversary and, unfortunately, one of her most valuable customers. "I have always appreciated and welcomed your business."

"Until this morning."

"Oh, now, surely you aren't going to all this trouble over what happened this morning. Surely you don't intend to cancel your account here and pay enormous amounts of money to out-of-town merchants and to the UP railroad because of a little misunderstanding."

"That's precisely what I intend to do." David smiled a slight smile. "I was certain you'd understand."

"But, Mr. Alexander, it was all a misunderstanding," she said again. "If I had known you wanted the supplies, I'd have put them on your account as always." Margaret ignored Lorna's gasp of outrage at the barefaced lie.

David's face hardened into lines closely resembling the look of fierce determination on the face of a mountain lion stalking its quarry. "I sent Miss Roarke and young Mr. Donegal here this morning to pick up supplies for me."

"I didn't—"

"Did you or did you not refuse to add the cost of the supplies to my account?"

"How was I supposed to know that was all right with you?" Margaret asked defensively. "Anyone could come in here and ask to have things charged to someone else's account." She looked around to the customers gathered in her store. "I didn't know the young woman. I pride myself on my diligence in protecting my customers."

"From riffraff?" David asked silkily. "That is what you called Miss Roarke, isn't it? Riffraff."

"Well . . ." Mrs. Jeffers hedged.

"And when Miss Roarke offered to pay for the supplies in cash, didn't you refuse to sell them to her?"

"I can refuse service to anyone who enters my store if I choose to do so," Margaret stated firmly. "It's my right."

"Yes, it is," David agreed easily. "You have every right to refuse to serve customers you deem unfit."

"See?" Margaret said to the crowd gathered close enough to hear. "I told you Mr. Alexander wouldn't be offended if he knew I was standing up for my rights as a store owner."

"Oh, but I am offended, Mrs. Jeffers," David corrected her. "In refusing to sell the supplies to Miss Roarke, you refused to sell to me. When you called her names, it was the same as calling *me* names. And when you refused to accept the 'dirty money,' it was my money you turned away. You have a right to do all those things," David told her. "Just as I have a right to buy my supplies elsewhere, and I will gladly pay more to do so."

"But I have your order right here." Margaret recognized the danger; if she lost David Alexander's business, she would risk losing the Trail T ranch's business as well. "The order is ready. It's been sitting here all afternoon just waiting for you to pick it up."

"Then I'm afraid you went to a great deal of trouble for nothing, Mrs. Jeffers, because I've come to settle my account." David extracted his wallet. "I trust you'll accept gold today. I wouldn't want to be accused of foisting dirty bills on you against your will." He stopped long enough to read the expression on Margaret Jeffers's face.

She nodded in mute assent.

"Good. Now, please be so kind as to tell me how much I owe—minus today's order, of course," David instructed her. "Oh, and strike my name from your account list."

Lorna stepped forward and politely told him how much he owed the store. "Your account totals seventy-three dollars, Mr. Alexander."

David placed that amount in gold on the counter.

"You can't do this." Margaret Jeffers now fully comprehended the enormity of what she had done. "You can't do all this just to stand up for that . . . that . . . *saloon hussy*."

"I have done it."

"She's not worth it," Margaret warned.

"That's not for you to decide," David reminded her.

"But you're one of my most valuable customers," Margaret protested.

"I *was*," David replied.

"What about the ranch account?" She couldn't restrain herself. She had to ask.

"Oh, yes, the ranch account." David paused as if he'd forgotten, then removed several more gold coins from his wallet. "If this doesn't cover the outstanding amount on the Trail T's ledger, send me a bill." He returned his wallet to his inside coat pocket. "And don't forget to strike the ranch from your ledger as well. Good day, Mrs. Jeffers, Miss Taylor." David nodded. "You know, Miss Roarke was right about the Satin Slipper," he said, standing at the door. "It does cater to a better class of customers." Seeing the outraged look on Margaret Jeffers's face, David left the store.

The crowd began to disperse, disappointed that there hadn't been screaming and name-calling, but aware that a major battle had taken place just the same. David Alexander was the undeclared winner.

He'd won the skirmish, David thought, as he walked back to his North Street office, but he found little pleasure in the victory. It would cost him. Not just money, though it would cost him plenty of that. It would cost Tessa, too. It would make it that much harder for her to be accepted into Peaceable's small-town society once this was all over. People would remember the showdown at Jeffers's Mercantile and that Tessa was the cause. He'd done the right thing, but now he had to worry about the damage to Tessa's case and the repercussions once the murder of Arnie Mason was solved.

He pinched the bridge of his nose. Arnie Mason. God, everything came back to Arnie Mason. David wasn't looking forward to another showdown with Tessa, who seemed determined to keep every shred of evidence to herself. But he needed help. She had to help him. The only evidence he had to go on was her word, a length of gold chain, and the note found in Arnie Mason's pocket inviting him to Tessa's room. David's quiet isolation in Peaceable had been shot to hell by Tessa's arrival in his life. His whole life had been turned upside down, and it was time he did something about it.

CHAPTER 9

When David reached his office he found the front door locked. The printed sign in the window proclaimed otherwise, as did the hours posted on a plaque that hung on the front door. The sign said Open, but the door refused to yield. Inhaling a deep breath, preparing himself for the worst, David inserted his key into the lock.

"Coalie?" Tessa's voice came from somewhere inside the main room of the office.

"No, it's David."

"What happened?" Tessa asked as soon as she heard his footsteps cross the threshold. "What happened at the mercantile? You didn't make a spectacle of yourself, did you?"

"No." David walked to his desk. "I did not." He removed his heavy coat and hunted for a place to hang it. He decided he wouldn't satisfy her curiosity easily this time.

The main room of his office was a garden of white.

121

It looked the way David imagined a cotton field down south might look, provided the cotton was processed into fabric and sewn into ladies' undergarments. Stockings, petticoats, pantalets, chemise, corset cover, and corset decorated nearly every piece of furniture in the office, including his desk; a wet petticoat lay draped across the polished surface.

He smiled ruefully. His office looked as exotic as the Satin Slipper.

"What the hell?" David muttered beneath his breath. On the floor nearby were his stacks of papers. He picked up a brief, checking it for watermarks and damage. A tiny drop of water dampened one of its corners. "Tessa!" He looked around for her.

"Well, what happened? What did you do?" In his absence, she'd turned his office—his sanctuary and place of business—into a laundry. She'd even gone so far as to hang sheets on a line of kitchen twine in a square around the stove, assuming they'd dry faster that way. Her voice drifted to him from inside the square of sheets.

"I paid my account in full and informed Mrs. Jeffers we won't be doing business with her in the future. Oh, and I told her I thought you were right about the Satin Slipper."

Tessa laughed. "What about the look on her face?"

"You were right about that, too." David chuckled. "It was worth it."

He heard a splash of water. She was obviously doing more laundry. "You did get the supplies first?"

"No." David leaned against the edge of his desk.

"Oh, David . . ." Tessa nearly wailed her dismay.

"What's the matter?"

"You canceled your account without getting our

supplies? That wasn't very smart. I thought you knew better."

"Did you want me to ignore what happened and forgo the pleasure of seeing Margaret's face?" David asked.

Tessa shrugged her shoulders. "To be honest, I'd thought you'd go back and demand the supplies," she told him.

"It was a matter of principle."

"But at least we'd have food on the table and tea to drink and soap for bathing. This is the last of it."

David heard another splash of water and saw, for the first time, the shadowy outline of Tessa's body behind the sheets as she stepped out of the tub. "You're bathing?" He dropped the brief. The pages fluttered to the floor, adding to the general disarray.

She sounded a little breathless. "What did you think I was doing?"

David swallowed hard, watching the shadows as Tessa patted herself dry. "I thought you were doing your laundry." David said the first thing that popped into his mind.

"I finished it. Just the uh . . . unmentionables. Besides, it's Saturday," she concluded as if that explained everything.

"What does Saturday have to do with anything?" Her logic bewildered him.

"I always take a bath on Saturday night. What's the point of putting clean clothes on a dirty body?"

He watched in fascination through the translucent screen as she bent at the waist to wrap a length of toweling around her hair. She must have thought she was in complete privacy, but he couldn't look away. He hunted for an excuse to stay in the room. "Have you mentioned your theory to Coalie?" David's voice was low, thick with emotion. He edged aside one corner of her petticoat and rested more of his weight against the desk. "He doesn't seem to subscribe to your view of cleanliness."

"He's a little boy," Tessa answered. "I've never known one who did." She straightened, lifting her arms to balance the makeshift turban.

David sucked in his breath, then shifted his weight from one leg to the other to accommodate the sudden swelling in his groin. The outline of her perfectly shaped breasts was silhouetted on the sheet. He shifted again, stood up, and began to pace the small space left to him.

"Is Coalie with you?" she asked.

"No, I sent him on an errand." He didn't elaborate, distracted as he was by her veiled movements.

"Oh." She sounded disappointed. "I thought I might talk him into using the tub while the water's warm." Tessa pushed at a sheet and stepped out. She wore her flannel nightgown. It was damp in places where it clung to her skin. David noticed immediately.

The air seemed to thicken around them. Modestly covered, she should have been completely at ease, but she wasn't. And neither, Tessa saw, was David. The unmentionables scattered about the room advertised in dainty white letters that she was naked underneath the night rail. At a loss for words, Tessa struggled to find something to ease the tension. "Would you like it?"

"What?" David was engrossed in the damp white patch marking the valley between her breasts.

"The bathwater," she explained, releasing her wet hair from the towel. "It's still warm."

So was he. And the thought of washing himself in her bathwater did nothing to cool him down. As he spoke, visions of the two of them sharing a bath clouded his brain. "I assumed you'd bathe in your room." He cleared his throat. "Or even the storeroom."

"Those rooms are too cold." Tessa looked up at him and found his handsome face lined in concentration, his dark gaze studying her closely. "And I would've had to carry the water all the way back there. This way, all I had to do was drag the tub in here." Her blue eyes sparkled with pleasure. "More heat. Less work. Simple."

"I never thought of it that way—carrying water back and forth from room to room." When he'd lived in Washington, there were hotel maids to carry water and draw his bath. He wondered, suddenly, who had provided that service for him at home. At the ranch there were no servants, just his mother; his sister, Mary; and Reese's wife, Faith. He'd never given a brimming tub of hot water much thought; it was simply there when he wanted it, waiting. The thought of Mary or Faith carrying water for his bath dismayed David, but the thought of his mother performing the task for her grown, able-bodied son shamed him.

Tessa witnessed the sudden flush of color that stained David's high cheekbones and thought she'd embarrassed him. Yesterday she'd have been delighted at the idea, but today, after all that had happened, it didn't seem right somehow. She set out to put him at ease. "My family always bathed in a tub in the kitchen."

"Your family?" He seemed surprised.

"Not together," Tessa hurried to explain. "We took turns. My mother bathed first, then we girls. After we finished, my father would bathe, followed by the boys." She smiled at the memory. "It was that way every Saturday night."

"In one tub of water?" The concept of sharing the bath with the entire family intrigued him. It seemed like such an intimate thing to do. Such a cozy family activity, to wash in water that had touched so many other bodies. With the exception of a few female companions through the years, David had spent his entire life taking solitary baths.

"Well, we did add more hot water once in a while." Tessa began to work the tangles from her long red hair. David noticed that she'd taken the liberty of borrowing the comb from his dresser set. That somehow heightened the air of intimacy between them. "Even after the others passed away and I left Ireland to come to America, we carried on the Saturday night tradition."

"You and Coalie?"

"No, my brother, Eamon. I lived with him after I arrived in America."

"The one who died?" David remembered her mentioning Eamon earlier.

Tessa's dreamy blue eyes suddenly became sad. But her gaze hardened just as quickly. "Yes. He was killed in an accident," she said quietly, her voice almost a whisper.

"Here?" David didn't remember reading about it in the *Peaceable Chronicle*.

"In Chicago." She tugged the comb through her hair. It caught in the snarls, but she pulled it through anyway.

David winced when he saw the red strands yanked by the teeth of the comb. "Let me." He took the comb from her hand. "Sit down." He grabbed the arm of the chair behind his desk and guided it in front of him. He tapped the back of the chair with the comb.

Tessa seated herself in front of him.

David pulled her wet hair away from her neck and draped it over the back of the chair, then began to work the comb gently through the heavy, wet tresses.

She closed her eyes and let him minister to her.

"Tell me about it," David encouraged. "Tell me about your past."

Tessa began to talk about Ireland, her brother, and the horrible morning the Chicago policemen came to the door. She ended her story with Eamon's wake. Yet she made no mention of Coalie or the journey to Peaceable.

He finished combing her hair and offered her the comb. "Tessa?"

She looked up at him.

"How did you get to Peaceable?"

"My brother had a return train ticket in his pocket. I used it," she answered truthfully.

"Do you have any idea who killed Arnie Mason?" He asked the question almost as an afterthought. The news that her brother had been to Peaceable bothered him.

"I don't know for sure who killed him." Her voice had taken on that hard quality again, each word carefully enunciated. "But I have an idea who might have."

Something in her expression alerted David, gave him the germ of an idea. "You don't think Coalie had anything to do with it, do you? You're not trying to protect him, are you?"

"Don't be ridiculous." Tessa got up from the chair

and began to rip the sheets off the lines and wrap them into tight balls. "Coalie's a little boy. He couldn't kill anyone. I know he couldn't."

"Not even to protect you?"

Tessa avoided his question. "What should I do with the water?"

"Forget the bathwater."

"Do you want it or not?"

I want you. The thought popped into David's head unbidden. But it was true. He wanted her. He wanted the Tessa he'd glimpsed when she talked about her family and her brother. When he took a bath in her water, he wanted it to be because she shared the tub with him. David studied her movements, the way the flannel gown clung to her body, swayed around her legs unencumbered by undergarments. The thick wave of desire struck him like a blow. It took all his concentration just to form a coherent sentence. "I don't want it. I'll go to the bathhouse later."

"Tessa," David asked softly, "what brought you to Peaceable?"

"I told you. My brother had a train ticket. I used it to come to Peaceable." She looked at David. "He had a train ticket and a paid rent receipt in his pocket. For a room at the Satin Slipper."

"How did you know what it was if you couldn't read it?" David asked.

"The nurse at the hospital told me when she gave me Eamon's things," Tessa answered, studying the bathtub. "I think I'll save the water for Coalie. Just in case . . ."

"Don't." David didn't want Coalie sharing Tessa's bathwater. That was an intimacy he'd reserved for himself. "I'll take him to the bathhouse with me." He left his desk, walked over to her, took the sheets out of her hands, and started folding them. "Tessa?"

She bent at the waist once again and began to drag the copper tub away from the stove across the wooden floor.

"Leave it," David ordered. "What is it you aren't telling me?"

"I left Chicago and all its memories," Tessa admitted. She straightened and faced him, looking for some sign of what he was thinking.

"Where does Coalie fit into all of this?" He asked the question that had been bothering him. "He loves you, and you obviously love him. What is he to you?"

"He's mine," she replied fiercely, but something about the way she refused to meet his eyes made him wonder.

"Your son?"

Tessa avoided David's direct gaze. She looked around, anywhere except at David's face. "I do love him. That's what matters." She took a deep breath, aware once again that she'd said more than she intended. "When will Coalie be back?"

David pulled out his watch and looked at it. "Anytime now."

"You didn't send him to the Satin Slipper?" Panic edged her words.

"No," he replied. Tessa was still afraid of someone at the Satin Slipper. Was it Lee? Myra? Charlotte?

Tessa relaxed. All her concern focused on Coalie. "He'll be hungry." She spoke her thoughts aloud. Coalie was always hungry. "What am I going to do about supper?" She turned to David, her blue eyes worried. "You didn't get any food. It isn't for me," she told him. "I can go without. It's for Coalie. I promised he'd never go hungry again."

"You don't have to worry, Tessa. I sent a telegram out today; the supplies are coming Monday morning. And I've arranged for our meals to be provided for us until then." He smiled. "Trust me."

Tessa stared at him, at his warm brown eyes, his smiling mouth, and the dark shadow on his firm jaw. His face had become very dear to her in the last two days, as dear as Coalie's. David Alexander had stood up for her in front of the whole town, supported her. He wanted to help. He had helped. He'd taken her and Coalie in, given them shelter and clothing. Maybe she should try to trust him, if only for Coalie's sake. He had earned a certain amount of loyalty, at least. If only she knew the nature of his relationship with Liam Kincaid.

She smiled at David. "I hope you remembered to order cat food for Greeley."

"Are you telling me how to take care of my cat?" David teased.

Tessa began gathering barely dry unmentionables off the furniture. "I wouldn't dream of telling you what to do." Her eyes sparkled like sapphires as she leaned over to pick up a pair of lacy drawers.

David sat stunned.

Tessa Roarke was teasing him.

CHAPTER 10

Tessa stepped out of her room on Sunday morning and crossed the hall to stand in front of David Alexander's door. She knocked but there was no answer. She waited a moment, then knocked again, harder and louder.

"What?" His voice was rough, sleepy.

"It's time to get up." Tessa's voice reached him through the door.

"What time is it?" David sat up and groped at the nightstand for his watch. He found it, flipped the cover open, and stared at the face until the numbers came into focus. "It's not even seven o'clock yet!" he announced before he snuggled back into the warmth of the bed, pulling the covers over his head.

Tessa listened at the door for a moment. "Are you up?"

"Go away," David grumbled. "Come back at a decent hour."

Taking a deep breath, Tessa tried the doorknob. It turned. She pushed open the door. "It is a decent hour.

You should have been up ages ago." She advanced toward the bed.

David pushed the covers away from his face and sat up.

Tessa's breath came out in a rush when she realized he was not wearing a nightshirt. She stared at his naked chest, fascinated by the ripple of muscles beneath his bronzed skin.

"It's Sunday," David told her, unaware of the effect his nakedness had on Tessa. "My day off. You know, day of rest and all that."

"What about church?" Embarrassed yet curious, she let her gaze wander to the planes of his handsome face. Noting the shadow of his beard darkening the strong lines of his jaw, Tessa quickly glanced at the floor.

"What about it?" Church services weren't high on David's list of priorities. Not since he'd moved to Peaceable. He preferred to sleep late on Sunday mornings and enjoy the relative quiet of the town when everyone else was at the Sunday services. He didn't like to be reminded that his family was a short train ride away at church in Cheyenne.

"Aren't you going?" Tessa asked. She had gone to Sunday mass all her life. The idea of anyone not going shocked her. Even the girls at the Satin Slipper attended Sunday services. They all dressed up and marched to the Methodist church and sat in the last pew, near the door. They were the last to enter and the first to leave every Sunday. Tessa, Coalie, and two other girls from the saloon walked to the tiny building on the edge of town at eight o'clock in the morning two Sundays a month when Father Joseph stopped and said mass in Peaceable before boarding the train for other churches along the way west.

"No," David said. "I'm not going to church. I'm going back to sleep." He slid down in the bed and pulled the quilts over his chest, but he let his gaze roam over her. From his position in the bed, he had a unique view of the underside of her calico-covered breasts. They were magnificent. "You're a little over-dressed," David teased. "But you're welcome to join me under the covers."

"I'm going to church." David's naughty invitation sent color rushing up to Tessa's face.

"Fine," David said agreeably. "Close the door on your way out." He pulled the quilt up over his face, covering his eyes.

"Oh, no, you're not!" Tessa marched out the door into the office.

David heard the creak of the pump minutes before Tessa returned to his room.

"Are you going to get up?" she asked as she approached the bed again.

He slowly pushed back the quilt, opened his eyes, and looked up at her. She stood next to his bed, holding a pitcher of water over him at a threatening angle.

"You wouldn't."

Tessa tilted the pitcher slightly. A drop of ice-cold water landed on David's top lip. He licked it off.

She leaned forward to watch as his tongue captured the moisture.

Bending over was a mistake. David moved with the swiftness of a cat. He reached out from beneath the covers and grabbed Tessa's arm. Water splashed against his chest as he jerked her toward him. She let go of the pitcher. David batted it away with his free hand. It bounced off the bed and landed on the floor with a crash. Shards of glazed pottery scattered across the woven rug and the wooden floor.

Tessa landed on top of David's hard body.

"Have you thought about what you're going to do next, contessa?" David asked, staring up at her. Her china-blue eyes were wide with surprise, and her pink, pouting lips, though slightly open, were quiet for a change. "No?" He placed his hands on her waist and pulled her closer. "Too bad. Because I have," he murmured an instant before his mouth found hers.

Tessa felt the heat of his body penetrating her green dress, but it was nothing compared to the heat of his mouth. She tasted him, feeling the rasp of his tongue against her teeth as it slipped between her lips into her mouth. She felt the urgency of his mouth and echoed it, moving her lips on his, allowing him greater access. Tessa moved her own tongue, then experienced the jolt of pure pleasure as it found and mated with David's. She tightened her grip on his wide shoulders, drawing little circles against his feverish skin, then trailed her fingers up the column of his neck and buried them in the thick black silk of his hair.

David caressed her back through the fabric of her dress. The green calico hampered him, frustrated him. He wanted to feel the softness of her flesh beneath the layers of clothing. He wanted to move his hands over her, count her ribs, and test the weight of those wonderful pear-shaped breasts, but all he could really feel was cotton. Too much cotton, masking the curves pressed against him. He moved his hand down her back, over one firm buttock, to the back of her thigh. He fumbled with her skirt until he'd raised the hem and could slide his hand underneath. He made his way through the petticoats until his palm rested against the curve of her bottom while his mouth moved over hers.

Rolling Tessa over onto her back, David reversed their positions. He stopped kissing her mouth long enough to press warm kisses against her jawline, her neck, and beneath one ear.

Tessa gasped when his probing tongue explored the contours of her ear. She was hot, breathless, light-headed. She whimpered, seeking his mouth.

David took that as a sign of encouragement. Becoming bolder, he found the lace-edged leg of her drawers, then slipped his hand up under it.

Tessa pulled away. "What are you doing?" she murmured against his lips.

"I want to touch you," David answered. "I want to undress you and spend the morning kissing you all over. Your lips, your eyes, your breasts." His dark brown eyes found each part of her as he listed his desires.

Tessa's eyes widened with each husky word, then darkened to a deeper blue as his meaning became clearer. Feeling the hot flush of color staining her face, Tessa pressed her forehead against his neck. She moaned a little and wiggled against his hand, urging him to greater liberties.

He touched her hipbone, fingers teasing the sensitive flesh.

"David!"

"Yes, Tessa." He bent closer and kissed her mouth, hard.

She kissed him back, now familiar with the texture of his lips and the hot taste of his mouth.

"Some people worship God in churches," David said, his warm breath fanning her face as he nibbled at her lower lip. "And some worship in other ways. I think this is why God created Sundays."

"Sunday," Tessa repeated, stiffening in his arms, as awareness of their situation drifted back to her.

David silently cursed his wayward tongue for reminding her of the day.

Flushing, she pushed at his chest. "It's the in-between Sunday. If you don't hurry, we'll miss the train for Cheyenne."

He eased his weight off her. She sat up, then scrambled off the bed. She stood beside his dresser and glanced in the mirror. The bodice of her dress was wet from his chest, her skirt creased.

"I'm not going to church in Cheyenne," David said. "You go."

"I can't," Tessa informed him. "Not without you."

"Why not?" David pushed himself up and leaned against the headboard. He stretched, then rubbed his chest.

"Because . . ." Watching him, Tessa stuttered, losing her train of thought. "Because you made me promise not to go near the depot or the stage office. I can't leave Peaceable without you."

"Go to church in town instead. I'll give you permission."

"It's the in-between Sunday," Tessa repeated. "The priest only comes to town two Sundays a month. On the other Sundays we have to go to Cheyenne or one of the other towns along the railroad. But Cheyenne's closest."

"Does church mean that much to you?" David swung his legs off the side of the bed. They were bare, as was the rest of him. He kept a grip on the covers, anchoring them across his lap. From the look on her face and the throbbing in his groin, David decided he wasn't going to get any more sleep.

"I never miss church."

David gave in. "I'll be ready in half an hour." He supposed it wouldn't hurt to ask God for help on Tessa's behalf.

"But we'll miss the train. We'll be late."

"I know what time church starts in Cheyenne," he informed her. "We're not going there." He was willing to take Tessa to church if that's what she wanted, but not in Cheyenne.

"But . . ." The Catholic church in Cheyenne was the largest in the area and the loveliest.

David held up his hand to halt her arguments. "We'll go west. Surely there's a church in one of the other towns along the line." He reached for his robe lying across the foot of the bed. "Tessa," he said when she made no move toward the door, "I'm as bare as a newborn baby beneath these covers. I can't get up until you leave."

"Oh!"

He smiled. "Yes, 'oh.' " His dark brown eyes crinkled at the corners. "Why don't you check on Coalie's progress?"

"Coalie's dressed already," Tessa replied. "He's gone to get our breakfast from the hotel." Still she continued to stand where she was, fascinated by the sight of him.

"A cup of coffee would be nice," David suggested. "And some water. Hot, this time. For shaving."

"All right." She backed toward the door.

"And, Tessa." His voice was husky, deep with meaning. "Much obliged for the morning kiss."

She flushed, looking at him, staring at his lips,

remembering their magic. Tessa swung around, then hurried out the door.

David heard the clatter in the kitchen as she banged around at the stove. He stood up and shrugged into his robe as he walked to the washstand. "Ouch, dammit!" David's curses carried into the main room, reaching Tessa's ears.

"Stop your cursing on Sunday. It's blasphemy," she called from the kitchen.

"I stepped on a piece of the water pitcher," David shouted. "I cut my foot, and it hurts like hell!" If he expected sympathy, he was disappointed. He hopped to the bed and sat on the edge.

Walking back to his door, she peeked in and watched as David propped his injured foot on his other knee and began a tentative search for the fragment. "You should be more careful," she finally said.

"You're the one who dropped the pitcher." He sucked in a breath when he touched the tiny shard.

"You saw me do it." Tessa smiled at him. "You made me do it." She entered the room and knelt beside him. Brushing his hand aside, she began gently probing the wound. "Let me."

"Stop! I'll do it." He cradled his foot.

"Don't be such a baby!" she snapped.

She found the sliver and pulled it out. A tiny speck of blood dotted the wound.

"Ouch! Dam—"

"Watch your mouth!" Tessa scolded. "It's a good thing we're going to church." She tossed a length of towel at him. "You can ask forgiveness for your foul mouth."

Tessa felt his dark-eyed stare and looked up to find him watching her.

David reached out and touched her hair, neatly coiled in a thick braid around her head. "What about you, contessa?"

"What about me?" She couldn't take her gaze away from his lips.

"Are you going to ask forgiveness for my mouth?" He leaned forward to kiss her. "For the things it does to you?"

She saw it coming, yet she made no effort to move away. "I told you to watch your mouth," she reminded him.

"You watch it for me," he answered, tasting her lips for the second time and finding them sweeter than before.

David was almost dressed by the time Coalie returned with breakfast.

Coalie set the basket of food on the table, and Tessa took out a sealed milk pail and a selection of pastries. She poured milk into cups for Coalie and herself, then poured a cup of coffee for David.

"I brought some breakfast from the hotel," Coalie announced as David entered the room. "All kinds of pastries. See?" He waved a doughnut around. The boy's green eyes sparkled at the display of sweets.

David's eyes sought Tessa's, his gaze locking with hers before he turned his attention back to Coalie. "I'm not much of a pastry eater. You and Tessa go ahead and enjoy them. I'll just have coffee." He nodded his thanks as Tessa set a cup and saucer down in front of him.

She seated herself next to Coalie and selected a sugar-coated confection. "You're sure you don't want any?"

He grinned at her, arching one eyebrow.

She felt the flush of color staining her face.

"No, thanks. I've already had my breakfast sweet." He noticed the becoming pink on her cheeks, then concentrated on her mouth, where a bit of powdered sugar clung to her lips. He ached to lick it off.

"What kind?" Coalie's question caught both of them by surprise.

"A very special kind," David answered.

"Hurry," Tessa responded, tearing her gaze away from David and turning to Coalie. "Eat your breakfast. We don't have much time."

Coalie gobbled up his doughnut, then washed it down with a gulp of milk.

"It's all right, son," David said. "You can slow down a bit. We're not in that much of a hurry." He spoke to Coalie, but his next words were meant for Tessa. "We have plenty of time."

Late in the afternoon, after mass and a huge Sunday dinner at a restaurant, Tessa, Coalie, and David boarded the train in Buford for the return trip to Peaceable. Coalie immediately dozed off, his head in Tessa's lap.

Tessa smiled up at the man sitting beside her. It was easy to pretend they were a family returning from a Sunday afternoon excursion just like so many other farm families.

"It was a lovely day," Tessa said.

"Yes," David agreed, "it was."

"Then you didn't mind taking us?"

"No, Tessa, I didn't mind," David admitted, "though I never dreamed we'd have to go all the way to Buford to catch up with the good padre."

"We could have gone into Cheyenne," Tessa reminded him.

"No." His tone of voice carried an edge. "We couldn't have. I have family and friends there I'd rather not see."

"Why not? Are you ashamed to have all your big-city friends see Coalie and me?"

"It's nothing to do with you," David answered. "It's me."

"What did you do that was so bad?" Tessa asked, wondering what his answer would be. She wondered if he'd admit to keeping secrets, maybe even admit to being friends with Liam Kincaid. "What's any worse than being accused of killing a man?"

David faced her, the expression in his dark eyes painful in its intensity. "Seeing the look in the eyes of your loved ones and knowing you've disappointed them. Knowing they're ashamed of you."

Tessa suddenly understood that David Alexander did have secrets. He spoke from bitter experience, and her heart went out to him.

CHAPTER 11

"Open up!" The pounding on the front door startled Tessa. "Open up, David Jordan Alexander. I know you're in there, and you've got some explaining to do."

Tessa debated whether or not she should open the door, then decided it would be all right, since the voice of the caller was female. She pinned her braid into place then pulled the sash of her borrowed robe tighter around her waist. It was early in the morning for visitors, but the woman obviously knew David Alexander and had no intention of leaving. Tessa padded across the office to the door. Horace Greeley trotted along beside her.

Tessa turned the key in the lock and swung open the door.

"Oh!" Mary Alexander stared. The woman in the doorway of David's law office was lovely. A thick braid of red hair circled her head like a coronet. Her ivory skin was smooth, unblemished, and her eyes were a lovely shade of blue. That she had been asleep was apparent, as was the fact that she'd spent the night—she was wearing one of David's silk robes. "I'd like to speak with my brother." Mary's voice was cool, full of teacherlike authority, as she stepped forward.

"He's not here." Tessa studied David Alexander's sister. There was quite a family resemblance, from the dark hair and brown eyes down to the dimple in her chin.

"I'll wait," Mary said, "if you don't mind."

Tessa stepped back to allow her entrance into the office. "Let me take your coat."

Mary shrugged out of her wool coat and handed it to Tessa.

She took the garment, walked across the office, and hung it on a hook. Tessa motioned toward the coffee-pot simmering on the stove. "David left coffee."

"Thank you."

Tessa walked to the cupboard and removed a cup and saucer and placed them on the table across from her own glass of milk before lifting the pot from the stove. "Sit down, please," Tessa said, as she poured the coffee.

Mary seated herself at the table.

Tessa put the pot back on the stove, then offered her hand to the other woman. "I'm Tessa Roarke."

"Mary Alexander. David's sister." Mary let go of her hand. "Then you must be . . ."

"The saloon girl accused of murder," Tessa answered, sitting down at the table.

Mary blushed. "I was going to say, 'David's new client.' "

"Oh." Tessa refused to show any embarrassment. "Yes, well, I guess I am."

"So the rumors are true?" Mary admired her poise.

"What rumors?"

"The rumors that you and David are . . . well . . . sharing these quarters." Mary sipped at her coffee.

"I am a client," Tessa said raising her chin. "I was released into your brother's custody. He brought us here because we had no place else to go."

"We?"

"Coalie and I."

"Who's Coalie?"

Tessa looked Mary straight in the eyes. "My little boy."

"Really? How old?" Mary showed genuine interest. "I'm a teacher. David asked me to lend him some beginning readers and a slate."

"He did?" Tessa asked. "And you brought them all the way from Cheyenne?"

Mary laughed. "I wasn't supposed to bring them; I was supposed to send them. David isn't expecting me. I planned to surprise him. To get the books he was going to have to talk to me. Where is he?"

"At the courthouse, I think. He said something about arranging my hearing date." Greeley jumped into Tessa's lap, and she began to stroke his fur. She faced David's sister, her expression earnest. "I didn't kill anyone, but no one except Coalie and your brother believes me."

Uncomfortable with the direction of the conversation, Mary tactfully changed the subject. "How old is your boy? David's note said beginning readers. I wasn't sure what age."

"Coalie's nine."

"Does he go to school in town?"

"Not yet," Tessa said. "I wanted to send Coalie to school this morning but I'm . . ." She looked at Mary.

She seemed sympathetic, trustworthy. "I'm afraid he might not be safe in school right now." Tessa attempted an explanation of sorts. "I mean with what's happened. There are some bad feelings around town."

Mary saw the glimmer of apprehension in Tessa Roarke's eyes. It was bad enough to be charged with murder, but to have to worry about the safety of her child as well . . . No wonder David had taken them in. Mary reached across the table and patted Tessa's hand. "I understand. There's no reason he can't learn his lessons at home just as easily as he would at school."

The door opened, and Liam Kincaid stepped inside, closing the door behind him. He looked around and found Tessa Roarke sitting at the table with another woman. He tipped his hat. "Morning," he said. "I was at the depot getting the liquor shipment for the Satin Slipper when your supplies came in on the train. I had 'em loaded onto my wagon. Thought it would save you some time and money if I brought them by."

"That's very kind of you—" Mary began.

"Get out!" Tessa sprang from her chair, startling Greeley, who bounced off her lap and ran for the safety of Tessa's bedroom.

Tessa paused long enough to grab the coffee pot before she advanced on Liam, weapon in hand.

"What?" Lee was astonished by her reaction. She looked as if she'd seen the devil.

"Get out! I said get out! We don't want any help from you," Tessa shouted. "Stay away from me! Stay away from Coalie!" Tessa swung the coffee pot. Coffee spewed from the lid and splattered one sleeve of Liam's coat.

"What the hell's the matter with you?" Lee side-stepped to avoid being hit by the enameled pot. "Just wait a minute. You've got this all wrong." He took another step. Forward this time.

But Mary entered the fray. "You heard her," she told the tall blond man. "She asked you to leave."

"Listen, lady," Lee began. "I don't know what's going on here, but I assure you—"

"I assure you you'll be sporting two holes if you come any closer." Mary spoke softly.

Lee glanced down to where Mary held a two-shot derringer. The silver muzzle glinted dangerously.

"Easy, lady. It doesn't take much to make those things go off." Lee mentally began measuring the distance between Mary's hand and his own.

"I know," Mary replied. She kept her gaze locked on Lee. She caught the glint in his eye and interpreted it correctly. "I wouldn't try it if I were you," she warned.

"Tessa? What's wrong?" Coalie's voice sounded from the hall.

Tessa whirled around. "Go back! Go to my room, Coalie! Lock the door!" Tessa blanched; her breath came in gasps.

"But, Tessa—"

"Do it!" Tessa ordered.

Tessa heard Coalie run to her room and slam the door. She held her breath as he locked it.

"All right?" Mary spared a quick glance at Tessa and saw that she'd begun to breathe easier.

Tessa nodded, noticing for the first time that David's sister had a gun pointed at Liam Kincaid. She said the first thing that came to mind. "Where did you get that?"

"My pocket. I always carry a derringer when I travel." Mary kept her eyes on the handsome man. "So I'm ready for any emergency. Where do you want him?"

"Outside," Tessa said.

"Okay," Mary directed Lee, "back up slowly toward the door."

Lee did as he was told.

"Tessa, open the door for him. But stay out of his reach."

Tessa hurried to open the door.

"Out you go," Mary ordered. "One step at a time."

Lee backed up another step, right into David Alexander.

"What the devil is going on here?" David demanded.

"Ask her," Lee suggested a moment before Mary came into David's line of vision. "I'm damned if I know. All I did was deliver a wagonload of supplies from the depot."

David looked around Lee and saw his sister brandishing her little silver gun. "It's always good to see you, Mary, but this visit is unexpected." He smiled at her. "Do you mind telling me why you're here?"

Tessa, right behind Mary, answered for her. "She came to see you. She brought some schoolbooks. It's a good thing she was here, too, because *he* walked right in as bold as brass without knocking."

"This is a business office," Lee said. "Open to the unsuspecting public."

"Be quiet, mister," Mary directed, motioning with the gun.

"That's enough of that." David took control. "Hand me the gun, Mary." He held out his hand.

"David . . ."

"He's right, you know," David told her. "This is a business." He glared at his sister. "You'll be lucky if this gentleman doesn't press charges against you."

"Gentleman? Hah!" Tessa snorted. "He doesn't know the meaning of the word. Chasing women and children across the country like he does, scaring the wits out of them, hunting them down."

"What are you talking about?" Lee demanded of Tessa, before turning to David. "What's she mean by that?"

"You know what I mean," Tessa informed him. "You and your blood money."

"Enough, Tessa." David was fast losing patience. "All right, Mary, if you won't give me the gun, put it away."

Mary reluctantly did as he asked, placing the weapon in her pocket.

David spoke to Tessa, then Mary. "You two, wait inside. I'll escort Mr. Kincaid wherever he wants to go." David motioned for Lee to move outside, then followed him out the door.

"Do you mind explaining what was going on back there?" David asked as soon as he and Lee were out of sight of his office. They turned the corner into the alley.

"Damned if I know." Lee shook his head as if trying to clear it. He leaned against the side wall of the bank. It was embarrassing to admit he'd been attacked by a woman wielding a hot coffee pot and even more embarrassing to be thrown out of an office by a woman with a two-shot derringer.

"What were you doing at my office?"

"I brought you a report on Arnie Mason from the

agency. I thought it might be helpful to your case. The supplies you ordered were sitting at the depot." Lee shrugged his shoulders. "They seemed like a plausible reason for a stranger to show up at your office. At the time."

David nodded in agreement. "So what went wrong?"

"I opened the door . . ." Lee paused to recall what else he had done. "I opened the door, I said good morning, and she came at me with a coffee pot."

"Who?"

"That hellion you call a client."

David smiled. "I get the feeling she doesn't like you. What did you do to her while she worked at the saloon?"

"Nothing," Lee swore. "She stayed out of my way, avoided me at every turn as if I had some catching disease."

"Well, something about you sets her off," David commented. "You must have done something. She must have seen you somewhere before."

Lee paused for a moment, weighing the information. "Look, David, I knew who she was even before I got to Peaceable. I followed her from Chicago."

"On agency orders?" David asked. "Is she under suspicion? Wanted for something?"

"She's clean as far as I know," Lee assured him. "Except for Arnie Mason. But she happens to be the sister of a Pinkerton man, a detective who was killed in Chicago a couple of months back."

"Eamon," David guessed.

"Yes, Eamon Roarke," Lee confirmed. "He was working on a case here in Peaceable. The same case I'm working on now."

"Was Roarke's death an accident?" David wondered.

"If it was, it was a damned convenient one. Eamon was on to something big. Stagecoach robberies, illegal whiskey, gun smuggling . . . just to list a few."

David whistled beneath his breath. "What about Tessa? What's she doing in Peaceable?"

"I don't know," Lee admitted, "but she left Chicago in a hurry. I followed her because I promised her brother I'd look out for her."

"What about her husband?"

"According to Eamon, she's a spinster."

"But the boy," David said. "She told me Coalie was her son."

"He's not her son," Lee explained. "There were just the two of them, Eamon and Tessa, from the time she came over from Ireland five or six years ago until he got killed."

"So she lied."

"Looks like. I know that boy isn't hers. He wasn't with her in Chicago. Just here in Peaceable."

"You know a hell of a lot about her and her brother," David commented.

"That's because Eamon was always telling me about his sister—Tessa this and Tessa that. I think he was trying to do some matchmaking 'cause he asked me for a picture to show his sister." Lee smiled at the memory. "Anyway, before he died, he made me promise to look out for her." Lee fixed his gaze on David. "And I've tried. I tried to be nice to her but I swear that woman hated me on sight. She avoided me at the Satin Slipper and was downright hostile to me when she couldn't. She's made it damn near impossible to look after her. I sure as hell don't want anything to do with anyone else's sister."

David raked his fingers through his hair. "I know what you mean." He looked at his friend. "And you don't have to look out for Tessa any longer, Lee. She's my responsibility now. I'll take care of her."

"Be my guest," Lee invited. "You're welcome to that other she-devil, too." Lee rubbed absently at a spot on his flat stomach. The spot the bullets would have entered had she decided to pull the trigger. It hurt just thinking about it. He shuddered. "I don't know who the hell she is."

David laughed. "I do."

Lee glared at him.

"My sister, Mary."

"That figures." Lee rolled his eyes.

David clapped him on the back. "How about lunch? I'll buy. We can say it was my way of appeasing you, to keep you from pressing charges against Mary after she pulled her gun on you."

"Nah, it's too risky," Lee answered. "Besides, I'm due back at the Satin Slipper before noon." Lee patted his pockets, feeling for his gold watch. "What time is it, anyway?"

David removed his and checked the time. "Twelve after eleven. Where's your timepiece?" Lee always sported an expensive watch.

"It's at the jeweler's," Lee explained. "I snagged the chain and broke it and the crystal. I told the watchmaker that chain was too delicate for my watch."

David hated the thought that came to mind, but he wondered suddenly who was lying and who was telling the truth. And he also wondered if the piece of gold chain in his top desk drawer belonged to Lee Kincaid.

* * *

"I think you should go with Mary to the ranch," Tessa said to Coalie when he unlocked her bedroom door and came out.

"I want to stay with you," Coalie told her.

"It's just for a little while." Tessa knelt on the floor in front of Coalie, pleading with him to understand. "I can't look after you properly until this is all over—this thing with the man at the Satin Slipper, the dead man." She hated to say his name. She hated to even think about him.

"I'll look after you." Coalie wrapped his arms around her neck and hugged her tightly. "It's my turn."

"Please, Coalie," she whispered. "If Liam Kincaid comes back I may not be able to protect you."

Mary looked first at Tessa, then at Coalie, studying them closely. There was no doubt Tessa loved the boy and that he returned her love, but there was no family resemblance. After witnessing Tessa's outburst and her fear and hearing her accusations against Liam Kincaid, it wasn't hard for Mary to put the pieces of the puzzle together. "Coalie's not your son, is he?"

Tessa whirled around, facing Mary, a denial on her lips.

"Did you take him away from his parents?" Mary demanded an answer.

"No," Tessa said softly. "I rescued him from a brutal drunkard who beat him every day."

"We run away," Coalie added. "Me and Tessa. We run away so I'd be safe."

Mary looked at Tessa with new awareness, her gaze full of admiration for Tessa's unselfishness and courage. "And now this Mr. Kincaid is following you?"

Tessa nodded. "I'm sure there must be a reward for

Coalie's return. Kincaid will want to collect it."

"I ain't going to no ranch," Coalie announced. "I ain't leaving Peaceable without you."

"Please, Coalie," Tessa pleaded. "What if Kincaid comes back? What if I can't stop him from returning you to Chicago?"

"David won't let him," Coalie replied confidently.

"What if David isn't here? Like this morning? What then?" Tessa hugged him closer. "Oh, Coalie, I love you. I don't want to lose you. I don't want you to be hurt or lonely or frightened ever again. Please say you'll go with Mary just for a while, to see if you like it." Tessa brushed away her tears.

"Aw, Tessa . . ." Coalie shifted his weight from one foot to the other. "Don't cry."

Mary stepped forward and put her hand on Coalie's shoulder. "It won't be for long, Coalie. It can be just a visit. You can meet the other children—Joy and Hope and the twins, Jimmy and Kate. And my brother, Sam, can teach you to ride a horse."

"It won't be for long?" Coalie looked to Tessa for confirmation.

"No," she said.

"And I can come back if I don't like it?"

"Of course. I'll come and get you myself. Nothing will stop me."

"You promise?"

"I promise," Tessa answered. "And when this is over, we'll go on with our plans to find a house and garden with a few sheep to tend, just like we dreamed."

"All right, then." Coalie agreed. "I do like horses. Always wanted to ride one."

Tessa took a shaky breath and stood up. "Then it's

settled." She bit her lip to keep from crying again.

"Let's shake on it," Coalie suggested. And the three of them—Coalie, Tessa, and Mary—clasped hands.

Mary waited until Coalie went back to the storeroom to gather his belongings before she voiced her concerns. "I'm not sure this is best. I'm willing to take him," she said, "only because I don't like seeing children threatened. But you have to do something for me in return."

"I'll do my best," Tessa cautiously replied.

"It's not so much to ask," Mary continued. "I just want you to persuade David to visit the ranch more often. We've missed him since he moved to Peaceable. He stays away purposely, and there's absolutely no need. We know he didn't do anything wrong, and we're waiting to listen whenever David's ready to talk about it."

"Did you tell him that?" Tessa asked softly.

"Well, no," Mary admitted, "but of course David knows better than to think we'd believe rumors and innuendo." How much did Tessa Roarke know about the scandal in Washington? she wondered.

Tessa looked Mary right in the eyes. "Does he?"

Mary was impressed by Tessa's insight. "How much do you know about my brother?"

"Not much," Tessa admitted. "But I know how it feels when people look at you with pity in their eyes, wondering all the time if you really did the things they heard. Maybe David thinks you look at him that way. Do you?".

Mary ignored the question, though she recognized the fact that Tessa had given her food for thought. "Well, I'd better be going. I'd rather not face David right now."

Tessa nodded. "You'll take care of Coalie?"

"I'll protect him with my life."

"Good," Tessa said, "because if anything happens to him . . ." She let the rest trail off.

"Nothing will happen," Mary assured her. She called to Coalie. "It's time to go."

Coalie joined them in the office, pulling himself up to his full height in a manly posture, years older than his age. "Are you sure this is best, Tessa?"

"No," she confided, "I'm not sure, but I think so." She tried to smile in encouragement. "I hope so."

Coalie nodded. "Okay."

Mary walked to the front door. Coalie followed. At the door, Mary turned back to speak to Tessa. "You know, when I heard about David taking a saloon girl on as a client, I was fully prepared to dislike you."

"I understand," Tessa said.

"But I was wrong," Mary continued. "You're quite a lady. Good-bye, Tessa Roarke."

"Bye," Tessa said. "See you soon."

Coalie ran back to her and hugged her once more around the waist. "It won't be for long," he reminded her. "Just till this is over. Don't cry."

Tessa sniffled.

"I love you, Tessa," Coalie said, trying to control his own tears. "Don't forget to come and get me."

"I won't," she promised.

"Good-bye, then."

"Good-bye." Tessa waited until Mary and Coalie were out of sight before she allowed all her tears to flow. She'd done the right thing, she told herself. It was best for Coalie. Mary would keep him safe at the ranch. He'd be treated as a member of the family. Mary had promised.

Coalie's future was secure. Tessa could breathe a little easier. He was safe and no matter what happened to her at the hearing, Coalie would have a real home and a family of his own. He wouldn't have to work to support himself.

Work. Tessa suddenly remembered the chores David was paying Coalie to do. She squared her shoulders and bit her lip. David might not like it, but she wouldn't allow those chores to go undone. He and Coalie had made a bargain. Tessa planned to see that the terms were fulfilled. She was going to do Coalie's chores herself. Then David wouldn't have any reason to complain about taking her on as a client.

And somehow she'd find a way to prove her innocence to David and to the rest of the citizens of Peaceable.

CHAPTER 12

Tessa was struggling to maneuver a fifty-pound bag of flour off the rear of the wagon when David returned.

"What the devil do you think you're doing?"

"Unloading supplies." Tessa grasped the bag and tried once again to lift it.

David took the bag out of her hands and hefted it onto his own shoulder. "I'll do it."

Tessa didn't look at him. She climbed into the back of the wagon and grabbed the corners of another sack. "I don't need your help."

"Maybe not," David conceded, "but that's what you're going to get." He watched as Tessa doggedly tugged on a bag of sugar. "Leave it."

Tessa ignored him.

"Dammit, Tessa, can't you do as I ask for once?" He balanced the sack of flour. "You and Mary are two of a kind. Mule-headed stubborn. Where do you want this?"

"Inside."

David carried the flour inside the office. Except for Horace Greeley, sunning himself on David's desk, the place was unoccupied. It was quiet. Too quiet after the earlier excitement.

He lowered the sack of flour onto the table and walked back outside to the wagon. "Where's Mary?"

"She's gone." Tessa busied herself sorting the supplies.

"That figures." David raked his fingers through his thick black hair. "Since I specifically asked her to wait here until I got back." He'd missed his sister and would've liked to spend some time with her. Her leaving so abruptly disappointed him, but Mary was known for doing the opposite of whatever he asked. David looked at Tessa. "Did she tell you why she was leaving?"

"She thought it best to go quickly." Tessa turned to face him. "Before I changed my mind."

Her eyes were red-rimmed and swollen from crying.

"You're crying because my sister left?"

"No."

Prickles of alarm lifted the fine hair on the back of David's neck. Few things had the power to make Tessa cry. But Coalie was one of them. "Where's Coalie?" He looked around. "Has something happened to him?"

"I sent him away."

"You sent Coalie away?" David stood up, then raked his fingers through his black hair. "Where?"

Tessa smoothed her hair back off her face and rubbed at the wrinkles in her skirt. "I don't know," she said evasively. "I told Mary to take him someplace safe. Away from here. I didn't ask where."

"But you love him," David replied. "Why send him away?"

"Because I love him," Tessa answered fiercely, grabbing hold of one of the crates. "Because I'll do anything to protect him."

"Protect him from what?"

She shoved the crate with all her might. "Liam Kincaid." Tessa glared at David. "He wants to take Coalie away from me."

David caught the crate before it slid off the back of the wagon. "Why would he want to do that?" he asked. "Why would a bartender want to take a boy away from his mother?"

He knew. David knew. Something in his tone of voice warned Tessa he had learned her secret. And now that he knew, would he continue to help her or hold it against her?

"Tessa, answer me. Why would Lee . . . Liam want to take Coalie away from you?"

"I don't know," she answered defensively. "I just know he does."

"I don't think so."

Tessa shot him an angry look. "I don't care what you think. He's after Coalie. I know it. He followed us from Chicago. He was on the same train."

"It could have been a coincidence. There were lots of people on the Chicago train." David had heard Lee's version of the story. Now he hoped Tessa would trust him enough to give him her version. He didn't want to believe she would deliberately implicate Lee any more than he wanted to believe Lee would point a finger at Tessa.

"And most of the passengers got off in Cheyenne," Tessa informed him. "Only three people left the train in Peaceable. Me, Coalie, and Liam Kincaid." She threw David a smug glance. "He followed us."

"You could have followed *him*," David suggested.

"Don't be daft. I came to Peaceable because I thought—" She stopped abruptly, ending the discussion.

David picked up one of the crates and carried it into the office, then returned to the wagon for another one. This was the opportunity he'd been waiting for. David knew he could press Tessa for the answers he needed. Tessa knew it as well. But he decided not to press her. He decided to be patient long enough for Tessa to tell him her story on her own. That was what he wanted. He wanted her to trust him. Taking a deep breath, David decided to change the subject. "Maybe it's best you sent Coalie away." He told her on his second trip. He'd tried to think of a better way to tell her, but the words slipped out with no warning. "Your hearing's a week from today."

Tin cans rolled in every direction as a box of canned goods slipped from her grasp. "So soon?"

"The circuit judge is making his rounds. He'll hear all the cases since his last visit, including yours."

"What will happen?" Tessa knelt in the bed of the wagon and began gathering the cans.

"The attorney for the territory will submit the evidence against you. We'll present ours. Then the judge will decide if there's enough evidence to hold you for trial." David picked up a can and handed it to her.

"Is there?" Tessa asked.

"I'm afraid there might be," David answered truthfully. "We'll need all the help we can get. I need *your* help," he added gently.

Tessa thrust the armload of canned goods at him, then picked up a small box. She jumped down from the wagon, box in hand, and started for the door of the office.

"We're not finished," David reminded her, his arms full of food. "Where are you going?"

"To make some tea." Tessa waved the box at him. "I wasn't planning to unload everything. I just wanted to find the tea. My mother always said problems seemed clearer over a cup of strong tea." She paused in the doorway, turning to look at David. "I need to see my way clear."

David followed her inside. He set the canned goods on the table next to the flour and watched as Tessa filled a kettle with water for tea. Now that Coalie was gone, she'd have to deal with him. He needed more answers.

"I'm sorry about Coalie, Tessa. I know you'll miss him. I'll miss him, too. But I think you're wrong about Kincaid." David watched her expressive face for a reaction. "He doesn't seem like the sort of person who would steal a child."

"People steal children for lots of reasons." Tessa spoke as if she knew. "Sometimes they steal them when their owners won't let them go."

"Owners?" David asked. "Don't you mean parents?"

"No. I mean owners—men who take little children from orphanages, then put them to work at all sorts of horrible jobs." The water began to boil. Tessa lifted the kettle from the stove and set it aside while she measured the tea.

"Coalie isn't your son. Why did you steal him?" David asked softly.

Tessa stopped.

"Give me a reason, Tessa. One simple reason." He recognized the look in her eyes. It was the same look she'd worn yesterday morning when he kissed her—cautious and wary, yet soft, vulnerable. He wanted to take her in his arms again and kiss away the fears, the apprehension.

"Because his owner beat him." She whispered the words quietly, defeated. She'd been holding them inside too long. "Because that angry brute of a man beat Coalie every single day of his life. For working too slow, for working too fast, for smiling, for crying, for breathing. I was afraid one day he'd kill him. I used to watch for Coalie from my window every morning. He delivered coal to our apartment." Tessa sighed. She knew she was taking a chance, but she was willing to gamble. By now Coalie was far away from Liam Kincaid. She would trust David with her story and hope he understood why she'd had to break the law. And hope too that David wasn't working with Liam.

"Of course," David murmured in awe. He should've guessed. "Coalie."

"Yes," Tessa said, "that's what he was called, 'the coalie.' The boy who delivers the coal. He doesn't remember his real name. Just Coalie."

"So he came to your apartment? That's how you met him."

"Yes. He was so thin. I'd always save him a pastry or two for breakfast. You know how Coalie loves sweets." She smiled. "Eamon and I lived above a bakery, you see, and I often bought day-old bread and pastries." Tessa spooned tea leaves into the teapot. "Would you like some tea?"

David nodded. "After all the trouble you've gone to to get it, why not? If you guarantee it will help me see my way clear, too." He managed a smile.

She added another spoonful of tea to the pot. "I tried to buy Coalie's work contract. I spent nearly all my savings. I couldn't bear the thought of waking up one morning to find another little boy delivering the coal. The man Coalie worked for was so mean and big."

"Like Arnie Mason?"

"Bigger." Tessa shuddered. "Coalie nearly always had a black eye and horrible bruises."

David walked to the table. He pushed the sack of flour to one end and stacked the crates on top of one another, clearing space.

Tessa placed the mismatched cups and saucers and two spoons on the table. "Sit down," she directed.

David seated himself in his usual chair.

Tessa carried the teapot to the table and leaned over him. She liked performing this homey task. She felt a tingle of excitement race through her when she brushed against his shoulder. Her hand trembled a little as she poured the tea.

She filled his cup, then sat down across from him and poured some for herself.

David took a sip of the tea, shuddering at the strong, bitter taste. It was awful, but he couldn't bear to hurt her feelings by telling her. He'd drink it. Somehow. "I left the sugar on the wagon," he remembered, "but we've got plenty of milk if you want it." Reaching for one of the cans, he pulled a small knife from his pocket, punched two holes in the top of the milk can, and poured some into his cup. "See?" He held the can so Tessa could see the picture of a cow on the label. "Evaporated milk."

She took a sip of tea. It was strong and bitter, but she forced herself to swallow it.

"Try it with this," David urged, passing her the milk.

Tessa poured a small amount into her cup, then handed the container back to David.

Greeley rose from his place atop David's desk, arched his back, and jumped down. He padded over to the table to investigate the enticing smell, leaping onto David's lap. David removed his cup, then poured some of the canned milk into his saucer for Greeley. The cat meowed appreciatively as David set the saucer to the side. Greeley leapt onto the table, trotted over to the dish and began to sniff the treat. Tessa watched, fascinated, as David stroked the orange fur covering Greeley's neck and the edge of one mutilated ear, sipping his tea while the cat lapped up his treat. She liked David's hands. They were big and strong, but gentle as well. She remembered the way she'd felt when he caressed her, and she envied the ugly orange cat.

"What happened with Coalie's employer?" he asked thoughtfully.

"He took my money, but he wouldn't let me have Coalie," Tessa answered carefully. "He cheated me. I didn't care about the money. Just Coalie. I had to do something!"

"So you decided to take him?" David guessed.

Tessa nodded without looking at him. "I packed my things and waited for two days until Coalie came to deliver more coal. I asked him if he still wanted to live with me. He did." She peeked at David to try to gauge his reaction. "We sneaked down to the train station, bought Coalie a ticket, and boarded the train going west."

"That's why you used your brother's ticket to come to Peaceable."

"Yes."

She realized now that she'd planned to leave Chicago from the moment she learned of Eamon's death. She didn't mind the city so much, but she missed the country. She longed for fresh air and freedom and a home of her own. She'd only stayed in Chicago because her brother needed her. The plan to spirit Coalie away had come to her when she discovered she ached at the thought of leaving him behind. She planned to escape the city and rescue Coalie at the same time. Together they would start a life for themselves in the country. Peaceable seemed like just the right place. The ticket from Eamon was a legacy that meant everything to her. It was the ticket to a new life.

Tessa hadn't understood the value of Eamon's belongings when the nurse at the hospital gave them to her. She'd barely listened when the nurse carefully listed each item as she handed it over—a train ticket to Peaceable, Wyoming Territory, twelve dollars in cash, and a receipt for lodging in a place called the Satin Slipper. But later on, in the lonely apartment after Eamon's funeral, Tessa remembered she had the means to leave. And a reason. She didn't want to stay in a Chicago apartment without her brother. She wanted a home and a family of her own, and she dreamed of finding a new life in Peaceable. With Coalie.

When she and Coalie arrived in Peaceable needing a place to stay, one of the men at the train station told them the Satin Slipper had rooms to let. And Tessa took that as a sign. Somewhere up above, Eamon was looking out for her.

Until she met Arnie Mason . . .

Tessa shifted in her chair. "Now that you know the truth about Coalie, what do you plan to do?" she asked David, her eyes mirroring the anxiety she felt at revealing so much. "Send him back to Chicago?"

David shook his head. "How can I, when I don't know where he is?" he asked, meeting Tessa's gaze. "Wyoming's a big territory," he elaborated. "I wouldn't know where to begin looking."

They both knew he was lying, that he need to look only as far as his family's ranch outside Cheyenne. But the fact that he was willing to pretend lifted Tessa's spirits.

"You're not going to tell Liam Kincaid?"

"No." David stared at her, his dark gaze penetrating. "If Liam Kincaid wants to know where Coalie is, he'll have to ask somebody else. I won't volunteer the information." David knew that Lee wouldn't ask about Coalie's whereabouts. He wasn't interested in the boy. He was interested in Tessa or, more specifically, in keeping his promise to Tessa's dead brother. "You don't have to worry about Liam Kincaid." David told her the truth. "I don't believe he's after Coalie."

"Is he after me?" Tessa asked. "Do you work with Liam Kincaid?"

"Not anymore," David answered truthfully, "though I did during the war. I can't tell you what Liam's doing, Tessa, but I can tell you not to worry about him. He's not your enemy."

She looked up at David, studying his face, probing. "Are you my enemy?"

David shook his head. "No." His lips formed a half-smile. "I promise I won't hurt you. I only want what's best for you. I want to take care of you."

Tessa shuddered in reaction. She didn't want him taking care of her. Or making promises he couldn't keep. She'd learned from bitter experience that the people who promised to take care of her always died. Tessa could take care of herself and Coalie. She didn't want David Alexander on her conscience.

David watched as Tessa sipped her tea. She'd come to Peaceable on the run. And from the moment of her arrival, all her efforts, all her concern had been for Coalie, never for herself. It was remarkable. She was remarkable. David knew her secret, and he admired her all the more for having kept it.

Tessa Roarke had taken an innocent child away from the man who hurt him. She hadn't ignored the situation but had taken matters into her own hands, despite the law and the hardships. And by working in the Satin Slipper Saloon, she had knowingly sacrificed her reputation to provide for that child.

David Alexander wished he had done the same. He took a drink of strong tea, trying to see his way clear once again, but his mind filled with memories of things he wanted to forget. . . .

It had been raining in Washington as he exited the theater through the stage door after spending several minutes chatting with the actors.

He would have liked to stay longer, discussing the finer points of the Shakespearean drama, but it was late and he had a long day ahead of him. Pulling his evening cape around him to ward off the rain and chill, David had stepped into the alley.

He saw her sitting on a wooden packing crate shivering in the downpour only seconds before he heard her crying. David walked over and touched her shoulder. Startled, she looked up. David recognized her—Caroline Millen, Senator Warner Millen's daughter. He remembered meeting her at one of Millen's social evenings; the senator had introduced them. It had been his daughter's first formal gathering, and Millen had asked David to escort Caroline to dinner. As he stood in the theater alley he studied her face. She couldn't have been a day over sixteen.

He spoke her name.

She stopped crying long enough to answer him.

He introduced himself, offered her his handkerchief, and asked her what she was doing outside in a downpour.

Caroline Millen had kept his handkerchief and skillfully avoided answering his questions. He had known something was wrong when he offered to drive her home, but he hadn't known how wrong.

David had found out a month later when Senator Millen barged into his town house, waving David's linen handkerchief and demanding satisfaction.

Pregnant and frightened, Caroline Millen had named him as the father of her child.

He tried to explain that he'd come across Caroline crying in an alley behind the theater, but the senator wasn't listening to explanations. His daughter was ruined, and someone was going to pay.

David had paid. He'd told the truth and he'd paid for it. He wasn't the baby's father. He didn't love Caroline, didn't even know her, and he absolutely refused to marry her.

But Warner Millen would have none of that. David would marry his daughter or be damned.

David refused, knowing that in the end Caroline too would regret such a marriage.

He should have known better than to cross the influential Washington politician. Senator Millen had the power to ruin him and he used it. The scandal had cost David his career, his social standing in Washington, and his reputation. He'd paid a high price for his principles, but Caroline had paid an even higher one.

After being sent away from Washington and her family, she'd given birth to a healthy baby girl, but the process had cost her her life. And the baby . . .

David closed his eyes and pinched the bridge of his nose in an effort to ward off the throbbing. When he learned the Millens had refused to accept their grandchild, David had tried to find her, but the Millens blocked him at every turn. They buried their daughter and her indiscretions along with her. And they allowed the baby to be sent to an orphanage.

Caroline had insisted on naming the child Lily Catherine Alexander, and the thought of a child bearing his name, growing up in an orphanage, thinking she was unwanted, haunted David.

He'd made every attempt to find her—had spent the past year writing letters, making inquiries. . . . David frowned. He'd done everything except marry Caroline Millen. And it hadn't been enough. Looking back on it now, he thought perhaps he should have made her his wife, but he'd been angry, hurt. At the time, he'd felt that marrying Caroline would be the same as admitting he seduced her. David hadn't been ready to do that. He was innocent. He didn't want to be named as a seducer of young girls or manipulated into a loveless marriage. So he had placed his pride above the welfare of an unborn baby, and he regretted it. He'd regretted it since the day he learned of the little girl's birth.

Lily Catherine wasn't his child, but that no longer mattered to him. He wanted her.

Why hadn't he stolen her away, as Tessa had taken Coalie? Why hadn't he done something besides wallow in self-pity? Why hadn't he taken care of them? He squeezed his eyes shut trying to forget.

"David?" He opened his eyes and found Tessa standing over him. "Are you going after him?"

For a moment, before he realized she was talking about Coalie, David thought Tessa had read his mind.

"Not if you don't want me to," David answered, "or unless we need him for the hearing."

"I'd rather he stayed where he is for now," Tessa replied softly. She'd miss him. She missed him already, but for the time being, Coalie was better off at the ranch. She was sure of it.

"All right," he agreed, thinking not just of Coalie but of the little girl in the orphanage. "But only for a while longer."

CHAPTER 13

Coalie's empty chair stood out like a beacon at supper that night. Tessa's gaze returned to the chair time and time again. It was also a very visible reminder that, with Coalie gone, she was alone with David Alexander. Very alone. The fact that they were made her nervous. Jumpy. If only he would stop watching her. He'd watched her all evening the way Greeley studied a mouse before pouncing.

Tessa pushed her chair back from the table and abruptly stood up. She picked up her empty plate, then held out her hand for his. "Are you finished?"

"Yes." David offered her his plate.

She practically snatched it out of his hand, then carried the dishes to the sink and set them in the dishpan under the water spout. Tessa scraped a bar of soap over the grater, brushed the slivers into the dishpan, and pumped the handle up and down as hard as she could. The cold water gushed out, bounced off the plates, and splashed up, soaking the front of Tessa's green dress. "Thunderation! See what you made me

171

do?" She whirled around to face him.

David nearly choked on his coffee. The wet fabric clung to her chest. David could see the trail of tiny indentions across her breasts and knew it was the lace at the top of her chemise. Fully dressed as she was, the wet calico did nothing more than hint at what lay beneath the fabric, but it was a vivid reminder of Saturday's bath ritual. The memory of her body silhouetted against the sheet tortured him. He had to force his next words around the lump in his throat. "You should change your dress; you might catch cold."

"And wash dishes in one of my brand-new dresses?" Tessa was appalled. "I will not!"

David finished his coffee and carried the cup to the sink. "Wouldn't you like to try them on for size?"

She would. She had wanted to ever since David unloaded the rest of the supplies. Tessa'd unpacked the boxes and crates, delighting in the variety of canned goods and the thoughtful luxuries he'd ordered. She had almost everything put away when he brought in the last two big cartons. David had set them on the table, glancing at the labels.

"These are for you," he'd told her. "I ordered a few things from Mary's seamstress in Cheyenne."

"More clothes?"

"You can't keep wearing the one green dress," he answered. "Oh, and there's a couple of pairs of denims for Coalie and some shirts."

Tessa looked stricken.

"Don't worry. Mary'll buy him some more. Go ahead," he urged. "Try the dresses on."

"No, I can't. I've work to do."

She'd stubbornly refused to open the packages earlier in the afternoon, but now she wanted to. She had reason to.

But still she protested. "The dishes . . ."

"I'll do the dishes," David promised.

Tessa looked askance at him.

"Come here."

Tessa moved closer to him.

"Turn around."

She did.

She felt his hands on her back as he quickly unbuttoned her dress and loosened her corset laces. It was a husbandly task. An intimate task. Yet it was something David Alexander had done for her a number of times. Something Tessa trusted him to do. She liked the warm feeling it gave her to know he'd done it without being asked. And up to now he'd always acted the gentleman.

"There," David said. "You're undone. Now you can go try on your new dresses."

"Thank you."

"Any time," he replied, smiling down at her. "Go on. I'll take care of this."

She hurried across the room and grabbed the stack of boxes off David's desk.

"Be careful," she warned when David dropped his cup and the forks and spoons into the pan with a clatter, "or we'll be buying more new crockery."

"I know how to wash dishes." He saw the skepticism in her expression and decided to prove it. He walked to the stove and removed the new copper kettle full of boiling water. Returning to the sink, he tipped the spout over the dishpan and poured, testing the water from time to time, until he got it hot enough.

Tessa watched, amazed. He did know how to do

dishes. "Why didn't you say something earlier?" she demanded. "I thought you must've had a woman come in to clean before I got here. I didn't know you did the work yourself." She pinned an accusing stare on David. "I've been washing all the dishes since I got here when we could've been taking turns."

David unbuttoned his cuffs, then turned to look at her. "I thought you wanted to."

"Hmmf," Tessa snorted, glancing upward. Only a man would say such a thing. "You thought I *wanted* to wash dishes?"

"Yes, and if you don't go try on your new dresses, I'll think you want to wash these." David smiled his most devastating smile and rolled up his sleeves.

Tessa watched as he revealed the bronzed muscles of his forearms. She remembered the feel of his arms pressed against her. Turning, she left without another word, hurrying to her bedroom, where she slammed the door.

David allowed himself to relax. It was a relief to have Tessa out of his line of vision. The strain of holding his body in check was more than any one man should have to bear. He couldn't seem to keep his gaze off her. He'd made a valiant effort, but he'd failed. She fascinated him.

It was all he could do to keep his hands off her. He wanted to taste her, to feel her. In the state he was in, David didn't know how he'd make it through the night knowing they were alone, just the two of them together. He wanted to make love to her all night long. Even now he envisioned her taking off the green calico dress and the wet chemise. He saw her loosening the long satin laces of her corset, pictured the lovely pale, almost translucent skin, of her neck and arms and her long, long legs. Plunging his hands into the hot dishwater, David scrubbed a plate with a good deal more vigor than was necessary.

"I like the little pink flowers." Tessa spoke from the doorway.

David whirled around, dripping sudsy water onto the floor. "What?"

Tessa giggled, a deep throaty giggle that took David by surprise. She moved to stand in front of him. "I said I like the little flowers on the plates." Her heart seemed to beat a little faster at the picture he made standing there so tall and unbelievably handsome with a white dish towel draped over one shoulder. "You looked as if you were going to scrub the flowers off."

"You look . . . beautiful." He reached up for the end of the towel and dried his hands.

The yellow wool day dress fit her like a second skin. The soft fabric lovingly molded her curves in all the right places, and the color accentuated her vibrant red hair.

Tessa blushed. She'd heard many compliments when she worked at the Satin Slipper, but none so sincere or so flattering as the one David Alexander had uttered.

"You don't think it makes me look too . . . too yellow, do you?" Tessa didn't really doubt that the shade was becoming. She simply wanted to hear David confirm his earlier assessment.

"I think you look as fetching as a spring flower," he assured her. "A daffodil." He changed his mind. "No, an iris. A lovely, elegant iris."

She spun around so he could view the back. "It fits perfectly. How did you know?"

"I told the seamstress you were about Mary's size,

only a few inches taller, and a redhead."

She glanced back over her shoulder. "I've never worn a bustle before," she admitted, "but I've always wanted to. Isn't it grand?"

David focused his gaze on the back of her gown, paying close attention to the curve where her firm little bottom should have been. He frowned at the bustle. He preferred Tessa's natural shape to the horsehair-enhanced version, but rather than spoil her pleasure in the fashionable bustle, David relied on his vivid memory. "It's a work of art."

"And look," Tessa ordered, raising her hem a fraction. "Shoes to match."

David looked at her trim ankles encased in dyed kid boots and the exposed portion of one calf in shimmering gossamer silk. The bill for her clothes would be outrageously high, made as they were on such short notice, but he wouldn't complain. He'd already decided they were worth every last penny.

"Did you know there were three dresses?" Tessa asked, her lilting brogue thickening in her excitement. "This yellow one, a brown one, and a blue one. With gloves and . . . you know . . . everything to match." She blushed again at the idea that he'd ordered more unmentionables for her. And lovely ones, at that.

"Everything except hats," David told her. He despised hats, especially ladies' hats with all the flowers and lace and bows and yards of tulle. He'd even seen some with stuffed birds on the brims. They ranked right up there with tea and—he stared at the back of her dress again—bustles. No hats. He'd telegraphed that message to the seamstress along with the others. He enjoyed the play of light on Tessa's fiery mane. It would be a crime to cover it up.

"Well, who needs more than one hat, anyway?" Tessa smiled brightly, too brightly. She tried not to feel disappointed. After all, he had bought her all these lovely things. She should have known David would forget to order hats. She'd noticed he seldom remembered to wear his own.

"You can order a few hats if you want," David offered impulsively, belatedly realizing Tessa liked feminine headgear and that he was being high-handed by denying her. "I'll even take you into Cheyenne." He hated the thought of going into Cheyenne, but if it would make her happy, it was worth it. Feeling generous, he continued, "You can pick them out yourself. There's a milliner in the city who makes hats of all descriptions, covered with bows and lace. Even stuffed quail and sparrows." He tried not to cringe when her eyes lit up.

"When can we go?"

"In a week or so, after the circuit judge leaves," David said, postponing it as long as he could. "I'll have more time then."

"Oh." Again she tried to hide her disappointment.

"I might be able to fit a trip in sooner."

"I can wait a week or so," Tessa assured him although she wasn't certain she wouldn't be in jail then.

"I'll see what I can work in between hearings," David promised.

Hearings. David realized what he'd said almost immediately, and he could tell from the expression on Tessa's face that she'd noticed as well. She had been accused of murder. Technically she was his prisoner, not his houseguest. She might not have any time after the hearing. She might not have any time at all.

"Tessa . . ."

"David . . ." Tessa stared at him, unable to look away. She recognized the need in his voice. Lifting herself up onto her toes, she sought his lips.

David met her halfway, closing the distance between them.

Tessa wrapped her arms around his neck. The dish towel fell to the floor, unheeded. She pressed her lips against his.

He reached for her, touching the base of her spine with one hand. He felt the softness of the yellow wool as he pulled her to his body. Holding her cradled against him, he lifted his other hand to the back of her head. He tangled his long fingers in the silken strands of her hair, scattering the pins in every direction. The heavy mass tumbled from the confines of her braided coronet to hang well below her shoulders. David gently separated the braid and ran his hand through her hair.

Loving the feel of his hands in her hair, yet wanting more, Tessa explored the seam of his mouth with the tip of her tongue.

He groaned aloud. Parting his lips to allow her entrance, David kissed her back with an urgency that couldn't be denied. He ate at her lips, tasting her over and over again, probing the depths of her mouth. He inhaled her breath, her little whimpers and cries of pleasure, as his tongue met, then mated with hers.

Tessa moved her hands from around his neck, caressing the breadth of his shoulders before working her hands between them. Finding the buttons of his shirt, Tessa undid them one by one, then slipped her hands inside the opening and touched the skin of his chest.

The feel of her hands against his flesh ignited the fires he'd kept carefully banked. Forgetting restraint, David tore his mouth away from hers, planting kisses on her eyelids, her cheekbones, down the column of her neck, and back again to her ear. He plunged his tongue inside the delicate shell.

Tessa shivered in reaction.

David released his tight hold on her, allowing his hands to roam over the back of her yellow wool gown searching for the fastenings.

She felt the cool rush of air against her back as David freed the hooks of her dress. Moving his hands to the front, he tugged it off her shoulders and down her arms. The bodice fell to her waist.

Placing a hand on either shoulder, David smoothed the straps of her corset cover and chemise aside. Tessa pulled her arms free. Smiling at the wonderful bounty she offered, he leaned forward and kissed the curve of each breast, then bent to pull the sheer silk garments lower.

Tessa gasped when his mouth found the hard nub of one breast. Her legs quivered beneath her. She groped for something to steady herself and found his wide shoulders. He licked, lightly at first, then harder, suckling her like a baby demanding nourishment. Tessa felt a rush of moisture between her legs, felt the incredible ache that begged for attention.

A hoarse shout followed by a burst of high-pitched feminine laughter outside the window echoed through the office.

"Damn!" David cursed beneath his breath as he straightened up and walked to the back door. It was unlocked. Lifting the window shade, he realized it was dark outside. Twilight had given way to night,

and in the brightly lit interior of the office he and
Tessa had been silhouetted against the shades for all
of Peaceable to see. "Son of a bitch!"

"Who is it?" Tessa whispered, suddenly feeling
exposed and vulnerable.

David strained to make out the figures walking arm
and arm down the alley. Listening closely he heard
the low murmur of conversation and the rhythmic
jingling of spurs. As he watched, the two shadows
stopped to kiss. David let the shade fall back into
place.

"Just a cowboy and his lady friend." He turned back
to Tessa.

She stood in the center of the room, the bodice of
her dress held protectively in front of her. Her eyes
were a dark sapphire blue, her lips red and swollen
from his kisses, her glorious red hair tousled by his
eager hands. She'd never looked more inviting. Or
lovelier.

David massaged the muscles at the back of his neck.
What the hell was he thinking of? Tessa Roarke was
his client, not his lover. He couldn't forget that. But
neither could he forget the feel of her in his arms or the
taste of her. He wouldn't let himself think about that,
he promised. He'd think about her case instead. He
couldn't make love; all his energy should be focused
on saving her. He couldn't risk her life for a few hours
of pleasure. David smoothed his hair back, restoring
a semblance of order, and buttoned the top button of
his shirt.

He would act honorably.

"David?" Tessa searched for a sign, some clue to
his emotions, but his face gave nothing away. He had
distanced himself from her. One minute they were

intimate, and the next, he acted as if he'd never kissed her. Tessa struggled to regain the closeness they'd shared. "Would you like to kiss me again?"

God, yes, he thought, I'd like to kiss you all over. All night. Forever. "I think we've done enough kissing for one night, Tessa." He finished buttoning his shirt and walked to the sink. The dishwater was cold.

"Don't," Tessa told him, her voice thick with emotion. "I'll finish the dishes."

"We had a deal," David reminded her, diligently scrubbing another plate. "I'd wash the dishes while you tried on your dresses."

Tessa tried again. "Which dress would you like to see next? The brown or the blue?"

David plunged the plate into the rinse water before facing her.

She let the bodice of her dress slip just a bit, so the tops of her breasts were exposed to his view once again. She licked her lips and took a step forward.

David forced himself to stay where he was, but every inch of his body strained to accept her invitation. He cleared his throat before he spoke. "I . . . um . . . think you should try the other dresses on in your room."

"You think too much." Tessa took another step.

He held up a hand to ward her off. Drops of water ran down his wrist and fell to the floor. "Because you don't think enough."

She stopped, stung by his words. Her expression hardened. The softness left her eyes; they became a colder shade of blue.

He hated the change. "Tessa, you don't understand. . . . I'm your attorney. You're my client."

"I understand that I was as much your client when

you kissed me as I am now," she told him. "And I understand that I might not have much time left. A week from now I might be in jail for the rest of my life." Tessa turned and stalked across the room and down the hall and into her bedroom, leaving him with a splendid view of the rigid column of her corsetted spine.

CHAPTER 14

Tessa couldn't sleep. She tossed and turned against the feather mattress, waiting, listening for the sound of David's footsteps in the hall. She hadn't heard anything except the rustle of the bedclothes against her body for hours. Had he left her? Had he gone out? Tessa remembered the last time he'd gone to the Satin Slipper when he'd told her about his drinking, how it made him want to love a woman all night long. Tessa punched her pillow one more time, then flipped back the covers. If he'd gone to the Satin Slipper, she'd kill him. If he wanted to make love to a woman, it wasn't going to be Charlotte or Myra. It was going to be her. She was the one who might go to prison for the rest of her life. Tessa knew David would fight hard to prove her innocence to the judge and jury, but she also knew that the people of Peaceable already believed her guilty of killing Arnie Mason. She felt, deep down in her heart, that she didn't stand a chance of going free. She understood that she might never get another opportunity to lie in David's arms and to make love with him. She desperately wanted her chance to experience the pleasure David offered. She was the woman he wanted, not Myra or Charlotte, and *she* wanted him. Why shouldn't she take advantage of her one chance at loving? Why shouldn't she have the man she wanted before she went to prison?

David looked up from his desk, the words on the pages of the Pinkerton dossier scattered across his desk blurring in the lamplight. He closed his eyes, then wearily pinched the bridge of his nose. It was no use. He couldn't keep his mind off Tessa. He wondered how she looked when she slept. What she wore. The memory of her back tortured him. He wanted to caress her soft skin, to kiss each vertebra, run his tongue up and down her spine, turn her over and pay homage to her magnificent breasts. David shifted in his chair, adjusting to accommodate the swelling in his trousers. It had been like this all night. He opened his eyes, forcing himself to read the meticulously written notes on Arnie Mason, the lists of petty crimes, extortion, and attempted murder. Just thinking of a man like that coming in contact with Tessa . . . Tessa. David closed the dossier and picked up a lawbook. Streams of dull legal phrases swam before his eyes. He reached into his desk drawer and removed a bottle of Scots whisky and a glass. David uncorked the bottle and filled the glass, then recorked it and replaced the bottle. He took a small ring of keys from his trouser pocket and locked the drawer, then threw the key ring across the room so he wouldn't be tempted to overindulge. It bounced off the wall and skidded across the floor.

Sipping his drink, David concentrated on the printed page. There had to be something here, some legal
precedent, some tiny loophole to prevent the Territory
of Wyoming from prosecuting Tessa Roarke. Tessa.
He groaned as her name conjured up pictures. Tessa
with her yellow dress bunched around her waist, her
breasts bared. Tessa, her lips swollen, her cool hands
against his chest. Tessa, stalking away, her beautiful
back displayed just for him. He imagined her lying
naked amid the lawbooks and papers on his desk,
begging him to love her.

"Dammit!" David muttered, raking his left arm
across the top of his desk, sweeping books and papers
off the shiny surface. The heavy law books thudded to
the floor. "Dammit!" He pressed his forehead against
the polished wood. He had to concentrate on his work.
He had to stop thinking about her.

"David?"

He lifted his head, blinking at her image. She moved
toward him, and David wondered if he'd conjured her
up from the depths of his memory.

"David?" Tessa repeated his name, then saw the
glass of whisky in his hand. "Are you drunk?"

"Nope. It's my first."

"Oh."

He stared at her long, shapely legs outlined against
the fine silk of her nightclothes. She wore a chemise,
brief silk and lace underdrawers, and nothing else.
The shadow of the triangle between her thighs beck-
oned to him. "You sound disappointed."

Her face flushed with color. "Maybe a little." Tessa
studied him, gauging his sobriety.

"I hate to disappoint you," David told her, shifting
against the leather chair, "but I've limited myself to

one drink." He raised the glass and saluted her. So much for her coming to gloat over the fact that she'd driven him to drink.

"Oh, I thought . . ." She shifted her weight from one leg to the other.

"You thought I might be drinking myself into a high temper on your account?" David interrupted.

"I . . . hoped you might," she told him.

"Not this time."

Tessa moistened her lips with the tip of her tongue.

Leaning back against the comfortable leather, David took a gulp of whisky.

"I guess you're not ready yet," Tessa said, trying to hide her disappointment. "Maybe if I come back later you'll be ready." She turned.

"Ready for what?" Her words puzzled him.

"To make love all night long, like you said."

"What?" The lead-crystal glass slipped from his hand and shattered against the floor.

"You know . . . You told me not to be afraid of you because you weren't a mean drunk," Tessa explained.

David didn't remember saying anything of the kind.

"You said that lots of drinking made you . . . and I thought maybe you wanted to . . . earlier tonight."

David stood up and pushed back his chair. The wheels crunched on the remains of the glass. The strong odor of expensive whisky drifted up from the floor. David ignored it, focusing his attention solely on Tessa.

She wanted this one night with David Alexander and she meant to have it. With her mind made up, and her conscience firmly pushed aside, Tessa wet her lips again, then smoothed her hands over the soft fabric of her chemise.

David ached to do the same. "You thought if I got drunk enough, I'd want to make love to someone?"

"Not just someone. Me."

"You?" David parroted, wondering if he'd heard correctly.

"Maybe you think I'm not good enough? Maybe you'd rather have Charlotte or Myra?"

"Yes. No," David blurted.

"Well," Tessa demanded, hands on her hips, "which is it?"

"Yes."

"You don't think I'm as good as they are?" She moved so close that David could feel the tips of her breasts brushing against his shirt, driving him out of his mind. And he gave in.

"No," he told her. He wrapped his arms around her waist and pulled her closer to his body. Tessa felt the hard length of him against her abdomen. "I think you're better. Much better."

"You're not going to the Satin Slipper?"

"Dammit Tessa, you know I'm staying right where I am," David said fiercely, "with you." He kissed the side of her neck, nuzzling the hair around her ear.

"Have you had enough?" Tessa asked, shivering in response.

"Not by a long shot."

Tessa pulled out of his arms.

"Where are you going?" David asked, grabbing hold of her chemise.

"To get you a cup," she told him. "You broke your glass." Tessa pointed to the mess behind his desk. Then a thought occurred to her. "Unless you'd rather drink straight out of the bottle."

"Contessa?" David's dark brown eyes sparkled.

"Yes?"

"Forget the cup. And the bottle. I won't need it." He pulled her back into his embrace. "I never did."

"But you said—"

David stopped her words with his mouth. He kissed her until her knees buckled. She clutched at his shirtfront. David bent and swung her up into his arms. He released her lips long enough to say, "Are you asking me to make love to you, contessa?"

"All night long," Tessa reminded him. "Just as you said."

David laughed. "What exactly did I say?"

"You don't remember?" A frown creased her forehead.

"Bits and pieces." David kissed the tip of her nose. "Refresh my memory." He sat down on the top of his desk with Tessa in his arms.

"You told me I didn't have to be afraid of you. You said that despite what people say about Indians and half-breeds like you, I should know you weren't a mean drunk. You said—"

"I must have been crazy," David commented, "to say all that." He kissed her again. "What about the whisky?" he asked.

"You said it doesn't make you want to fight or be cruel or slap women around. You said—"

"Too much, apparently," David remarked. "Skip to the good part. What's this about all night long?"

"You said whisky made you want to take a woman in your arms and make love to her all night long."

"I said that?" David couldn't believe it. "To you?"

"Yes. To me." Tessa frowned again, wiggling in his arms. "Who else?"

David tightened his arms around her. "Nobody else." He pressed his lips against her shining hair.

"David?" Tessa squirmed against him, demanding his attention. "Are you going to make love to me or not?"

"I'm not." David looked down at her and saw the darkening of her blue eyes. "I'm not going to make love to you, contessa."

Tessa opened her mouth.

David covered it with his own, answering the question he read in her eyes, kissing her until they were both gasping for breath. "I think," he teased, "that we'll enjoy it a hell of a lot more if we make love to each other."

"All night long?"

"What's left of it, anyway." David slid off the desk. "Grab the lamp," he instructed.

Tessa reached up, found the cord of the overhead lamp and pulled it down on a level with his face. David blew the flame out.

"Now," he whispered, "we can get down to business without giving the rest of the town a show." He gently lowered Tessa onto the shiny wooden desk top, then moved to stand in front of her.

"What are you doing?" Tessa felt his fingers at the pearl buttons of her chemise.

"I thought we'd start in here," David answered, unbuttoning the garment to her waist, "and work our way to the bedrooms."

"Can we do that?" Tessa sucked in her breath as David raked the tip of her nipple with his thumb.

"Why not?" He caressed the other breast. "We've got the place to ourselves." His voice grew huskier. "And we've got all night."

*   *   *

"David?" Tessa lay sprawled across the top of the desk, her chemise gone, her long legs draped over his shoulders. She couldn't see his face in the darkness, but she felt his lips on her, felt the cool leather back of his chair against the soles of her feet, heard the creak of its wheels as he shifted his weight.

"I'm here, Tessa my sweet." His warm breath tickled the hair of her mound. Strands of his thick black hair brushed her inner thigh.

"What are you doing?"

He heard the wariness in her voice and reassured her. "I'm kissing you."

"Not there." She felt him nuzzle her.

"Yes, here," he said. "I'm going to kiss you everywhere."

"Can you do that?"

Tessa felt rather than saw his sensual grin. "I can if you let me."

She decided to let him.

Tessa gasped when he kissed her. She squirmed beneath him as he used his mouth to give her the most extraordinary pleasure. She alternately pleaded with him to stop the wonderful torture, and demanded he never stop—until the unbearable tension ended suddenly in a wave of exquisite pleasure that washed over her. Tessa arched her back. She called his name without knowing she did it. David stood up to hold her. Tessa wrapped her arms around his waist as she clung to him, pressing tiny kisses on his warm flesh and shivering with reaction.

She continued to shiver long after the spasms left her limp and pleasantly sated.

David realized she was cold. He scooped her up in

his arms. Tessa relaxed against him, looping her arms around his neck.

"Where are we going?" she asked.

"To bed."

"Oh." She smothered a yawn.

David chuckled. "Don't go to sleep on me now, Tessa. We're just getting started." His voice was laced with tenderness. He discovered that despite the life she'd led at the Satin Slipper, Tessa had never before felt the exquisite sensations he'd aroused within her moments before. She had more to learn about lovemaking, more pleasure to experience. David felt honored to teach her.

He carried her to his bed.

Tessa snuggled into the covers, watching as David peeled off his shirt. He lit a lamp, turning the wick down low. "I want to see you," he told her, "and I want you to see me." He kicked off his boots, then shucked his tight pants.

Her eyes widened in surprise as he revealed himself to her. Sleek and bronzed in the lamplight, he was magnificent. His wide shoulders tapered into a hard, ridged stomach. A light sprinkling of black hair trailed from his navel, pointing downward to . . . She closed her eyes. A hot blush stained her face red.

David grinned. "Open your eyes, Tessa," he commanded softly. "Look at me."

She opened one eye, then the other.

"See what you do to me." He walked to the bed, pulled the covers back, and slipped between the sheets next to her. "Feel what you do to me." He pressed his large body into hers.

"You're so warm," Tessa told him, placing her hands against his chest. "I've never felt anything like this."

"Touch me, Tessa," David directed, taking her hand in his, guiding her down to the hard length of him.

Tessa marveled at the contrast. The steel hardness encased in velvety softness, the rough crinkle of hair at the base, the smooth, gentle slope at the summit. David removed his hand. She no longer needed his guidance. She explored him on her own.

David groaned aloud, biting his full lower lip as she tested his limits. He squirmed beneath her hand, whispering her name over and over, like a litany. She ran a hand down his inner thigh. David reacted instantly. He caught her hand in his, moving it up to his chest. "No more." His voice was hoarse, strained. "I can't stand it."

Leaning on an elbow above him, Tessa trailed her hand across the expanse of his chest, then up his neck, to his mouth. She traced the fine contours of his lower lip with her fingertip. "What should I do next?"

Smiling at the innocent question, David hooked an arm around her neck and pulled her down to him. He captured her lips with his own, kissing her with a thoroughness that sent her coherent thoughts flying. "Make love with me," he murmured between breaths.

Rolling her to her back in one sure motion and positioning himself between her legs, David slipped inside her. He pushed, trying to bury himself in her moist cavern, and met resistance. "What's this?" He looked down at her face, saw the way her teeth worried her bottom lip, and he understood. "God, Tessa, I didn't know . . . I never dreamed . . ." David slowed his movements, gentling his touch. He struggled to find the words to thank her for giving him her maidenhead. "You're wonderful. Magnificent." He praised her as he moved his hips, easing his way inside her. His heart felt near to bursting at the flood of sensations and the wave of tenderness he felt for her.

Tessa squirmed against the pressure building inside her.

David kissed the corner of her mouth. "It's all right. I can wait until you're ready. There's no need to hurry."

But there was. Tessa's heart pounded in her breast. She moved against him, yearning to explore the wonderful feeling, wanting to quench the fires within, sensing that only David could help her.

"Tessa, don't move," David pleaded. "Please don't move. Not yet."

But she did. She hugged him. Pulling him as close as possible, Tessa pressed her lips against his breast, finding his nipple, feeling the rapid thundering of his heart.

And David was lost. Unable to control the emotions urging him onward, he withdrew a bit, then plunged his length into her welcoming depths.

Tessa felt a twinge of pain a moment before he began the rhythmic stroking. Then she forgot all about the pain, forgot about everything except David and the pleasure spiraling inside her. She arched against him, then locked her long legs around his waist.

"Hold me," David demanded hoarsely in her ear. "Don't let me go."

Tessa obliged, holding him through the storm as he buried himself deep within her one last time. Tessa heard the wonder in his voice as he called her name and felt the pulse that shook his whole body. She answered his cry with a cry of her own only seconds before their world exploded in a shower of colors, like the fragments of a rainbow.

Tessa opened her eyes, hugging David tightly as he rolled to her side.

He held her close. "Oh, Tessa . . ." he whispered, kissing the sensitive skin beneath her ear. "My sweet, sweet, Tessa. I promise I'll take care of you."

"Don't," Tessa whispered back. "Don't make promises." She snuggled closer in his arms. "You might not be able to keep them." She sighed deeply, then closed her eyes and slept.

CHAPTER 15

David opened his eyes. Horace Greeley sat perched on his chest. Tessa lay cradled against his side, her body nestled against his, her head pillowed on his shoulder. Greeley flicked his tail in agitation, leaned forward, and sniffed Tessa's hair.

Arching his back, the cat stretched and then ambled across David toward Tessa in an effort to reclaim his favorite spot in the bed.

Realizing Greeley's purpose, David intercepted him. He picked the cat up and moved him away from Tessa. "Get your own girl. This one's mine."

David scratched the underside of Greeley's chin. It was true: Tessa was his. He listened to the contented purr rumbling in Greeley's chest, wishing he could do the same. But things had become more complicated. Tessa had given him her virginity, become his lover as well as his client, and now David wasn't sure what to do.

God, what a mess! He'd been so convinced she had made love before. After all, Arnie Mason was murdered in her bed. But Tessa had been a virgin. Until last night. David watched her sleeping. She was loving and beautiful and brave. He turned his head and pressed a kiss against her shining red hair. She was everything he could want in a woman. And he wanted her. God, how he wanted her. But he couldn't have her. Not again. Not until she was free. It wasn't fair to her, and it wasn't fair to him. He was her defense attorney, but he wouldn't be able to defend her properly if he couldn't think about anything except making love to her.

David was struck by the tremendous responsibility. Their lovemaking had been a mistake. It should never have happened. David could have prevented it, but didn't. Instead, he'd welcomed her with open arms, and she hadn't disappointed him. He was a fool.

He was haunted by the idea of Lily Catherine in an orphanage somewhere back east. He couldn't stand the thought of Tessa going to prison, Tessa possibly bearing a child, his child, in prison. He couldn't take the risk. What had happened between them could not happen again.

But, David realized, he wouldn't have changed last night for anything in the world. The loving was spectacular. Better than anything he'd ever experienced. There was no doubt about that. But he was confused. Had she come to him out of gratitude or had she given herself out of love? Would she have chosen him if she were free or had last night been the result of a moment of weakness? He wasn't sure. He only knew that before they made love again, Tessa had to be able to choose. She had to be free. David didn't want her to come to him out of gratitude. He didn't want payment. He wanted love.

He carefully eased his body out from under her, then lifted Greeley off his chest and rolled to the side of the bed. He couldn't make love to Tessa again while she remained in his custody, but he could try to make her life as pleasant as possible. He pulled on his pants and headed into his office.

Tessa awoke to the smell of bacon frying. Her nose twitched at the delectable scent. She opened her eyes, rolled to her side, and stretched. Memories of the night came flooding back. Tessa reached for David. The sheets were cold, and the bed was empty except for Horace Greeley.

"David?" Tessa sat up in bed. Sunlight streamed in the bedroom window. "Where is he?" she asked, hugging the orange tom, nuzzling his fur. "Where's our big handsome man?"

She felt light, giggly. She wanted to laugh and cry at the same time, to embrace the world and everyone in it. It was wonderful, this thing between men and women. David was wonderful, incredible. Tessa reached for his white shirt on the foot of the bed, slipping it on to cover her nakedness. She flipped back the covers and stood up.

Crossing the bedroom, Tessa opened the door, and padded down the hallway, buttoning his shirt along the way.

She paused in the doorway.

David stood at the stove. He wore black trousers and socks. Nothing else. The rest of his body was bare. He held a plate of freshly scrambled eggs and a few strips of bacon in one hand and a steaming cup of tea in the other. The cup and saucer rattled against the side of the plate as he caught sight of Tessa.

"Good morning." His words warmed her. The look in his eyes made her stomach flutter. "I cooked breakfast." He moved with the grace of a cat and deftly set the plate in front of Tessa's chair. "I thought you might be hungry." He offered her the cup of tea.

Tessa walked to the stove. "Thank you." She blushed as she took the cup of tea from him. Her movements were slow and awkward. Tea sloshed over the brim of the cup into the saucer.

David cleared his throat. He let his gaze roam over her. His shirt, open at her throat, covered the essentials but left her long, shapely legs exposed. Her feet were bare, her toes curled against the cold floor. "Why don't you sit down?" David suggested. He pulled out her chair and patted the seat.

"Are you going to join me?"

He wanted to. God, he wanted to. "No." He didn't quite meet her eyes. "I've already eaten."

She set her cup on the table next to her plate. "Oh."

"I like what you do for my shirt." David didn't realize he'd said the words aloud until Tessa's face turned a deeper shade of red. He sat down across from her.

She toyed with the top button. "I didn't think you'd mind. After last night . . ." She looked around the room.

"I don't mind." David had promised himself he wouldn't think about last night, but not thinking about their lovemaking was impossible. His gaze followed Tessa's around the room. He'd swept up the broken glass, but that was all. Her clothing was still scattered across his desk and on the floor, lying where it had fallen when he undressed her.

He cleared his throat again. Looking at his desk, David realized he'd never be able to work at his desk again without remembering how she looked and sounded lying naked on top of it. "Uh, Tessa, about last night . . ."

"Oh, David." Tessa's blue eyes sparkled with emotion. "It was wonderful!" She smiled at him tentatively. "I never dreamed men and women could do such things." She speared a mound of eggs. "Can we do it again? This morning?" She was eager to explore his body and the depths of his passion in the light of day.

"No." David's voice was flat as he forced the refusal.

"Why not?" Tessa was curious.

"Because, it can't happen again. It shouldn't have happened last night."

The forkful of fluffy yellow eggs stopped midway to her mouth. She didn't like the tone of his voice. She'd heard it before. In the jail. "Are you sorry?" Tessa's blue eyes sparkled with a different emotion now. Tears shimmered near the surface.

David got up from the chair and began to pace. "Not sorry, exactly." For someone known for his eloquence, he was doing a sorry job of explaining the situation to Tessa. His words came out sounding harsh and abrupt.

"Did I do something wrong?"

He turned back to look at her, saw the worried expression on her face. "No, Tessa, I did something wrong."

"What?"

"You were a virgin!" David burst out. "For God's sake, Tessa, I took your virginity."

"You did no such thing." Tessa dropped her fork; it clattered against the plate. "You didn't take it. I gave it to you," she said fiercely.

"Well, dammit, you shouldn't have!"

"That's what you say now." Tessa stood up. "It's not what you said last night."

"I didn't know last night!" He ran his fingers through his hair. "What the hell was Arnie Mason doing in your room? I thought—"

"You shouldn't have." She flung the words at him. "I told you from the beginning that I didn't go with the gentlemen."

"You worked at the Satin Slipper."

"I served drinks, not myself."

David laughed, a harsh sound that hurt Tessa's ears. "Did Myra know she had hired a virgin? By God, you could have made her rich! Why did you work there?"

"Coalie and I had to eat," Tessa reminded him. "And we needed a roof over our heads. But I never went with the gentlemen."

"I know that," David said. "So why the devil did you go with me last night?" He raked his long fingers through his hair.

"Because I wanted to."

"Why?"

Because he made her feel beautiful and special and loved. Because she wanted him to feel the same way. Tessa realized suddenly that she wanted David Alexander, not just in the physical sense but in every way. Somewhere between the first time she saw him standing in the mass of curious spectators and last night, she'd fallen in love.

"What difference does it make?" Tessa asked. "It's done." He had spoiled it. The most beautiful experience in her entire life, and David had ruined it by saying he regretted it.

"It makes a hell of a lot of difference to me." David stopped pacing. "I don't want to be accused of seducing a poor innocent girl or fathering her child."

Tessa recoiled as if he'd slapped her. In fact, slapping her might have been kinder. "What did you say?" Her voice was as frigid as an Arctic wind.

"You heard me." David read the expression on her face. The surprise. The shock. The pain.

"Is that how you see it? Do you think that's all that happened between us?" Her eyes widened until they looked like huge sapphires against a pale background.

David didn't, but he couldn't admit that, not even to erase the pain. It was better for her to be hurt now than pay a higher price later. So he ignored her question, unable to tell her how much their lovemaking had meant to him because telling her would bring her into his arms once again. And David was very much afraid he wouldn't be strong enough to let her go.

She stood stock still. "Is that how you make love to Myra or Charlotte at the Satin Slipper?" Tessa demanded, fighting to keep her composure, fighting to keep the tears from flowing.

"Tessa—"

"Answer me. Do you do the same things to other women? Touch them the same way? Kiss them the same way?"

"Leave it alone, Tessa," David said softly, "a gentleman doesn't kiss and tell."

"And you're a gentleman, aren't you, Mr. Alexander? The perfect gentleman." Tessa hurled the words at him. "What about last night? What happened to you then? Did some of the savage come out? Did you forget to be a gentleman with me?"

Her barb hit home.

"Yes." He paled, stepping back as if she'd wounded him. "Yes, I forgot everything except taking what you offered. Everything except burying myself inside you." His words evoked the images. David groaned, feeling himself swell with anticipation.

"What is it you're afraid of, Mr. Alexander?" Tessa taunted. "Me or yourself?" She snatched her nightgown off the back of David's leather chair.

"Both." David, one step behind, reached out and grabbed her, pulling her into his body. "Both of us, dammit. And what we do to each other!" Leaning down, he covered her mouth with his own. Tessa's nightgown fell to the floor, unnoticed.

The kiss mirrored his frustration and his need— hard and punishing at first, then softer, gentler, more loving. David buried his hands in her hair. He touched the red strands, tangling his long fingers in their silkiness, holding her head at the perfect angle to meet his questing mouth and tongue.

Tessa's arms went around his waist. She kissed him back, meeting his tongue with her own, melting against him, offering him her body and her love.

David felt the soft cushion of her breasts against his chest, felt the buttons of his shirt pressing into the muscles of his stomach. David deepened the kiss, placed his hands on her hips and fitted her against him. God, he wanted her! Needed her to stop the ache.

But he couldn't have her. He couldn't take her.

"No, Tessa." David broke the intimate contact. He moved his mouth away from hers, then took her arms from around his waist. "Stop." He put her away from him, out of his reach, then moved around the office, gathering up her stray clothing.

"What's wrong?" Tessa murmured.

"We can't do this." He thrust the clothes into her arms.

"I don't understand," Tessa said. "You want to. I want to. Why can't we?" Didn't he realize that they may never have another chance? Didn't he realize what might happen to her, that she could die in prison?

"Because I need to be thinking about your hearing, not how wonderful you feel beneath me. I should be thinking about winning your freedom, not making love." David stared down at her. "And so should you. Dammit, Tessa, do you want to go back to jail?"

"How can you ask me that?" Tessa demanded. "No, of course I don't want to go back to jail. I worry about it during the day. I dream about it at night. I think about my case. I think about being convicted of murder and being sent back to jail nearly every minute of every day." She looked up at David and saw the harsh lines at the corners of his mouth, saw the frustration in his eyes.

"I'm not going to let that happen." David wanted to shake her for her lack of faith in him, and at the same time he wanted to hold her and kiss her and tell her how much he admired her courage.

"You may not be able to prevent it," she said.

And they both knew it was true.

"Then help me, dammit." David's voice was raw with emotion. He wasn't going to lose Tessa, not when he'd just found her. He moved closer and put his hands on her shoulders.

It was a mistake.

Tessa leaned into him, her lips poised for kissing.

He touched his lips to hers before he could stop himself.

She reached up and wrapped her arms around his neck, increasing the contact.

The moment her breasts pressed against him, David came to his senses. He broke off the kiss. "No." His voice sounded firm. "We're not going to repeat what happened last night. We're not going to tempt fate and risk having you become pregnant."

A thought occurred to Tessa. "The girls at the Satin Slipper don't have babies."

"The girls at the Satin Slipper know how to protect themselves," David told her.

"Do you know how to do that?"

"Yes."

"Then protect me," Tessa replied logically.

"I can't," David said. He moved toward his desk. He needed distance. He needed to put something substantial between them. "I didn't protect you last night. It may already be too late. And I'm not going to take another chance."

"David . . ."

David stopped, alerted by the husky quality in Tessa's tone of voice.

"Look at me."

He turned.

She had to try just one more time to see if he would love her. "What's wrong with stealing a few hours of happiness? In a week or two, I may be in prison for the rest of my life." Tessa dropped the clothes on a chair and unbuttoned another of the buttons on the shirt she wore.

"Tessa . . ." David managed a strangled croak, watching as she slipped another button through the buttonhole.

"I want you to love me." Tessa approached him, running her finger down the middle of his chest to the arrow of coarse, dark hair that disappeared into the waistband of his trousers.

It took an almost Herculean effort, but David forced the words around his tongue. "Not while you're in my custody." He watched her. "Dammit, Tessa, help me. Give me something to go on."

Tessa undid the last button, then shrugged her shoulders letting the shirt fall down her arms. "Here." She studied the strained look on David's face, his impassive stance, and knew he was battling himself as much as her. "You'll need this to get started." She handed him his shirt, then turned, gathered her undergarments, and walked naked into her bedroom.

David stood frozen in place, watching her exit. The lock on her bedroom door clicked into place.

Walking to his desk, David grabbed the handle of the top drawer. Locked. "Damn." He paced the confines of the office, searching the floor for the key to his scotch drawer.

CHAPTER 16

The atmosphere in the office of David Alexander, attorney-at-law, grew increasingly colder as the day wore on. Tessa emerged from her bedroom about midmorning, wearing the bright yellow wool dress he'd bought her and set to work straightening the office and cleaning away the remains of breakfast. David looked up from the books and briefs scattered across his desk as Tessa prepared a lunch neither one of them wanted to eat.

He joined her at the table. She didn't speak. She placed a plate of food on the table for each of them, then sat down across from him. She didn't eat, David noticed, but poked at the vegetables on her plate, rearranging but not tasting them.

David thought about the lively meals he'd shared with Tessa and Coalie in the past few days. He hated this quiet. It reminded him of all the solitary meals he'd eaten since coming to Peaceable. He put down his fork.

"Thank you," he said, finishing his lunch and pushing back from the table.

"You're welcome," came the mechanical reply.

"You don't have to go to all this trouble for me," David said. "I can eat at one of the restaurants."

"I don't mind." Tessa stared down at the boiled potato on her plate. She had always enjoyed cooking, and since leaving Chicago, she'd had little opportunity. David needed someone to take care of him, to see that he ate properly and got enough sleep at night. She enjoyed taking care of him.

"Still," he protested, "you don't have to do it. I can afford to have meals cooked and brought in."

"It gives me something to do with my time." She looked up and found his dark gaze studying her. "I'm used to being busy."

He was thoughtful for a minute. "I can probably spare some time to start your reading and writing lessons tonight after dinner."

"I don't think that would be a good idea," Tessa told him, forcing herself to sound uninterested.

"Why not?" He asked the question out of curiosity; he wanted to know what she was thinking.

"Because I can't be close to you anymore without wanting to touch you," she answered honestly.

David felt as if she'd punched him in the gut.

Unable to tolerate the tension any longer, Tessa left the table and went back to her bedroom. She came out a few minutes later with an envelope. She handed it to David. "This might help you prepare for the hearing."

David looked up at her. "Tessa, you hardly know me. You shouldn't be so trusting where I'm concerned."

"Why not?" Tessa asked. "You've been telling me to trust you for days."

"That doesn't mean you should. It only means I want you to." David didn't understand why he was so determined to warn her; he only knew he had to do it. He somehow felt he owed her that much honesty. She didn't know him the way he knew himself. He was a liar, he'd been a spy during the war, and he had been accused of seducing an innocent girl. His past was full of half-truths and scandal. He didn't deserve her trust. He wasn't the trustworthy type. He was her lawyer, for God's sake. Didn't she know better than to trust a man like him? David studied her face, searching for a clue to what she felt.

He found it in the steadfast gaze of her china-blue eyes.

"I do trust you," Tessa said softly. "Please open the envelope. I want you to know everything."

David opened the envelope. Inside there were three photographs. He recognized the people in two of them. "Where did you get these?"

"Two of them were in my brother's coat pocket when he died." Tessa leaned over his shoulder. "Those two." She pointed out the pictures of Liam Kincaid and Arnie Mason.

David studied the photograph of Lee Kincaid. A frown creased his forehead as he thought about his last conversation with Lee. Tessa's brother had asked for the picture. Lee neglected to mention the fact that he'd obliged him.

"Why didn't you show me these before?"

"I know Liam Kincaid is your friend."

David arched an eyebrow, questioning. He and Lee had been so careful. But she had known all along. And Tessa suspected Lee.

"I saw you talking to him at the bar in the Satin Slipper. The night I sneaked back to get these pictures. I was hiding beneath the stairwell."

"You little idiot, you risked being caught twice." David couldn't keep the note of pride out of his voice.

"It was worth it," Tessa said triumphantly. "I got the pictures and my mother's rosary."

"I got the rosary," David reminded her.

Tessa ignored him. She preferred not to think about how he had gotten her rosary. She had it back in her possession and that was all that mattered. "I recognized Liam from this picture. I know he followed me to Peaceable, but I think he was after Arnie Mason, too. I think he wanted both of us." She paused, looking at David, gauging his reaction to the news. "I know he's a friend of yours, but I think maybe he killed Arnie Mason."

Interesting. Tessa had been afraid of Lee, but not of Arnie Mason. David was silent.

Tessa continued, "I don't understand why Eamon had these pictures in his pocket." She took the envelope and pulled out the picture of Arnie Mason. "It's not a very good picture, but I recognized him when I saw him at the Satin Slipper."

"Did he know you?"

"I told him who I was," Tessa replied. "I told him I was Eamon Roarke's sister and that I'd come to Peaceable to take Eamon's place at the Satin Slipper."

Good God, David thought, no wonder Arnie Mason had gone to her room! David had read the Pinkerton dossier on Arnie Mason. He knew what the man was capable of doing, what he'd done in the past. Arnie Mason had probably gone to see how much Tessa knew about her brother's business. If he was right about Mason, Tessa had walked blindly into a den of thieves.

"Did you tell Mason you'd come to take Eamon's *room* or his *place*?" David realized the wording of her statement was very important. It could have made the difference between Arnie Mason killing her or letting her live. "Think, Tessa," he urged. "It's very important."

Tessa closed her eyes, concentrating on her first meeting with Arnie Mason. "I said I'd come to take Eamon's place."

David grinned. "That's it!" He stood up and swung Tessa around. "That's it!"

"What?"

"Tessa," David explained, "this is a police photo. A picture taken of criminals. Arnie Mason was in prison." He pointed out the numbers painted across the front of Arnie Mason's shirt. "That's what the numbers mean. If I'm right, he didn't go to your room just to . . ." David paused, wondering how to tell her. Then, deciding there was no easy way, he told her straight out. "He went to your room to silence you." Seeing her blank expression, he added, "To kill you."

"Oh." Tessa's knees nearly buckled. She was quiet for a moment or two before her anger began to build. "I thought he was a friend at first, but then I realized Eamon would never make friends with someone like that. He was mean and brutish. Coalie was afraid of Arnie. He'd heard some bad things about him and warned me to stay away, but it was too late. I'd already been friendly to him and he thought . . ."

David clenched his fists. It was a good thing the son of a bitch was already dead. "That's why he went to your room that night."

"Yes," Tessa admitted. "He wanted to . . . you know . . . He tried to force me."

"What happened?"

"I fought him off." Tessa paused, remembering. "Then I saw a shadow moving behind him. The next thing I knew, Arnie was dead. Lying across me. Bleeding all over me."

"What did you do?"

"I shouted for help."

And I heard you, David thought. I heard you.

Tessa continued. "I looked up and saw Coalie at the foot of the bed. He'd been sleeping in the alcove behind the curtain. I screamed for him to get help. He ran out the door. Then, suddenly everyone came running in. I tried to explain, but some of the girls were screaming that I'd done murder, that I'd killed him. They wouldn't listen to me."

"So, Coalie came to get me while the deputies arrested you." David's voice was grim. He had the truth. Now all he had to do was prove it. And he had the proof if he could just persuade the judge and jury to put aside their bias against a saloon girl and listen to the facts. Someone had gone to a great deal of trouble to set Tessa up, but that someone had made a mistake. It hadn't been necessary for the murderer to lure Arnie to Tessa's room; he was going there anyway—to kill her. And whoever set Tessa up had written Arnie a note inviting him to Tessa's room, not knowing Tessa couldn't read or write.

"Why didn't you tell me all this before?" David asked the question, but he already knew the answer.

"I was afraid you wouldn't listen to me, that you wouldn't take the word of a saloon girl. And if you found out I'd stolen Coalie, you'd think I was a liar as well as a criminal."

It was the same prejudice he'd have to battle to save her.

David worked at his desk the rest of the afternoon, his feelings torn. He was relieved that Tessa had finally told him the whole truth about the night of the murder. That meant she trusted him. But he still wasn't confident he could save her . . . and it was now more than a matter of professional pride. He had to find someone to help put the pieces of the story together at the hearing. The logical choice was Lee, but David wasn't sure Lee would be able to testify unless his work in Peaceable was finished.

David took a deep breath. The only other logical choice was Coalie. Coalie could tell why he and Tessa left Chicago, and why they kept to themselves at the Satin Slipper. Coalie knew Tessa hadn't had a relationship with Arnie Mason because he had slept in the same room; he was, in fact, asleep in the curtained alcove when Arnie entered the room. But there was a problem. David didn't want to ask Coalie to testify, and Tessa was bound to object.

He stood up and grabbed his coat. He needed to talk to Lee.

Lying across her bed, Tessa breathed a sigh of relief when she heard him leave. She needed some room and some time to herself without David there. The living quarters were impossibly cramped under the circumstances.

Tessa wanted to laugh and cry at the same time. She was in love with David Alexander—her lawyer, but also for the time being her jailor. She was in love and living in another tiny, cramped apartment when all she ever really wanted was a home of her own and a family to share it.

Sweet Mary, how much more would she be forced to endure? Tessa almost laughed. She was in love with her jailor, her lawyer, and he didn't return her love. He wanted her; she knew that. But most of all, he wanted to take care of her. Lord, how she hated that phrase. All her life people had promised to take care of her—her mother, her father, her brother. Then they'd died and left her alone with the memories of empty promises.

Tessa didn't want anyone to take care of her. She could take care of herself, and she could take care of Coalie as well. What she wanted, what she needed most, was someone to love her and to share her life, someone who would accept Coalie as his own and give her other children to mother. She needed David. She wanted David and Coalie together and a home of her own, a little house with a yard and roses and maybe a few sheep scattered around, a place where she could lavish love and attention on her family. When this was over, when they'd found Arnie Mason's murderer, when she was free to choose her own way of life, maybe then David would love her. . . .

If they found the murderer.

Tessa squeezed her eyes shut, blotting out her surroundings. She didn't want to think about Arnie Mason's murder any more. She tried not to think at all.

She pressed her precious silver and onyx rosary, her mother's rosary, to her lips. She had finally found the man she could love. It was unfortunate that he was also her attorney, responsible for gaining her freedom. She needed all the help she could get.

Tessa felt the hot tears form behind her eyelids, then the dampness as they rolled down her cheeks, felt the lump in her throat as she struggled to recite the old familiar words. "Hail, Mary, full of grace. . . ."

She curled her body into a tight ball, whispering into the soft cotton quilt.

"You've got to tell me what you're working on." David confronted Lee at the bar of the Satin Slipper. "It's important."

"You know I can't do that," Lee answered.

"You have to." David sat on one of the barstools. "Tessa didn't kill Arnie Mason. I know that."

"Of course she didn't," Lee agreed, polishing glasses with a white towel. "She couldn't have."

"Then who the hell did?" David asked. "I have a pretty good idea, but that's not enough. You know this town. I don't just have to prove Tessa's innocence; I have to give them a murderer. Otherwise they'll hold her over for trial out of prejudice and ignorance. I have to find the murderer, and you have to help me." David leaned over the bar. "Tessa's life depends on it."

"I want to help you, David. But if I tell you what I'm working on," Lee reminded him, "*my* life could be in danger."

"If you don't tell me, my friend," David said through clenched teeth, "I guarantee your life will be in danger."

"It's against regulations," Lee hedged.

"Hang regulations! I know the regulations. And you know I won't endanger your life if I can help it."

"I'll need a few days to make some arrangements. Then I'll tell you," Lee answered.

"When?" David demanded. "I need to know."

"Soon."

"Dammit, Lee, how soon?" David demanded. "Tessa doesn't have much time."

"Neither do I," Lee muttered. He stared at a point over David's shoulder. "Damn! She's seen you."

"Who?"

Lee looked to his right and nodded. "Myra."

"Oh, hell." David barely got the words out of his mouth before the owner of the Satin Slipper approached him.

"Hello, lawyer man." Her voice was whiskey-rough, calculated to entice. "What brings you here this early in the afternoon?" She moved closer to David until she was almost standing beneath his arms. "I see you're not drinking." Myra eyed Lee disapprovingly.

"I've only been here a few minutes," David said. "I'm waiting for the coffee to finish brewing."

"Coffee?" Myra ran her right hand down the front of David's shirt, her scarlet fingernails tracing the threads around one buttonhole. "Lawyer man, you know I don't make any money serving coffee." She turned to Lee. "Pour the man some scotch."

"Yes, ma'am." Lee hurried to comply.

"I don't want scotch," David said. "It's too early."

"It's never too early for good scotch," Myra scoffed. "Besides, it's on the house, lawyer man." She moved her hand upward until the scarlet nail of her index finger reached his chin. "Anything else you want?"

David shrugged his shoulders. "Not today. Sorry."

Myra's eyes narrowed. "Not today, not tonight, not ever." She withdrew her hand from his face. Smiling at David, she kissed the tip of her finger. "Could be you're getting what you need elsewhere—from the little Irish girl." She moved to touch her finger to his lips.

David reached out and intercepted her, the strong, lean fingers of his hand closing around the delicate bones of her right wrist. "What have you got against her, Myra?" David moved the pad of his thumb against her wrist, feeling the abrasion encircling it.

"I don't have anything against her, lawyer man." Taking encouragement from the movement of his thumb against her pulse, Myra rubbed herself against him. "I knew her brother while he was here in Peaceable. We were very close. It's a shame he died so young." She shuddered. "Horrible to think of him run down by a wagon. That's why I gave the poor girl a job and a place to stay. I felt sorry for her."

"I'm sure Miss Roarke appreciates your concern." David loosened his grip on Myra's wrist. "I'll be sure to tell her."

"You do that." Myra stepped back. "You tell her for me."

David released her arm.

"I'll be here if you need me, lawyer man." She blew him a kiss. "For anything. Anything at all."

"Nice act," David said when Myra moved out of earshot.

"Yep," Lee agreed. "I was just thinking the same thing." He set a cup of coffee down in front of David.

"Was Eamon Roarke run down by a wagon?" David sipped at the black coffee.

"Uh-huh. Right in front of the detective agency. Witnesses said the driver fit Arnie Mason's description."

"You think Arnie Mason killed Tessa's brother?"

"That's about it," Lee answered.

David placed his cup back on the saucer. He bit back a wry laugh.

"What's so funny?" Lee demanded.

David looked him in the eye. "Not funny. Ironic." David took the picture of Lee out of his pocket and slid it across the bar. "Tessa gave me that this afternoon. Her brother had it in his pocket the day he died, along with a police photo of Arnie Mason."

Lee glanced at the picture. "Christ!"

"You think Arnie Mason killed Eamon Roarke. Tessa thinks you killed Arnie."

"Me?" Lee was all innocence. "You know me. Do you believe I killed him?" He shook his head in dismay. "I swear that woman hates me." Lee handed the picture back to David.

"She also thinks you were trying to take Coalie back to Chicago."

"What would I want with the kid?" Lee asked, genuinely puzzled.

"A reward for his return," David replied.

"Damn," Lee muttered. "So when I followed her and the boy from Chicago, she thought—"

"You were after Coalie."

"No wonder she attacked me." Lee whistled low, pulled the towel from over his shoulder, and started polishing the bar. He paused and looked at David. "And you, my friend? What do you think?"

David slipped the photograph into his coat pocket. He looked up and met Lee Kincaid's worried gaze. "I don't think you killed Mason."

"Thank God!" Lee exhaled. "With Eamon gone, I don't have too many friends left." He smiled at David.

"And I'd sure hate to lose one."

David returned his smile. "Then I'd say this calls for a celebration. What time is it?" he asked Lee. "Oh, wait, I forgot—your watch is at the jeweler's." David patted his pocket searching for his.

"I've got mine," Lee said, reaching for his pocket watch. "The jeweler put a new crystal on it and repaired the clasp on the chain. I picked it up from the store this morning."

David watched carefully as Lee removed his time-piece from his waistcoat pocket. The flashy gold watch dangled from a delicate gold chain. A chain that didn't match the one David had in his top desk drawer.

CHAPTER 17

Tessa was waiting when David returned to the office.

"You've been to the Satin Slipper." Her heart constricted when she smelled the perfume on him.

"Yes," David answered. He placed a big basket on his desk, then took off his coat and hung it on the rack. His nose wrinkled in distaste as he caught a whiff of Myra's scent. He hastened to explain. "It isn't what you think. Myra turns into a cat and rubs herself against me every time I go into the saloon." Tessa's eyes were red and swollen. She'd been crying. "I had a few questions for Lee Kincaid."

"I see."

"I don't think you do," David said. "Look, I stopped by the hotel restaurant and picked up some supper." He gestured toward the basket. David knew Tessa missed Coalie. He understood that she was lonely and often bored within the confines of the small apartment with only him and Horace Greeley for company, so despite his best intentions to limit his social contact with her, David had brought home a picnic for two. All the way from the hotel, he'd told himself he should keep his distance from Tessa, but with each step that brought him closer to her another part of him reminded him how much he missed her, how much he wanted to share with her. He didn't want to stay away. He couldn't. It took so little to make Tessa happy, and despite everything David realized he wanted to make her happy. "I thought we could have a picnic."

"In November?" Tessa didn't believe him. "In freezing weather?"

"We'll have it indoors and pretend it's spring." David walked to his bedroom and returned a few minutes later with a quilt. He spread it on the floor in front of the stove.

Tessa stared as he unpacked the basket, placing all of the containers on the quilt.

He looked up at Tessa. "We need plates and utensils. I couldn't talk the hotel into loaning me any more." He gave her a halfhearted smile. "I keep forgetting to return them." He knelt down on the quilt.

Tessa wanted to laugh. So that accounted for the mismatched plates and cups. He probably had plates from every eating establishment in town. "Wouldn't it be simpler just to buy some?" She walked to the cupboard, took down two plates, and handed them to him. "What about cups?"

"Not yet. But you can bring some warm water." He held up his hands, wiggling his fingers. "For our fingers." David unpacked a bottle of wine and two glasses. "I got this from Lee." He noticed the way Tessa tensed at the mention of Lee's name. "He gave me the wine to spite Myra and threw in the glasses for good measure."

Tessa gasped. "But she counts all the glasses. If they're missing it will come out of his pay." She handed him the silverware.

"Lee didn't seem to mind." David smiled in remembrance. A bottle of Myra's finest scotch whisky nestled in the bottom of David's picnic basket as well. Lee had given it to him. On the house. "Sit down." He patted a corner of the quilt. He finished unloading the basket, except for the scotch, and tugged off his boots.

She laughed as he wiggled his toes in front of the stove. Opening the door, she dumped another scuttle full of coal into the stove's potbellied interior. "Better?"

"Quite toasty." He wiggled his toes again, just to hear her throaty laughter. He wasn't disappointed. "Why don't you join me?" He uncorked the wine and poured two glasses, then uncovered the fried chicken. He stared up at Tessa, arching one brow in disapproval.

She sat down and stretched out her legs.

"Now we wait," he said, smiling, "for Greeley to join us." He began to count.

"You're timing him?"

"Uh-huh." David reached for her ankles. Grabbing one, he struggled with the buttons on her shoes.

Tessa laughed.

A streak of orange suddenly burst out of the storeroom and trotted into the office to inspect the picnic. Horace Greeley ambled over to David. He sniffed David's fingers, then butted his orange head against David's hand, demanding affection.

"I wanted to see how long it would take old Horace here to smell the chicken and come running." David stopped trying to unbutton her shoes and moved his boots aside. Reaching for her plate, he filled it with fried chicken and potato salad. He handed it to Tessa, then filled his own.

Tessa watched his long fingers as he patiently tore pieces of chicken into tiny, cat-sized pieces for Greeley.

"No!" Tessa shrieked when David placed the chicken on the quilt. She scrambled to her feet, hurried to the cupboard, and returned with a saucer. Shooing the cat away, Tessa scooped up the meat and arranged it on the saucer. Greeley protested, weaving his way between Tessa and the dish, but she wasn't putting up with his nonsense. She picked him up and hugged him, then set him down beside his saucer. "If we'd known you were coming," she told the orange tom, "we'd have set a place for you."

"Now you see why I eat in restaurants." David chuckled. "He gets more of my food than I do."

"He's a growing boy," Tessa commented, patting the cat affectionately.

"I thought you didn't like mangy cats," David teased.

"I don't," Tessa smiled, her eyes sparkling. "But this cat is far from mangy. He has a way of growing on you."

"And his owner?" David prompted.

"Tolerable." Tessa washed her hands in the warm water.

"Just tolerable?" David handed her a glass of wine, then returned his attention to her shoes, but he wasn't having much success removing them.

"Very tolerable." Tessa took the glass, then stood up.

"Where are you going?"

"Buttonhook," she explained. "This is a picnic. I want to wiggle my toes and feel the grass under my feet before it's over." She went to her bedroom and returned with the buttonhook for her shoes. She handed it over to him.

"Thanks," David said, wielding the buttonhook effectively. He loosened her shoes, then slipped them off and placed them next to his boots. Finished, he dipped his fingers in the finger bowl, dried them on a napkin, and reached for more chicken.

Tessa stretched out on the quilt, propping herself up on her elbow and resting her head against the palm of her hand. She nudged David's feet with one of hers. "Move over," she ordered. "I want my toes to be toasty, too." Scooting closer to the stove, she placed her stocking-covered feet over his, seeking the heat. "Oh, dear . . ." Tessa giggled.

"What is it?"

"Now I can't reach my plate."

"Not to worry." David grinned. "I'll feed you." He picked up a piece of white meat and tore it into strips. "Open up," he directed, tantalizing her with the delectable piece of chicken.

She did.

David popped a strip of chicken into her mouth. He realized his error when Tessa's tongue touched the tips of his fingers. He groaned, shifting his position on the quilt to hide his sudden arousal. He took a swallow of the white wine. "Maybe this wasn't such a good idea."

Tessa frowned, disappointed. "I think it's a lovely way to eat supper." She smiled up at David. "I've never been on a picnic before."

David drained his glass. "Then we should do it more often." He wanted to see her smile again. He wanted to taste her again, to drink the wine from her lips. He raised his wineglass, but she hadn't touched hers. "Don't you like the wine?"

"I've never had wine before." She sniffed her glass and wrinkled her nose.

David chuckled. "Don't smell it. Taste it."

Tessa took a hesitant sip. She liked the tart sensation on her tongue. She smiled. "It's good."

He drained his glass, then refilled it.

Horace Greeley finished his meal then moved over to David's lap.

Tessa laughed as the greedy cat butted at David's hand trying to intercept the food.

"This is not for you, fella." He tore another piece of chicken off the bone and held it out to her. "This is for the lady."

She took the food in her fingers and nibbled at it. Greeley hurried over to investigate. David grabbed him.

"Watch it, boy, or you'll be back on the streets fending for yourself," he warned the tom.

"Is that where you got him?" Tessa studied the motion of David's hand as he fingered the cat's torn ear and massaged the thick orange fur.

"Yep. I found him when he was a kitten."

"Tell me," Tessa urged. She loved the sound of David's voice, loved the way it rumbled in his chest, not unlike the purring of the cat. "Tell me how you found him and how he got his name." She reached for her plate. David passed it to her. "You talk. I'll feed myself. I'm hungry."

"I found him in Washington, at the train station," David remembered. "A group of nasty little boys had sicced their dog on him." He scratched Greeley's chin. The cat purred enthusiastically. He stretched out next to David's body, closing his green eyes until they were mere slits. "He was so tiny and helpless. Just a patch of spitting orange fur hiding beneath the steps of the platform."

"What did you do?"

"I ran the boys and the dog off, then crawled under the platform to rescue him. I was afraid he'd dart out onto the tracks if I left him there." David fingered the damaged ear. "The boys had hurt him. Ripped his ear. It was bleeding. I didn't really think I could save him." David wanted her to understand. "But I had to try."

"Do you do that often?" Tessa wanted to know. "Do you make a habit of rescuing creatures in distress?"

"No."

"Really? I wonder."

She spoke so softly David looked up to see if he'd heard correctly. She stared at him, her blue-eyed gaze penetrating his defenses. It was as if she'd looked into his soul. "I'll bet when you were a little boy you always brought home wounded animals and baby birds."

"How did you know that?" David challenged.

"It's obvious," Tessa pointed out. "First you rescued Greeley. Then me." Her smile was smug, knowing.

"No," he said. "Greeley was second." He inhaled a deep breath. "You were third."

"Who was first?"

He'd known she would ask. She couldn't help but ask. But once he'd mentioned it, David had second thoughts about telling her the story.

"You don't have to tell me if you don't want to," Tessa told him. She pushed her plate to the side.

"I do." The moment he said the words, the doubts were gone. He did want to tell her. He needed to tell her. Tessa would understand.

"Her name was Caroline Millen."

"Oh." Tessa wasn't sure she wanted to hear the rest. "A woman from your past."

"No." David shook his head. He nudged her foot with one of his larger ones, then reached out and grasped her hand. He needed to touch her. To hold her. "A girl from my past. Little more than a child, really. She'd just turned sixteen. I found her, too."

"Where?" Tessa prompted.

"Outside a theater in Washington." He frowned. "I'd gone backstage to speak to the actors, so I left by the stage door. It was pouring rain," he remembered. "I stepped out into the alley and saw her sitting on a packing crate in the middle of a thunderstorm, crying. I went over and touched her. When she looked up, I recognized her." He gave Tessa an ironic smile. "Her father was Senator Warner Millen. I'd been to their house for dinner; we were acquainted socially. I thought highly of him. In fact, I'd been invited to Caroline's first adult party and had escorted her to dinner."

Tessa wondered if it had been a thrill for the young girl to be escorted into the dining room by a handsome man like David. She envied the faceless girl back east. Tessa knew what it was like to be held in his arms. She knew how it felt to make love with him, but she wanted more. She wanted to have the right to sit beside him, even dance with him in public, in front of crowds of people.

"Tessa? Would you like some?"

She turned her attention back to David. He had poured more wine into his glass. He held the bottle poised over hers, waiting.

"Yes, thank you." She lifted her glass. "Go on," she encouraged when David seemed satisfied to remain quiet. "You were dining with her in Washington."

"Only once," David said. "But I recognized her that night at the theater, and she recognized me." His laugh was harsh. "That was my misfortune." He paused to take a swallow of wine.

"What happened?" Tessa sipped her wine, waiting none too patiently for him to continue.

"I offered her a ride home in my carriage. She accepted. I took her home. I walked her to the front door, and I never saw her again."

"That's it?" Caught up in the story David had made sound like a fairy tale, Tessa was disappointed with the abrupt ending. It was supposed to have a happy ending or a tragic one. All stories did.

"No." David managed a wry smile. "A month or so later Senator Millen stormed into my town house demanding that I marry his daughter. She was pregnant, and she had told her parents I was the child's father."

"But you weren't."

"I'd seen the girl only twice—once at her home and once outside the theater. That's what I told the senator."

"But he didn't believe you, did he?" Tessa understood.

"No, he didn't. Caroline had named me, and the senator was determined I would pay for ruining his daughter." David put down his wineglass. "I tried to explain that I'd never had intimate relations with her." He looked at Tessa. She saw the pain in his eyes, the memory of betrayal. "I thought the senator was my friend. I never dreamed . . . He was willing to accept me as a son-in-law if I married Caroline, but if I didn't, he said he'd ruin me—destroy my reputation, my career in Washington, everything I'd worked to gain. I couldn't believe it."

"You refused to marry her, didn't you." It was a statement, not a question. Tessa knew the answer, knew part of the story's ending.

"Of course I refused. I didn't love the girl, I didn't even know her, and I wasn't about to marry her." David sounded frustrated. "But sometimes I think things might have turned out better if I had."

"Don't think about what might have been," Tessa told him. "It hurts too much." And it hurt her too much to hear him doubt himself. To wonder if maybe he should have married Caroline Millen.

"The senator kept his promise to ruin me. All would have been forgiven if I'd agreed to marry Caroline. Until I refused, I was son-in-law material, a fine, upstanding attorney. After I said no, I was the dirty, no-good half-breed who had raped his daughter." He gripped her hand tighter.

"I'm so sorry." Tessa drew in a breath at the raw emotion in his voice. She felt his pain. The pain of being accused of a terrible crime and knowing you're innocent.

"My career in Washington was over." David drank the last of his wine, then inhaled deeply. "So I packed my clothes and my shingle and came home to Wyoming." He scratched the top of Greeley's head. "That's how this fella got his name. I was a young man going west, just as the real Horace Greeley had suggested. My cat was going with me, so I thought the name Horace Greeley was appropriate."

"You came to Peaceable?"

"I opened an office in Cheyenne first, but the city's growing. It's full of businessmen and politicians who travel to and from Washington. The scandal followed me. Nobody wanted an attorney with a reputation for seducing innocent girls and abandoning them to the mercy of their parents. I stayed a few months, then bought the office here in Peaceable. I wanted to forget. This town needed another attorney. They didn't care about the mess in Washington." David moved the cat to one side. He picked up his fork and poked at his food. "So here I am. End of story."

"What happened to Caroline?"

"She died," David answered. "She gave birth to a little girl and gave the baby my last name. She died, still protecting her lover's identity."

His words were full of bitterness.

"You did care for her," Tessa told him.

"Care for her?" David repeated. "I didn't know her. Christ, I can't even remember what she looked like."

"But you think about her."

"Every day of my life," David admitted. "I think she might still be alive if only I'd tried to help her. She was desperate. Young and pregnant and afraid of her father's wrath. I should have done more for her. I should have cared enough to marry her, but I didn't. I believed in love. I didn't care enough for Caroline to offer her a home and accept her child as my own." He looked at Tessa. "I didn't care enough to sacrifice my freedom, and I wasn't there when her parents turned their backs on her and shipped her off to have the baby all by herself."

"Why should you have been there?" Tessa asked him. "You weren't the baby's father. You were innocent. She lied about you to try to help herself, so she obviously didn't care about you. Why should it matter so much to you?"

"Because no one should die believing she's been forsaken," David said fiercely. "I saw too much of that on the battlefield." He turned to Tessa. "Don't you see? She trusted me to do the right thing."

"She used you," Tessa corrected, "hoping you'd feel responsible. There's a difference."

"It doesn't matter," David said. "It doesn't change anything. Caroline Millen is dead. Senator and Mrs. Millen are alone. And somewhere in an orphanage back east, a little girl with my last name feels she's been abandoned."

"So?" Tessa asked him, ignoring his look of outrage at her seeming heartlessness.

"What do you mean, 'so'?"

"If you feel that way, what are you going to do about it?" Tessa demanded.

"What can I do about it?" David asked. "I'm not the baby's father."

"But you want her."

"Yes, I do."

"Then find her," Tessa ordered. "Bring her home."

"I can't take care of her by myself," David admitted. "I don't know anything about babies or little girls. And do you really think I could find a woman to take both of us on, a half-breed Indian and an orphan?"

"Why not?" Tessa told him, her eyes sparkling with emotion. "You did it. You were willing to take on a redheaded Irish girl and an orphan boy when no one else in town cared." She reached out and placed her hand against David's cheek. "I'd take her," she told David. "I'd love her, and I'd never let her go."

David looked down and met Tessa's earnest blue-eyed gaze. He moved his face against her hand, then pressed his lips against her palm. Looking at Tessa, he knew he felt the same way. He didn't intend to let her go. Or Coalie, or Lily Catherine, either. He wanted them all.

He hoped he could find a way to win them.

CHAPTER 18

"It's time." Lee rapped on the glass pane in the back door after midnight four nights later.

David sat at his desk completely dressed, overcoat and all, waiting. As he'd waited every night since their talk at the Satin Slipper. He heard the knock, picked up his gloves and boots, and tiptoed to the back door. He slipped outside and sat down on the wooden step to pull on his boots. "I'm ready," he said to Lee when he finished.

"Let's go."

David turned to lock the back door, then pulled on his gloves. Tessa lay inside sleeping. He hated leaving her alone, unprotected, but he had no choice. He had to see for himself what Lee was investigating. David followed Lee down the dark alley where two horses waited.

"How far is it?" David climbed atop his mount.

"A couple of miles outside of town," Lee replied. "I've been watching the place for about a week now." He looked at David, guessing his feelings. "You should be back well before daybreak. You won't have to leave Tessa alone too long."

They rode in silence until they reached Lee's observation point. Lee hobbled the horses before leading the way. David fell into step behind him, crouching low to avoid detection. The chill air made breathing difficult, talking more so. They reached the crude shelter and crept inside, waiting.

David sat on the frozen ground and wrapped his arms around his knees, pulling his long legs up against his chest for warmth. He flipped the collar of his coat up around his ears and covered his nose and mouth with his dark wool scarf. Lee followed suit.

"This shouldn't take long," Lee whispered. "It's too cold for them to want to linger outside. The mail train was robbed yesterday outside Laramie. They'll come here to divide the cash."

"How much did they get?" David asked.

"About six thousand dollars."

Less than an hour later Lee's prediction came true. David watched as three men rode up to an abandoned shack, dismounted, and went inside. All three carried bulging saddlebags.

"According to Eamon Roarke, Arnie Mason led the ring. He robbed several mail and payroll trains, but the ring is also into anything else that's profitable. They've run stolen cattle through here. Also guns and illegal liquor."

"Liquor." David breathed the word. "Where do they take it? To the reservations?"

"You've got it. They'd have been pretty secure if they hadn't decided to dabble in smuggling liquor," Lee answered. "That's what tipped Eamon off."

"Of course." David whistled low. "The best place to hide large amounts of stolen cash and large quantities of liquor is in plain sight. A saloon."

"And not just any saloon," Lee agreed, "but the largest, most profitable one in town."

"The Satin Slipper." David placed his gloved hands over his nose and mouth, blowing into them to warm his face.

"Why do you think I've been tending bar there?" Lee asked. "I worked at several others in town asking questions before I applied at the Satin Slipper. Myra's clever." Lee had to smile in admiration. "She's the brains behind the operation. I've only caught a glimpse at the books, but she's hiding the money there somewhere. Circulating small amounts at a time through the saloon."

"What happened with Arnie Mason? Did he want a larger portion of the profits?" David asked. "Did she panic?"

"Arnie was mouthing off," Lee explained. "Getting drunk, boasting about having the run of the saloon and Myra. But she isn't the sort to panic. She thought she had Arnie under control."

"Until he followed Eamon Roarke back to Chicago." David picked up the trail of Lee's thoughts. "And killed him."

"Exactly," Lee confirmed. "Eamon got too close to the truth. He knew Myra was beginning to get suspicious of him. That's why he returned to Chicago."

"When Arnie took it upon himself to run Eamon down, he became a liability to Myra."

"He didn't follow orders," Lee said, "and Myra knew that if Eamon was really a detective, the agency would send another investigator and another and another until Eamon's killer was caught. It was just a matter of time."

"But Tessa showed up, with Coalie in tow, before you did," David said, "and announced that she was Eamon Roarke's sister, come to take his place." He took a deep breath. "Christ!"

"She's lucky to be alive."

"Yes," David agreed. "She escaped being murdered only to be framed for it." He shuddered at the thought of Tessa lying on a table at the undertaker's.

"At least now you should be able to prove she didn't kill Arnie."

"Yes," David agreed, "but first I've got to get the jury to listen. It's not enough just to present the facts and tell the truth. I've got to get their sympathy. Then I can prove Tessa didn't kill anyone."

"How are you going to get their sympathy?" Lee asked out of curiosity.

"I've got a plan," David told him. "But Tessa's not going to like it." He studied the toes of his boots. She wasn't going to like it one bit.

Lee took out his pocket watch and opened it. He turned his back, then struck a match so he could read the dial. Finished, he extinguished the flame and pocketed his timepiece.

David turned his attention to Lee. "What about you? How are you going to prove that Myra Brennan is behind all this?"

"Catch her accepting the cash."

"As if it were so simple," David commented.

"In this case, it is," Lee said. "This is where I leave you." Lee got to his knees, stood up, and stretched.

"Where are you going?" David wondered what Lee was up to.

"Down there." Lee pointed to the shack. "I'm the go-between." He chuckled. "I'm Myra's pickup man." An ironic smile turned up one corner of his mouth when he looked at David. "Convenient, eh?"

David followed Lee back to the horses. "Be careful, you rogue. You're getting too old for this," he teased. "We're both getting too old for this."

"Yeah." Lee chuckled. "Ancient at thirty-three."

"That's old for your line of work," David reminded him, "but not for mine."

"Yeah, I know." Lee was serious. "I've been think-ing of settling down same as you." He released the hobbles and mounted his horse.

"I'm not—"

"Oh, yes, you are," Lee corrected. "I've got eyes, my friend, and ears, and I can see you've got it bad." He clamped his hat down on his blond head. "But if you don't watch out, somebody's liable to snatch Tessa right out from under your nose." He turned his horse around. "Give her a kiss for me when you get back," he said to David. "She's the reason Myra trusted me with this pickup." Seeing David's puzzled expression, Lee explained. "Myra decided that since Tessa hated me, I couldn't be a Pinkerton man. I couldn't have known or worked with her brother." He shrugged his shoulders. "Big mistake. But then, who can figure women?"

Lee waved good-bye, then carefully picked his way down the dark trail leading to the shack.

David climbed atop his mount and turned his horse in the opposite direction, back to Peaceable.

David had to rouse the young man in the livery to stable his horse. He didn't like the idea of the stableboy knowing he'd been riding in the early morning hours, but his only alternative was to leave his horse tied to the rail outside his office, exposed to the cold night air, and he couldn't bring himself to do that.

The stableboy grinned at David as he took the horse's reins. "Been out to your ranch, Mr. Alexander?"

"No." David didn't bother to lie or to elaborate.

"Oh, I get it," the boy continued, "gone to see a lady friend?"

"Something like that." Better to let the town think he had a woman friend outside of town than to have them speculate on his sleeping arrangements at the office. And David had no doubts the gossips in town would hear about his midnight excursion. He flipped a silver coin at the boy. "Give him a good rubdown and an extra measure of oats." He patted the horse on the neck, left the stable, and walked to his office.

Pausing at the back step, David tugged off his boots and stood in stocking feet while he fumbled for the door key. He eased open the door and tiptoed inside, boots in hand.

Immediately he sensed a presence, then caught a movement from the corner of his eye. Dropping his boots, he quickly jumped aside, but he wasn't fast enough. A numbing blow landed on his shoulder, jolting him, radiating pain down his arm. "Dammit! That hurt!"

"David?" Tessa's whisper sounded loud in the quiet room.

"Yes, it's me," he answered. "What the hell'd you hit me with?" He leaned against the door, closing it. He recognized her soft tread a minute before she lit the lamp.

"This."

He turned. Tessa stood beside him. She held the heavy skillet up for him to see.

"You nearly brained me with that thing." David felt the cold sweat of reaction pop out on his brow. "I thought you were asleep."

"I thought you were a thief breaking in."

"I unlocked the door," David pointed out. "I used a key."

"Anybody could have unlocked that door with a skeleton key," Tessa said.

"But it wasn't just anybody." David levered himself away from the door. "It was me." He tried to shrug out of his coat. It was impossible without help. "Christ! I think you broke my shoulder." The pain forced him to utter the words between clenched teeth. "Help me out of this," he said. "Please."

Tessa placed the cast-iron frying pan back in the cupboard and hurried over to help David with his coat. "Come sit down." She led him to a chair near the stove and pushed him down into it. "I'll put on water for tea."

"Yes," David sarcastically agreed, "we mustn't forget the magic elixir. The cure-all."

Tessa ignored him. She went to the cupboard, took down the kettle, filled it with water, and plunked it on the stove. "You brought this on yourself," she scolded him. "What were you doing sneaking around in the middle of the night?"

"I wasn't sneaking around." David took offense. "I had a business meeting."

Tessa sniffed at his clothing, trying to detect the telltale odor of cigar smoke, liquor, and cheap perfume. But all she was able to smell was the manly scent of him mixed with the clean fragrance of the cold night air and the sweat of horses. "At three o'clock in the morning?" She tugged his coat sleeve down his injured arm.

"It was a late meeting." He shifted in his chair so she could pull the coat out from behind him. She didn't miss a trick, David thought. His mother was going to love her.

"Obviously," Tessa replied. "With your friend Liam Kincaid?"

"I can't answer that," David hedged. "Not yet."

"You don't have to." Tessa tossed his coat aside and began unbuttoning his shirt. "You don't have to tell me anything." Her words said one thing, her tone of voice another.

"Tessa, I'll be happy to tell you anything you want to know after tomorrow, but right now I can't. I'm sworn to secrecy until this is all over." David sucked in his breath as her cool hands unbuttoned the top of his union suit and slipped inside it to touch his chest. He tried to think of something to say, anything to change the subject. "What are you doing up at this hour?"

"I couldn't sleep," Tessa admitted. "I guess I'm a little nervous about the hearing on Monday. I thought I heard something moving around outside." She pushed his shirt and the top of his union suit off his shoulder and down his arm.

"It was probably Horace Greeley."

"Out in this cold? Not likely," Tessa contradicted him. "Your cat is curled up in my bed, asleep."

Just where he wanted to be, David thought.

She walked to the cupboard and took out a box of matches, then went back to the office and lowered the oil lamp suspended overhead. She touched a match to the wicks and turned them up higher, bathing the office in the yellow glow of the lamp. "Move over beneath the light so I can see better."

"If you could've seen better, you wouldn't have hit me with the frying pan," David grumbled. He scooted his chair directly under the lamp. "Ouch, dammit, that hurts!"

Tessa probed the flesh of his shoulder. "I don't think it's broken." She felt for the shoulder joint. The area was swollen and tender. "You need some liniment for the bruise. It's going to be sore for a few days," she predicted.

"Thank you, Dr. Roarke," David said wryly. "I could have told you that. It's sore already."

"You're lucky it's only a bruise," Tessa reminded him. "I could have really hurt you." She gently caressed the injured area.

"You did really hurt me."

To his amazement, Tessa shouted at him, then burst into tears. "You scared me half to death," she accused. "All I could think of was Arnie Mason creeping into my room."

"Come here," David ordered, feeling like a complete ogre. He extended his uninjured arm.

Tessa knelt beside him, allowing him to soothe her frayed nerves.

David patted her hair, smoothing the wayward strands off her forehead. "It's all right. It's all right, my love. Arnie Mason is dead. Very, very dead. He can't hurt you anymore."

Tessa turned her face against his knee so she could see him. "But whoever killed Arnie is still alive." She swallowed hard. "And he could come after me.

Sometimes at night I close my eyes and see Arnie Mason's face. I see the way he looked lying there. I can't get it out of my mind. Tonight I dreamed about him."

"You should have come to me," David told her, still rubbing her thick curls. "I won't let anyone hurt you, Tessa."

"I did come to you," she told him. "And a fine lot of good it did me." Her eyes sparkled wetly as she ruthlessly blinked back the tears. "I went to your room, but you weren't there. Then I heard a noise. Lucky I had a heavy skillet."

"Yeah, lucky," David commented. He knew she didn't really need him for protection so much as for reassurance. She'd done all right with the frying pan. But still, Tessa'd gone to him for protection for the first time since he'd known her, and he'd been out with Lee hunting criminals. "You're the bravest woman I know. I'm sorry I wasn't here when you thought you needed me." He awkwardly fumbled in his back pants pocket for his handkerchief and offered it to her. Feeling her warm breath against him, David shifted in the chair and concentrated on the throbbing in his shoulder rather than the pounding in his groin. "Would you like me to make the tea for you?" He felt helpless in the face of her unexpected show of weakness.

Tessa blew her nose on his handkerchief. She pushed herself to her feet. "I'll make it." She managed a half-smile for David's benefit. "Would you like some?"

"Only if you'll pour a little scotch into it," David answered. One day he'd have to work up the courage to tell her how much he hated tea. "My shoulder hurts like the very devil."

"It's your own fault," she told him. "But I'm sorry I hit you so hard."

"I'm not. You did the right thing. What if I had been a prowler?"

"I'd have brained you." A couple of tears slipped down her face.

The sight of them deeply disturbed David. "But you didn't." He got to his feet and walked to the stove. "Come on. I'll help you make the tea," he said, lifting the kettle of hot water off the stove.

"No, really," Tessa protested. "You rest. I'll do it. I'm fine now." She struggled for composure.

"If you're sure . . ." David walked over to his desk and sat down in the big leather chair.

"I'm sure," Tessa told him. She went to the cupboard and took down the box of tea, two cups and saucers, two spoons and the sugar bowl. David liked his tea hot and sweet. "Where do you keep the whisky?"

"The key's hanging on a hook above the door," David answered. "The scotch is locked in my desk drawer."

Seeing her surprised expression, David offered a partial explanation. "I didn't want Coalie to see the bottle sitting around."

"I understand," Tessa said. She located the key and handed it to him.

David debated for a moment longer before telling her the whole truth. "And you were here." He stared down at his desk. "I didn't want to be tempted to drink myself into a stupor every night," he admitted.

"But, David, I don't mind if you drink as long as it makes you . . . you know . . ." She couldn't put her thoughts into words. She busied herself carrying the cups and saucers to the table, then going back to the cupboard for the sugar bowl and the box of tea.

"It makes me drunk," David told her. "That's all."

"But what about wanting to make love to a woman all night long?"

"You make me want to do that," he confessed. "You make me want to make love to you all night long. Nothing else." David unlocked the drawer, retrieved the bottle of scotch, and set it on his desk.

"Oh." Blushing, Tessa spooned tea into the kettle.

David smiled. "Yes, 'oh.'" He mimicked her. "Come here." His voice was deep, husky with emotion.

"I don't think that's a good idea." Tessa recognized the look in his dark eyes. She wanted to. Very much. But not tonight. Not with her hearing a day away. She wasn't going to add to David's burdens. She'd thought about it a lot since the night they'd made love. David was right. What if there was a child? His child?

"Why not?" He whirled the chair halfway around.

"Your shoulder."

David extended the bottle of whisky. "Fill half my tea cup with this and pretty soon I'll forget all about my shoulder."

She reached for the bottle.

David reached for her. He clasped her wrist and pulled her toward him.

"David . . ."

"All I want is a kiss," he coaxed. "Just one kiss to ease the pain." He couldn't control the urge. He'd been thinking about kissing her ever since Lee had teased him. At the moment he couldn't think of anything else. He wanted to feel her lips against his, feel their breath mingle. He wanted to take her in his arms and make love to her, but since he couldn't do that, he wanted to kiss her.

She leaned forward and met him halfway.

He nibbled at her lower lip, then soothed the tiny bites with his tongue. He licked the seam of her lips to gain entry. Tessa parted her lips. Her tongue met his. David foraged. He used his tongue to rake the inside of her mouth, her tongue, and the slick-hard surface of her teeth. David stroked her, his tongue recreating the intimate act, reminding her, making her remember all they'd shared. Passion took flame. Tessa whimpered with need as he deepened the kiss, crushing her to him. She kissed him back, meeting him thrust for thrust. Searching, seeking the source of her pleasure.

David spread his legs. Tessa stepped into the opening. He placed one arm on her hip, exerting just enough pressure to push her down onto his leg. She sat in his lap, bracing herself against his shoulders. He cradled her like a child while he kissed her like a lover.

Aching with the need to mold her breasts against his chest, Tessa wrapped her arms around his back, kneading him like a cat. He left her lips and moved to kiss her cheeks, her eyelids, her nose, the slender column of her neck. She tilted her head back, welcoming his sensual exploration.

His kisses grew wilder, deeper, more passionate. Tessa gripped his shoulders and held on.

David groaned in pain, then tore his mouth away from hers, gasping for breath.

Realizing she'd hurt him, Tessa let go.

David throbbed. All over. The pain of his arousal surpassed even the pain of his bruised shoulder. He stared at Tessa. Her fiery red hair hung loose about her shoulders. Her blue eyes were dark with passion, her mouth swollen and red from his kisses, the firm line of her jaw showing signs of whisker burn. She'd never looked more desirable. He'd never wanted her more.

He kissed the tip of her nose. "Maybe you were right. Maybe a kiss wasn't such a good idea. I don't want to stop with a kiss, but my shoulder..." He used his injured shoulder as an excuse to let her go.

Tessa stood up, self-consciously running her hands down the front of her flannel nightgown to still their quaking and help soothe the aching need of her body. She wanted to be touched, needed to be touched, and she wanted David's knowledgeable hands to do the touching. "Why don't I pour the tea before it gets cold?"

David nodded. "That's a good idea," he agreed. "We'll drink a cup of soothing tea and go to bed." That was the plan, though David had little hope that it would work.

Tessa poured the tea into the cups, adding a hefty splash of whisky to his, then sat down at the table. David got up from his chair at the desk and joined her, sitting in his usual spot.

They drank the tea in silence. David finished his first and lowered his cup. It clattered against the saucer. He yawned widely. "I'm ready for bed."

"Me, too." Tessa set her half-empty cup aside and stood up. "Leave the dishes. I'll get them in the morning."

"All right." David felt awkward, clumsy. He didn't want her to leave, but he couldn't ask her to stay.

"Well..." Tessa hesitated. "I'll go to bed now." She looked at David, at his shirt and his undergarment pushed over his injured shoulder. "Will you be okay?"

"I'll manage."

"Well, good night."

"Good night."

David waited until he heard her bedroom door close before he pushed himself to his feet. He checked the doors and windows, banked the coals in the stove, extinguished the lamps, and stumbled off to bed. He listened for the sound of the key turning in Tessa's lock. But it didn't come. He realized that for the first time since she'd come to stay with him, Tessa Roarke had left her door unlocked.

David heard her cries an hour or so later. He'd been lying in bed unable to sleep for the throbbing in his shoulder. He rolled over onto his uninjured side and pushed the sheets and the quilt back out of the way.

He padded barefoot across the hall to Tessa's room and knocked at the door. "Tessa?"

She didn't answer.

David turned the doorknob. The door swung open silently on well-oiled hinges. "Contessa?" He spoke softly, reaching out to touch her shoulder.

She was dreaming. Bad dreams. Her body jerked against the covers. She cried out in her sleep. It tore at David's heart to see her anguish.

He grabbed a handful of bedclothes and flipped them open. Horace Greeley growled in protest.

"Move over," David ordered the tomcat. "I'm coming in." Nudging Greeley aside, David slid between the cool sheets.

"Ssh. Ssh, love, don't cry. It's all right now. I'm here," David whispered. He looped an arm over Tessa's hip and pulled her against him, her bottom pressed against his aroused member, spoon fashion. He kissed the silky strands of her hair, gritted his teeth against the throbbing of his body, and closed his eyes. He slowly counted to one thousand three times before his wishes were finally granted.

The throbbing eased. David fell asleep with Tessa held firmly in his arms.

CHAPTER 19

David woke up with a start on Monday morning and found himself surrounded by warmth. Tessa's warmth. Greeley's warmth. Tessa's body was molded to the front of him, Horace Greeley curled at his back. His shoulder still throbbed painfully. David eased out of bed, trying not to disturb his companions, who continued to sleep soundly.

He looked out the window. The sun peeked over the horizon. David's eyes stung from lack of rest. According to his calculations, he'd gotten less than three hours of sleep. It would have to be enough. Tessa had suffered from a second night of bad dreams, and he had crept into her bedroom once again to hold her.

He looked down at her as she slept. Her hearing would start in a few hours, but it was still early. David decided to let her sleep as long as possible. She needed the rest. He needed it. He wanted nothing more than to climb back into bed beside her and pretend he belonged there beside her every morning for years to come. But that wasn't to be. He had work to do. He quietly tiptoed out of the bedroom. Tessa need never know he'd spent the night holding her again, comforting her while she slept.

By eight o'clock David had bathed, shaved, and dressed in a wool suit. Moving about the office as silently as possible, so he wouldn't wake her, David made a pot of coffee for himself, then heated water for Tessa's bath and put the kettle on for her morning tea. He sat at his desk sipping coffee and jotting trial notes, postponing the inevitable.

David took out his watch and looked at it for the third time in fifteen minutes. He couldn't delay any longer. He had to wake her.

He went into her bedroom and touched her shoulder. "Tessa, wake up. It's time."

She sat up abruptly, dislodging Greeley. "What?"

"You've got to get up." His dark eyes were full of concern. "Your hearing starts at ten."

Tessa took a deep breath, trying to steady her racing heart. "David?"

"In the flesh." He managed a crooked smile. "Don't worry, everything will be all right."

She pushed the covers back and swung her legs over the side of the bed. "Are you sure?" She stared up at him, her gaze darting over his face. "What if they don't believe us?"

"They will," David promised. "I'll make them."

She stood up. Her knees buckled.

David reached out a hand to steady her. "I'll bring your bathwater and a cup of tea."

"What should I wear?" Her voice held a note of panic.

David opened the armoire, quickly evaluating her

choice of dresses. "Wear the dark blue." The dark silk dress with high white collar and white cuffs made her look like a schoolteacher or a preacher's wife. It was the perfect choice. If she wore that, the judge and jury would be hard-pressed to see any resemblance to a saloon girl.

"I may need help getting dressed," Tessa said.

"Call me if you do," David offered. "I've become quite adept at wrangling with ladies' unmentionables lately," he teased, hoping to coax a smile out of her.

"Thank you."

"Don't mention it."

When they stepped outside the office an hour later, David was glad he'd had the forethought to rent a buggy for the brief jaunt to the courthouse. He hadn't wanted to parade Tessa through the streets of Peaceable once again. And the buggy offered her some protection from the curious spectators who lined the streets. David handed Tessa up into the vehicle, settled himself beside her, then flicked the reins, urging the horse into the traffic headed toward the courthouse.

The courthouse yard was more crowded than the streets. It overflowed with people dressed in their Sunday best. David maneuvered the buggy near the hitching rail. He climbed out, then reached up to help Tessa. The morning sunlight glinted off her brilliant red hair as David lifted her down. The crowd issued a collective gasp at the sight of her. Newspapermen surged forward, yelling questions at David and Tessa while photographers situated along the edge of the courthouse yard hid beneath their camera drapes taking pictures. Tessa moved closer to David. He placed a protective arm around her shoulders, cursing himself for not providing a hat and veil to go with the blue dress.

"Extra, extra!" A newsboy hawking papers ran up to David. "Trial begins for woman held in brutal barroom slaying!"

David snatched a copy of the morning edition of the *Peaceable Chronicle*, tossed the boy a coin, and rapidly scanned the headlines.

"Miss Roarke, can you tell our readers why you killed Mr. Mason?" A reporter blocked Tessa's path.

"She didn't kill Mr. Mason," David said. "Get out of the way." He glared at the newspaperman. "Please."

"His body was found in her room. Is it true she slit his throat?" He pulled out his notebook.

"No! Now, get out of the way." David stepped in front of Tessa, shielding her from the reporter with his body. He took her hand, pulling her behind him as he cleared a path through the crowd.

Another reporter entered the fray. "How do you feel about Mr. Alexander representing you, Miss Roarke? It's rumored in Washington that he molested a young lady from a prominent family. What do you have to say?"

"Leave me alone," Tessa ordered. She heard a rip as someone stepped on the hem of her skirt. "David!" She let go of David's hand long enough to shove the reporter. "Get off my dress, you clumsy oaf!" She snatched her skirt out of the way.

David stopped.

"Is it true you and Miss Roarke have been openly cohabiting? Are you intimately acquainted?" The first reporter stood in their path, refusing to give ground.

David grabbed the newspaperman by his shirtfront,

practically lifting him off his feet. "Did I hear you correctly?"

"You did." The man appeared undaunted. "I got the information from a . . ." He glanced at his notebook. "A . . . Mrs. Jeffers at the local mercantile."

"I'll just bet you did," David muttered through clenched teeth. "And how much is your newspaper paying for such information?"

"That doesn't concern you, Mr. Alexander."

David tightened his hold on the man's shirt, yanking him closer. "The hell it doesn't." He lifted his clenched fist, intending to ram a few teeth down the reporter's throat.

"David, no!" Tessa placed her hand on his arm. "It doesn't matter what they say."

"It matters." David lowered his fist, but he didn't release the man's shirt.

"No, it doesn't. He's going to write what he wants about us, anyway," Tessa reasoned. "If you hit him, you'll just give him more to write."

"Listen to her, Mr. Alexander." Sheriff Bradley hurried toward David and Tessa, pushing his way through the throng of people. He tipped his hat to Tessa. "Let the man go, Mr. Alexander."

"Yes, do, Mr. Alexander. Unless you want to be sued," the reporter said, a smirk on his weaselly face.

"Sue me," David told him. "It'll be worth it."

"You hush up," Sheriff Bradley warned the reporter, "unless you want to spend the night in my jail." He turned to the crowd. "Show's over. You folks step back and give Mr. Alexander and his client room."

No one moved.

"Do it," the sheriff directed, "or I'll haul the whole lot of you off to jail."

The citizens of Peaceable and the out-of-towners moved back, clearing the way to the door of the court-house.

"David," Tessa pleaded, "let go of him."

David released the reporter. "If you utter a word," he warned, his voice strained with fury, "I won't be responsible for my actions."

The newspaperman finally recognized the danger, the barely leashed rage. He tipped his hat at Tessa.

David surged forward.

Tessa intervened once again. "No." She tugged on his arm.

He turned to look at her and saw the steely glint in her blue eyes.

"Don't you dare," she warned softly. "He just wants to sell more papers."

David took a deep breath, forcing his body to relax, trying to regain control. He took Tessa by the elbow and followed the sheriff.

At the doorway of the courthouse, Sheriff Bradley clapped David on the back. "Well," he said, "good luck." He spared an encouraging look for Tessa. "You've run the gauntlet. Everything else is routine. The worst of it should be over."

The worst of it hadn't even begun. David discovered that fact as soon as he ushered Tessa into the courtroom. What should have been a simple preliminary hearing turned into a circus with townspeople and reporters clambering for ringside seats. It seemed everyone in Wyoming had come to see a woman stand trial for murder.

Judge Emory sat on the bench.

David groaned. The somber judge was known for his

harsh sentences, especially in cases involving women. Rumor in the legal community had it that the judge believed women should be seen, not heard. And to make matters worse, Judge Emory had no liking for David Alexander. He knew of the Washington scandal, and he had an adolescent daughter at home.

Sitting beside Tessa at the defense table, David hazarded a glance at the county attorney, Jeremy Cook. Jeremy gave him a smug, self-satisfied smile that warned David to be wary; the territory's case against Tessa Roarke was strong.

The hearing began promptly at ten. The bailiff announced Tessa's case. The crowded courtroom buzzed with excitement.

David listened in growing frustration as Jeremy Cook presented the territory's evidence, establishing the fact that a murder had been committed on the night Arnie Mason died. Since the victim was found in Tessa Roarke's room at the Satin Slipper, he said, it was reasonable and probable that Miss Roarke had committed the crime. It was the opinion of Jeremy Cook and the territory of Wyoming that Miss Roarke should be held over for grand jury indictment.

Judge Emory stared at David. "What's the plea?"

David stood up and faced the judge. "My client pleads not guilty, Your Honor."

Judge Emory rapped his gavel on the desk top. "I rule that Miss Tessa Roarke be held over for grand jury indictment." He rapped the gavel a second time. "The grand jury will convene in one hour." The judge stood up.

The people in the courtroom all got to their feet.

Judge Emory left the bench and retired to an office across the hall.

"What's happening?" Tessa whispered.

"Your case is going to trial today," David whispered back. "The members of the grand jury will be sworn in, and an indictment against you will be handed down."

Tessa didn't understand the terminology, but she understood the frustration in David's voice. It frightened her.

"Don't worry," he tried to reassure her. "I hoped it wouldn't come to this, but I'm prepared for it." He managed a crooked little smile for Tessa's benefit. "We're prepared for the trial. It will be all right." Even as he said the words, David fervently prayed everything would be all right. He hoped he could convince the jury that Tessa was innocent. He hoped Lee was ready. He hoped . . . David covered her hand with his larger one, feeling the chill of her fingers through the fabric of her gloves. He squeezed her hand gently, reassuringly. "Trust me."

She did. What was more, she loved him. Tessa knew David would do his best for her. She smiled for him. "I do."

"Miss Roarke?"

She turned at the sound of her name and looked up.

Sheriff Bradley stood over her. "If you'll come with me."

"Where?" Tessa asked, alarmed. "Why?"

David's voice was soft, calm, collected. "The sheriff has to take you into custody. It's procedure. He'll bring you back as soon as the judge is ready."

"Can't I stay with you?" Tessa asked David.

"I'm afraid not." David didn't want her to leave. He didn't want the sheriff to take her. "You must go with the sheriff." He touched Tessa's cheek with one finger. "Be brave a little longer."

Tessa stood up and gathered her courage. She faced the sheriff. "Are you taking me back to jail, Sheriff Bradley?"

The lawman took her by the elbow. "Nope. Jail's full, Miss Tessa." He winked at David. "Full of those pesky reporters. I thought I'd take you to my house. The missus should have dinner on the table about now. I'm hungry. How about you?"

"I don't think I can eat anything, Sheriff Bradley." Tessa declined the offer of food, but she appreciated the sheriff's invitation. She knew his jovial manner was meant to put her at ease. She doubted whether many of the county prisoners were invited to the sheriff's house for dinner. "But a cup of tea would be nice."

"Then, tea it is." Sheriff Bradley escorted Tessa into the aisle.

She hated leaving David. Their time together was limited and she wanted to spend as much time with him as possible. Tessa wanted enough memories of David to last a lifetime, if need be.

She looked back at her attorney. "David, will you be okay? I think we have some bacon left and fresh eggs at the apartment if you're hungry. I baked bread yesterday. You can make a sandwich. And of course, there's coffee and—"

"Tea," David said. "I know." His dark-eyed gaze roamed over her face. She was beautiful. She grew more beautiful and more precious to him every day. A corner of his mouth turned up in a semblance of a smile. He ached to kiss her. "I'll be fine, Tessa." It was just like her to focus all her attention and concern on someone else.

"You didn't have any breakfast," she reminded him.

"I'll grab something at the hotel restaurant," he promised. "Now go with Sheriff Bradley. I need to make some notes before the trial begins."

"You won't forget to eat?"

"I promise."

Tessa allowed the sheriff to lead her down the aisle. "Will your wife mind very much if you bring me home with you, Sheriff Bradley?" she asked the lawman. "I'd hate for you to get in trouble with your wife."

"Well," the sheriff answered, "shortly after your little dispute at the mercantile, I had a talk with the missus about how looks can be deceivin'." He grinned at Tessa, a wide, big-toothed grin full of humor and goodwill. "From what I hear, you conducted yourself like a real lady. Not like some we could mention. That's good enough for me. And the missus never has cared much for Margaret Jeffers and her highfalutin ways." He opened the courthouse door and allowed Tessa to precede him. "I think the missus will like you just fine."

David stuffed a stack of papers into his satchel. He waited until the sheriff escorted Tessa out the door. He walked to the window and watched as they crossed the street.

If Tessa's behavior at the mercantile and in the courtroom could change the sheriff's first impression, there was hope for the jury. She wasn't a murderess. She didn't act like a murderess or a woman of loose character. She looked delicate and fragile and every inch a proper lady. She would impress the jury. David knew that firsthand. She'd already impressed the hell out of him.

But if the jury appeared to doubt Tessa's story, he would have to rely on Coalie.

Tessa wasn't going to like it. She'd fight tooth and nail to keep Coalie from testifying if it came to that, but David didn't plan to give her a choice. Not when he was fighting for her freedom and her life. He'd simply present her with a *fait accompli*.

With that thought in mind, David exited the courthouse through the rear door and walked down the street. He stopped first at the jeweler's, then continued on to the telegraph office to send for Coalie.

CHAPTER 20

"You can't!" Tessa whispered furiously. They stood outside the courtroom, waiting for the townspeople and the reporters to disperse before they made their way to the rented buggy. "I won't let you do this."

"Tessa, you've got no choice."

"You promised," she accused. "I should have known better than to put faith in your promises."

"I promised I wouldn't go get him," David corrected. "And I won't. Mary will bring him here tomorrow morning."

The day-long session of court had ended. Finally. At five in the afternoon, the jury had handed down an indictment of Miss Tessa Mary Catherine Roarke on a charge of the murder of Arnie Mason. Judge Emory called the attorneys into his chambers and announced that Tessa Roarke was to be released into David's custody once again, but for her safety, that bit of information would remain confidential. As far as the crowds of reporters were concerned, Miss Roarke was being held at the Peaceable jail.

The trial would begin at ten the following morning.

"You gave me your word," Tessa reminded him.

David ground his teeth in frustration; a muscle tic jumped in his jaw. He'd expected Tessa to be angry and perhaps a bit disappointed in him when he told her he'd sent for Coalie, but he'd also expected her to understand why he did it.

"It's just a precaution, Tessa. I don't know how things will go. Jury trials are unpredictable." He ran a hand through his hair. "Damn, I'd hoped this wouldn't be necessary, but I'm not taking any chances."

"Coalie's a little boy," Tessa reminded him. "He shouldn't be exposed to this." She turned her full anger on David. "I thought you cared about him. How can you expose him to this . . . this circus?"

"I do care about Coalie. I care very much," David told her. *But I care about you more.* The thought popped into his head and wouldn't go away. Once the trial was over, he intended to show her just how much he cared for both of them. "I wouldn't have had to do this if the trial hadn't turned into a circus," David explained. "Don't you see, Tessa? You're the first woman in this county to be indicted for murder. The first to stand trial. The first to face a jury of your peers made up of men and women. This is news. And unfortunately we're caught up in the middle of it."

"But I didn't kill Arnie Mason," Tessa said.

"At this point it doesn't matter whether you did or not. He's dead, and the citizens of Peaceable want a killer to stand trial. The newspapers want to sell papers. And the county attorney and the judge want to make a name for themselves in a precedent-setting case."

"What do you want?" Tessa's gaze was penetrating, direct. She demanded an honest answer.

"I want your freedom."

"Wouldn't you like to make a name for yourself as well? To go back to Washington a winner?" Tessa lashed out at him. She wanted him to admit he cared for her, that he wanted her, even loved her a little. But she knew better. David Alexander would rather run from his feelings and suffer in silence than admit he needed her. "Is that why you took my case?"

Nothing could have been further from the truth. It hurt to know she thought him capable of using her to advance his career. He didn't give a damn about Washington or even about his career. He knew what was important in life now. He knew what he wanted. He wanted Tessa. Damn her! Couldn't she love him? Just a little bit? David gripped her elbow harder than he intended and propelled her toward the buggy. "I've spent the past year trying to escape notoriety," he told her. "I've separated myself from my family and most of my friends so I wouldn't have to face them day in and day out, wouldn't have to see the doubt on their faces. I came to Peaceable to escape scandal." He lifted her up into the buggy, then climbed in beside her and gathered the reins. "I don't need this. I don't want this." He looked at her. "I never wanted my privacy invaded or my name splashed across the front pages of any more newspapers. If I'd known things were going to happen this way, I never would have taken your case!"

"What are you going to do?" Tessa taunted. "Foist me off on another attorney? One who doesn't mind making a name for himself?" She meant to wound him just as he'd wounded her, and she knew where to strike. "Or do you intend to run away again? Abandon me and Coalie to the wolves the way you abandoned Caroline Millen and her baby?"

David whitened. The bronze color left his face. He recoiled as if she'd landed a mighty blow. A mortal blow. Icy contempt filled his dark brown eyes.

"No, contessa." The title was a sneer and the tone of his voice a mockery of politeness. "I plan to win this damned case. I plan to hand you your freedom on a silver platter so you can leave Peaceable and get the hell out of my life once and for all." David met her gaze. Her blue eyes filled with emotion and became a deeper, darker shade until they reminded him of bruises against her white face. David tried to stop the flow of words that rolled off his tongue, but he couldn't help himself. He thought of Coalie and what she'd said, and he couldn't prevent himself from issuing a warning.

"You asked me what I want. Well, Tessa, I'll tell you. I want freedom. Yours and mine. I want my apartment and my office and my cat. I want my life the way it was before you turned it upside down. I want to get back to normal."

David saw the look on her face and knew he'd hurt her. But he'd meant to hurt her. He'd wanted her to feel the same heart-rending pain he felt. "And I'm going to use whatever means necessary to get what I want."

An uneasy truce existed by the time they arrived at the office. Tessa shed her coat at the front door and slipped into the routine she and David had established. She prepared a supper neither one of them wanted to eat.

David cleaned up the dishes afterward while Tessa put on a kettle of water for tea.

They worked together as they'd done for the past few days, but there was a difference. The sense of companionship had disappeared. They were separated by a chasm too wide for either of them to cross.

David finished the dishes, then worked at his desk, making notes and poring over the pages of his lawbooks. Tessa sipped her tea and embroidered on a sampler the sheriff's wife had given her to "occupy her hands."

They didn't speak. They simply waited until it grew dark enough for one of them to escape to bed.

The knock on the front door startled them. David got up from his desk to open it. Lorna Taylor and Jewell Bradley stood on the sidewalk, each holding a covered basket.

"We hope we haven't come too late," Jewell said, "but this is the first opportunity I've had to slip away."

"What can I do for you ladies?" David asked, stepping back and allowing the women to enter the office. He closed the door behind them.

"We've come to see Miss Roarke." Lorna looked up at him. "And to bring you a little something."

Tessa rose from her chair. "Please come in." She ushered the ladies toward the table. "Won't you have a seat? I just made a pot of tea."

"That would be nice," Lorna said, placing her basket on the table before seating herself.

Jewell followed Lorna's lead. Opening her basket, she removed a pan of fried chicken and a plate of big fluffy biscuits. "We tried to get here before you had time to fix supper," Jewell said to Tessa, "but those pesky reporters have been making a nuisance of themselves in front of the jail."

"Why?" Tessa asked.

Jewell chuckled. "Why, my dear, that's where they think you're being held. Judge Emory let 'em think you'd be at the jail to throw them off the scent."

Tessa looked to David for confirmation.

He nodded in agreement.

"We had a devil of a time getting here," Lorna told them, "but it was quite an adventure." She poked Jewell in the ribs. "Just like when we were girls."

"Yes," Jewell agreed. "My Jimmy stalled 'em while Lorna and I slipped out the back way with your supper. A couple of the reporters spotted us, but we gave them the slip by walking behind the funeral parlor." She spoke in an eerie whisper. "Then we skirted the cemetery." She shivered with delight. "I haven't had so much fun in years."

"This is kind of you." Tessa took down two cups and saucers from the new set of dishes David had bought and set them before the women.

"Aw, pooh," Lorna scoffed, unpacking the items from her basket, which included an apple cake, a jar of strawberry preserves, and a plate of fried peach turnovers. "It isn't kind at all. It's the least we can do after the way this town has treated you. It's the same as we'd do for any neighbors. The same as we'd do for our friends." She smiled at Tessa and David.

"And," Jewell added, "it's our way of thanking you for standing up to the town bully." Her brown eyes sparkled merrily at the memory of Margaret Jeffers's setdown. "I was ashamed of myself for not coming to your aid."

"Me, too," Lorna admitted.

"But you didn't have to do anything," Tessa protested, filling their cups with tea.

"Come over here and sit down." Jewell looked up and caught David hovering in the background. She motioned to the vacant chair. "Have a piece of cake. I know you've already eaten supper, but there's always room for dessert." She patted her ample stomach.

"Yes, David," Tessa said, "please sit down." She got him a cup and saucer and poured tea into it.

"I really need to work," he told them. "There's a lot to do before tomorrow's session."

"We don't mean to keep you from your work," Lorna said. "We know how important it is." She smiled at Tessa.

"That's right," Jewell agreed. "We just wanted to show our support for you, Mr. Alexander, and most of all, for Miss Tessa." Jewell met Tessa's gaze. "My husband, the sheriff, doesn't think you're guilty, and I've seen for myself what a true lady you are. And, well, what I'm trying to say is that we'd be right pleased to call you our friend and neighbor."

"That pleases me very much," Tessa replied. "I don't know what else to say."

"You don't have to say anything else," Lorna told her. "Just know that I'll be in that courtroom tomorrow supporting you, and Jewell will be at home preparing your lunch and supporting you as well."

Tessa's blue eyes sparkled. She dabbed at them with the corner of a tea towel.

David smiled broadly, then crossed over to the table and sat down. "Well, ladies," he announced, lifting his cup of steaming tea. "I'd say this calls for dessert and a little celebration."

"Here, here," Lorna and Jewell chorused as they raised their cups and clinked them softly against David's. "To Tessa Roarke, bully-slayer, and to winning her case!"

Tessa looked at the three of them, then burst into happy tears.

The other women laughed in relief, while David deftly guided the conversation away from talk of the trial. They spent the next half hour amusing Tessa with stories of Peaceable's history and its residents.

"That was nice of Lorna and Jewell, wasn't it?" Tessa closed the door behind her two new friends and turned to David.

"Yes, it was." He had moved to his desk after offering to see the ladies home.

"What? And spoil our adventure?" Jewell had scolded. "You stay here with Tessa."

"We'll be fine," Lorna assured him. "We might even give some more nosy reporters something to write about." They'd laughed at that, then headed down the street toward the jail.

But when their visitors left, the strained silence between David and Tessa returned. They looked at each other, but couldn't find the words to apologize. Tessa walked over to where David sat. She cleared her throat, waiting for David to say something. "Well, I guess I'll leave you to your work."

"Fine." He barely glanced at her.

Tessa continued to stand beside his desk.

"What is it?" he asked abruptly.

She turned and silently presented her back to him.

He looked up from his book, recognized the long row of tiny hooks and automatically unfastened them.

Finished with her dress fasteners, he untied the knot of her corset strings and loosened the laces.

"Thank you." Her voice was cool, crisp.

David grunted in reply, then returned to his book.

He heard her sometime after midnight, crying in her sleep again. David punched his pillow and pulled the quilts higher around his ears. He wouldn't go to her. Not tonight. He couldn't. It hurt too much to hold her and pretend. David punched his pillow a second time, harder than before, rolled over, and tried to force his body to sleep. But his control and his willpower failed him. He lay awake listening to the sound of her anguished dreams long into the night.

Coalie arrived on the early morning train. He practically dragged Mary down the street to David's law office, then burst through the door before Mary had a chance to knock.

David worked at his desk as usual. Tessa stood at the sink rinsing her breakfast dishes. David hadn't eaten. He made his breakfast a cup of strong black coffee.

"Tessa!" Coalie spared a glance for David, then made a beeline for Tessa. He flung his arms around her waist.

"Oh, Coalie." Tessa dropped her cup in the dishpan, turned, and wrapped her arms around Coalie, pressing his body against her. "I missed you so much!"

Coalie wiggled out of her grasp before Tessa wanted to let go. He walked over to David and stuck out his hand.

David shook Coalie's hand. "Hello," he said. "It's been quiet here without you." Very quiet, David thought, especially during the past eight hours.

Coalie turned to Tessa. "Tessa, you should see the ranch. It's so grand. It goes on forever and ever, and all the people are so nice. Reese and Faith and little Hope. Even Joy. She's a girl." He frowned, then rushed on with his story. "But Sam's the best. He's teaching me how to ride. A real horse." Coalie's face was alight, his big green eyes sparkling.

"That's nice." Tessa tried to muster up some enthusiasm, but failed. Miserably.

"I'm going to school, too," Coalie told her, hopping from foot to foot with barely contained excitement. "Mary's teaching me." He glanced at Mary. "I'm learning the alphabet."

"That's wonderful." Tessa didn't make it sound wonderful. She made it sound as painful as having teeth pulled.

Mary looked from her brother to Tessa. The atmosphere in the office was tense. The tension between them seemed almost unbearable. "Coalie's excited now," she explained, "because he's with you again, but he was miserable the first few days."

"Mary said I was homesick," Coalie told Tessa. "But I wasn't sick for long." He noticed the tension for the first time and hurried to reassure Tessa that he was as strong and healthy as ever.

"I'm sure Mary took good care of you." David patted Coalie on the back, then hugged his sister. "I missed you, imp," he said, fondly.

"It's your own fault," Mary told him. "You can come to the ranch to see us anytime." She pinned her gaze on David. "Why haven't you?"

"You know why." He didn't elaborate, so Mary let the subject drop.

Tessa stood silently. She looked at David, studying his face. He probably blamed her for that, too, just as he blamed her for turning his life upside down.

Coalie explored the office. "You're low on coal." He pointed to the coal bucket near the stove. "You want me to get some for you?" he asked, eager to please Tessa.

"Oh, no," Tessa assured him. "You don't want to get your new clothes all dirty hauling coal." She realized that Coalie was clean and well fed and dressed in a new suit.

"I don't mind." Coalie shrugged.

David smiled. "I'm sure you don't." He knelt down and faced Coalie. "But I've got something more important for you to do today."

"I know. Mary told me. You want me to answer questions at the courthouse. I'm to tell the truth, no matter what." Coalie looked up at David and recited from memory.

"Coalie, you don't have to do it," Tessa said. "He can't make you." She glared at David, daring him to contradict her.

"I know I don't," Coalie assured her. "Mary—"

"Told you." Tessa gritted her teeth at the phrase. Was there nothing Mary hadn't done?

"Yeah. She said I didn't have to do it if I didn't want to. She said David could convince the jury without me." Coalie walked around the room touching familiar objects. "But I want to, Tessa. I want to help you the way you helped me."

Tessa tried to reason with the little boy. "But, Coalie, if you tell everybody what happened in Chicago and how we ran away to Peaceable, then they'll know I took you away from your boss. They'll know I stole you. What if they try to send you back?"

"David won't let them send me back," Coalie answered with all the confidence of a nine-year-old who knows he's right.

Tessa turned to Mary. "Did you tell him to say that, too?" She knew Mary was trying to help, but she was jealous.

"No." Mary understood Tessa's hostility. "Coalie came to that conclusion on his own." She smiled down at him. "He apparently has more faith in David's ability than you do."

That wasn't true. After yesterday's confrontation with him, Tessa had every faith in David. She knew he'd get her off. She knew he'd protect Coalie. That was what frightened her. He wanted her out of his life, but what if he wanted to keep Coalie? She couldn't stand the thought of losing both of them.

Tessa walked over to stand in front of David. "If they take him away from me because of this, I'll never forgive you."

"They won't," David said. "He won't testify unless it's absolutely necessary. I promise you that."

"Keep your promises," Tessa told him. "They don't mean much to me." She turned her back on David and Mary, took Coalie by the hand, and walked down the hall to her bedroom.

"She's angry," Mary said after Tessa and Coalie left the room.

"Very," David agreed.

"Because you may need Coalie to testify." Mary knew her brother well. She could see that Tessa's anger bothered him more than he liked to admit.

"I will need Coalie to testify." David began to pace. "God knows I don't want to put a child on the witness stand, but I know Jeremy Cook. I know what he's going to do." He paused. "Judge Emory is presiding, and Jeremy Cook is going to try to use Emory's notions about women to his advantage. He's going to paint Tessa as a fallen woman, a saloon girl who thought nothing of murdering a man." He stared at Mary, silently pleading for her to understand his position. "I've got to offset that image of Tessa with something else. I've got to get the jury's sympathy, and Coalie's the only character witness I've got."

Mary moved to stand next to her brother. She reached up and patted his shoulder. "You can do it, David. I know you can."

David snorted. "You apparently have more faith in me than Tessa does." He repeated Mary's earlier words.

"She's angry now, and scared," Mary said. "When she's thinking more clearly she'll understand."

He sincerely hoped so.

David didn't know whether to laugh or cry at the inescapable irony of his situation. He'd finally fallen in love. He had finally found the woman he'd been searching for all his life. He'd found her in the Peaceable jail, charged with the brutal murder of one of the saloon patrons. Tessa Roarke, a beautiful Irish colleen. Every man's dream. And every attorney's nightmare.

The gods did have a sense of humor, for David Alexander was both man and attorney, and at the moment he felt the gods were toying with him. If he was to have Tessa for his very own, he had to fight her. And then fight for her.

To save her he had willfully damaged the trust she was beginning to feel for him. Then, because she'd hurt him, he'd flung hurtful words at her, words he couldn't take back. But once the trial was over, the results would be worth all the pain and effort. Once Tessa and Coalie were free and safe, David knew he could make things right. He had to. He was desperately, hopelessly in love with Tessa Roarke. And he wasn't about to lose her.

CHAPTER 21

"Hear ye, hear ye. The November term of the district court of the territory of Wyoming, county of Laramie, city of Peaceable, is now in session. Judge Harland Emory presiding," the bailiff intoned. "All rise."

The case of the *Territory of Wyoming vs. Tessa Roarke* on the charge of murder began in earnest.

David glanced at his pocket watch as he listened to the closing portion of Jeremy Cook's opening statements. Thank God it was coming to an end. Jeremy had been more long-winded than usual, rattling on and on for over twenty minutes.

"And so, ladies and gentlemen of the jury, the territory of Wyoming will prove that Tessa Roarke did willfully murder Arnie Mason in a fit of rage. The territory of Wyoming will prove that the defendant not only knew Arnie Mason but knew him intimately. Though she sits here pretending to be a lady, we know her for the murderess she is, a jealous, scheming girl from the Satin Slipper who killed a man for no other reason except that he refused to marry her and give her boy a name." David grimaced as the prosecutor finished with a dramatic flourish, his voice rising with each word like that of a fire-and-brimstone preacher. David now knew what to expect. Jeremy Cook didn't have much of a case and knew it. He planned to convict Tessa on the basis of rumor, innuendo, and sensationalism.

David jotted down a note on a sheet of paper, folded it, and motioned for one of the clerks. He waited until the clerk had read the note and exited the courtroom before he stood up to begin his opening statement. David walked toward the jury. "Ladies and gentlemen of the jury, I know you've all listened carefully to Mr. Cook's remarks. I'm not going to repeat them, nor will I refute them point by point. I'm simply going to tell you that Tessa Roarke did not kill Arnie Mason or anyone else." He leaned closer as if confiding in the jurors. "I know it looks bad. Mr. Mason was killed in Miss Roarke's room at the Satin Slipper. Everyone in town knows that, but I caution you to remember that looks can often be deceiving. Innocent people are sometimes caught in compromising situations through no fault of their own. Miss Roarke is just such a person. She's innocent, ladies and gentlemen of the jury, and I intend to prove it. Thank you all. I know you'll be fair and do your best." David nodded toward the jury, then walked back to the defense table and sat down next to Tessa.

"Is that all you're going to say," Tessa whispered, "after everything he said about me?"

"That's it," David whispered back.

"But—"

David explained his strategy. "Tessa, the jury is tired of listening to that windbag rattle on. I said what was important, and I did it quickly. There's no sense antagonizing the jury by forcing them to endure another endless monologue."

"All right, Mr. Cook," the judge said. "Call your first witness."

Jeremy Cook called Deputy Harris to the stand. The deputy repeated the oath, then sat down and began to answer the prosecuting attorney's questions.

"Deputy Harris, will you tell the court what you found when you entered Miss Roarke's room on the night of the murder?"

"I found Arnie Mason lying on Miss Roarke's bed. He was bleedin' from a cut across his throat."

"What was Miss Roarke doing?"

"She was sitting on the corner of the bed, screamin' for help." Deputy Harris scratched his head, thinking. "She was all bloody. There was a knife on the floor. All the girls were sayin' she'd killed Arnie Mason."

"What girls?"

"The whor . . . uh, . . . the women who work at the Satin Slipper."

"Did you believe them?" Jeremy Cook settled into his routine, walking around the courtroom, gesturing from the witness stand to the defendant's table, and to Tessa.

" 'Course I did," the deputy replied. "Who wouldn't? Seeing all the blood and everything."

"Then, in your professional opinion, Tessa Roarke stabbed Arnie Mason?"

"Not just stabbed," Harris replied. "Cut his throat. Split his gullet just like butcherin' a hog." The people in the courtroom gasped in collective horror. Deputy Harris drew a line across his throat with one finger, illustrating the point.

"Is this the weapon you found in the defendant's room?" The prosecuting attorney held up a wicked-looking knife for all to see.

"Yes, sir."

"No more questions, Deputy Harris," Jeremy Cook concluded.

David took over. "Deputy Harris, you say Miss Roarke was sitting on the corner of her bed screaming for help. Is that right?"

"Yes, sir."

"Do you have any idea why Miss Roarke was screaming for help?"

"I guess because Arnie Mason was lyin' half on top of her. When I got there, she was tryin' to kick his body off her." The deputy stared at David. "He was bleedin' all over her."

"So Mr. Mason was lying face up?" David asked.

"No, sir," Deputy Harris corrected. "He was lyin' face down."

"Didn't you find that unusual?"

"No, sir. Not at the time. But now that you mention it, it does seem strange, seein' as how she cut his throat."

"Thank you, Deputy Harris. No more questions for now." David scribbled several notes on his tablet.

The prosecuting attorney called several more witnesses: the undertaker, the doctor, the sheriff, and two women from the Satin Slipper. Jeremy Cook hastily built his case. David carefully unraveled it.

"The territory of Wyoming calls Miss Charlotte Winston."

Charlotte the harlot took the stand. She echoed the deputy's testimony to the letter. Cook completed his questioning. Charlotte got to her feet, preparing to leave.

"One minute, Miss Winston." David stood up and walked around the defendant's table. He moved within a few feet of Charlotte. "I have a couple of questions."

The crowd in the gallery laughed.

"Miss Winston, will you tell us what happened after the deputies came to Miss Roarke's room at the Satin Slipper?"

Charlotte smoothed a lock of brown hair away from her forehead and straightened her hat—a hat covered with bows and lace and dyed bird feathers, David noticed. "Well, the deputies took Tessa—I mean, Miss Roarke—outside. Then they took her to jail."

"Then what happened at the Satin Slipper?" David asked softly. "Was Miss Roarke's room locked to keep people out?"

"No, sir. There ain't any locks on the doors at the saloon, except Myra's."

"Go on." David leaned closer to her. "Tell us what happened next."

"Myra . . ." Charlotte paused, licking her lips nervously. "I mean, Miss Brennan—"

"Owner of the Satin Slipper Saloon," David interjected for the benefit of the jury. "Please continue."

"Yes, sir. Miss Brennan told some of the girls to go get a mop and some rags and fresh bed linen."

"Then what happened?" David prompted.

"Well, after we cleaned up the mess, Miss Brennan told us to help ourselves."

"To what?"

"Tes . . . Miss Roarke's belongings."

David paced, measuring the distance between the witness stand and the defense table. "I see." He turned to face Charlotte. "Did you help yourself to any of Miss Roarke's things?"

"Yes, sir." Charlotte shifted in her chair, sitting up straighter.

"What did you take?"

"I didn't *take* anything," Charlotte said. "It wasn't like we were stealing. Miss Brennan *gave* it to us."

"It wasn't Miss Brennan's to give," David said. "Now, please answer the question. What did you take?"

"I got some of her dresses. The yellow one and the green one. And I got a couple of nightgowns and a silver and black necklace," Charlotte answered. "I lost it, though. Too bad. It was real pretty."

David ground his teeth at Charlotte's description of Tessa's rosary. "Did Miss Brennan give Miss Roarke's room to anyone else at the Satin Slipper?"

"Yes, sir. That morning."

David pinched the bridge of his nose. Getting Charlotte to volunteer information was next to impossible. "Do you know who got the room?"

"Mr. Alexander, you know who got her room," Charlotte reminded him.

"Yes, I do," David admitted, "but I'd appreciate it if you'd tell the rest of the people here who got the room."

"I did," she mumbled.

"Louder, please, so everyone can hear."

"I did."

"Thank you, Miss Winston," David said. "Now, I have just one more question. Did you like Tessa Roarke?"

"Huh?" Charlotte seemed genuinely puzzled by the question.

"Did you like Miss Roarke? I mean, she was one of you. You worked together. You both went with the gentlemen customers—"

Tessa gasped aloud.

"I don't know whether I liked her or not," Charlotte answered honestly. "I didn't really know her. She kept to herself. She and her boy. She didn't whor . . . go with the gentlemen, like the rest of us. She just served drinks. That's all."

"Thank you again, Miss Winston. I have no more questions at this time." David held out his hand. "You may step down." He helped her down from the stand, then walked back to the defense table and sat down.

Tessa reached out and placed her hand on top of his.

David looked at her.

She didn't speak. She simply squeezed his hand in a gesture of approval and encouragement and love and a dozen other emotions she couldn't put a name to.

David's heart thumped at her touch. He smiled at her.

"The territory of Wyoming calls Miss Myra Brennan to the stand." Jeremy Cook made the announcement.

The spectators in the courtroom recognized drama when they saw it. Almost everyone in town had witnessed the confrontation between Myra and David Alexander on the sidewalk the day Tessa Roarke was released from jail. And nearly everyone in town had seen Tessa dash into the saloon, intent on reclaiming her property.

Dressed in an exquisite black satin moiré dress in the latest Paris fashion, Myra Brennan walked to the front of the courtroom, raised her right hand, and repeated the oath. She carefully seated herself in the chair Charlotte had vacated.

"Please state your name and your occupation for the record," Jeremy said.

"Myra Belle Brennan. I'm the proprietor of the Satin Slipper Saloon here in Peaceable." She spoke softly, carefully.

"Do you know the defendant, Miss Roarke?" Jeremy Cook strolled over to the table where David and Tessa sat and pointed a finger at Tessa.

"Yes, I do."

"And did you know the victim, Mr. Arnie Mason?"

"He came into my establishment fairly often," Myra answered. "I suppose you could say I knew him."

"Will you tell the court how you met Miss Roarke?"

"Yes. Of course." Myra moistened her lips with the tip of her tongue. "She came to my place of business a month or so ago looking for a room to rent."

"And you rented her a room?"

"Of course. I felt sorry for the girl."

Sitting beside Tessa, David felt her body stiffen in reaction to Myra's statement.

"Was Miss Roarke alone?" Cook asked.

"No."

"Who was with her?"

"The kid," Myra replied. "I mean, her little boy. She'd just come from Chicago."

"Did anyone travel with her besides the boy?"

"Well, I don't know for sure . . ." Myra paused dramatically. "But I think maybe Arnie Mason did. He'd just come from Chicago, too," she hinted slyly.

"Objection!" David stood up.

The judge rapped his gavel on the desk. "Overruled. Continue, Mr. Cook."

"Did Miss Roarke ever work for you?" Jeremy asked. "You've told us that you gave her a room at the Satin Slipper out of the kindness of your heart."

"I paid for the room," Tessa whispered to David.

"I know," David whispered back.

Tessa nodded toward the jury. "Make sure they know," she told him, whispering furiously. "I don't take charity from anyone, especially her."

"Mr. Alexander?" Judge Emory spoke from the bench.

"Yes, Your Honor?" David glanced at Tessa, warning her to keep silent.

"Does your client have a problem?"

Tessa nodded.

David shook his head. "No, Your Honor."

"Then cease your whispering," the judge ordered. "Please excuse the interruption, Mr. Cook, and continue your line of questioning."

"Thank you, Your Honor." Jeremy's smug expression irked David. It was the expression of a boy who delighted in tattling on other children. "Now, Miss Brennan, did Tessa Roarke ever work for you?"

"Yes, she did."

"How was she employed?"

"She served drinks to the patrons of my establishment."

"And that's all?"

"Well," Myra began, "that's all I required her to do. What she did with her men friends after she finished work was her business."

Tessa squirmed in her chair. David shifted his weight, deliberately sitting on her skirt to keep her still.

"One last question, Miss Brennan. Did you ever see

Miss Roarke in conversation with Arnie Mason?"

Here it comes, David thought. Let her get too confident. Let her make a mistake.

"As a matter of fact, I did." Myra sat straight in her chair, smiling at the jury, enjoying her moment in the sun.

"Will you tell us about it?"

"I once saw her arguing with Arnie about the boy. I saw her talking to him on numerous occasions."

"When did the argument take place?" Jeremy was practically licking his lips in anticipation.

Tessa kicked David under the table, hard enough to leave a bruise on the side of his leg. "She's lying!" Tessa whispered.

"I know," David replied. "Now, ssh!" He nudged her foot with his.

"A day or so before the murder," Myra replied. "I don't remember for sure."

"But you did see the defendant in conversation with the victim?"

"Well, yes," Myra told him. "I distinctly remember seeing her hand Arnie Mason a note a few hours before she killed him."

Tessa kicked David again. "Aren't you going to stand up and object again?" Tessa's angry whisper was barely audible.

"No," David whispered. "Let's give her enough rope to hang herself. Be still!" He closed a hand over Tessa's. "Listen."

Jeremy Cook, sensing victory, asked a final question. "Do you know what the note said?"

"No, I don't." Myra smiled at Tessa. "She got quiet when I passed by, but I'm sure I heard her say something like 'Don't be late.' "

"You're positive?"

"Absolutely." Myra stared at David Alexander, then very slowly placed a fingertip against her lips and kissed it.

"Clever," David muttered, "but not clever enough."

"Thank you, Miss Brennan." Jeremy Cook turned to David and inclined his head. "I've finished with this witness."

Judge Emory spoke to David. "Any questions for Miss Brennan, Mr. Alexander?"

"Not at the moment," David answered.

"What?" Tessa gasped.

"But I'd like to reserve my right to cross-examine Miss Brennan at a later date." David ignored Tessa's outburst.

Judge Emory did not. "As we've been at this for quite a while, I suggest we recess for a late dinner." He checked his watch. "We'll reconvene at two o'clock." He fixed his eagle-eyed gaze on Tessa. "And, Mr. Alexander, I suggest you speak to your client about courtroom etiquette." He stood up.

The people in the courtroom all rose.

"David," Tessa demanded before Sheriff Bradley made his way across the room, "you aren't going to let her get away with saying those things, are you?"

David took her by the shoulders and turned her to face him. "Tessa, listen to me. Listen carefully. I know what I'm doing." She started to speak. "No, don't say anything yet. Just nod or shake your head, yes or no. I know Myra was lying, but right now I can't do anything about it," he explained. "I'm stalling for time. I don't want to put Coalie on the stand any more than you want me to, but I may not have a choice. Do you understand?"

Tessa shook her head.

"If things don't go as I planned I'll have to put either you or Coalie on the stand, and the jury will be a lot more sympathetic if they hear the truth from a child." David tried to smile. "I know you don't like the idea. But Myra's testimony is the most damaging."

"But she lied about everything," Tessa burst out.

"Not everything," David corrected. "Almost everything, but she told just enough of the truth to make her statements damaging to us. The jury will believe her. I sent for Lee Kincaid."

"You want Liam Kincaid to testify for me? Are you crazy?" Tessa ranted.

"Yes," David answered. Crazy about her.

"Yes to which question?" Tessa demanded.

David couldn't prevent the smile that turned up the corners of his mouth. She didn't miss much, he thought. Might even make a damn good attorney one day, once she learned to read.

"Miss Tessa?" Sheriff Bradley waited a respectful distance away. "I sure hope you've got your appetite back 'cause the missus baked a ham this morning for your dinner. I invited Miss Alexander and Coalie, too." He winked at David. "Do you think you could manage a bite to eat?"

Tessa gave the sheriff a brilliant smile. "Sheriff Bradley, today I think I could eat a horse. By myself."

The lawman offered Tessa his arm.

She took his elbow and allowed him to escort her to dinner at his house.

David looked down at his tablet as he packed his satchel. What he saw surprised him. He'd filled two pages with the words "Will you marry me?" And she hadn't been able to read it.

CHAPTER 22

When court reconvened at two o'clock, Mary sat in the first row of the gallery behind David and Tessa. Lorna Taylor sat next to her. Coalie waited at the sheriff's house with Jewell Bradley.

The prosecuting attorney, Jeremy Cook, had called his last witness in Myra Brennan. It was time for David to present Tessa's side of the story. He called his first witness.

"The defense calls Sheriff James Bradley," David announced.

Sheriff Bradley stepped forward, swore to tell the truth, then sat down in the witness stand.

David's approach to the questioning process was the opposite of Jeremy Cook's. Where Jeremy was a showman, David relied on logic. He had great respect for the common sense of the jurors.

"Sheriff Bradley," David asked, "were you present when Miss Tessa Roarke was arrested for the murder of Mr. Arnie Mason?"

"No, sir. I wasn't."

"Who arrested her?"

"Deputy Harris," the sheriff answered.

"When you first saw Miss Roarke what condition was she in?" David questioned. "How was she dressed?"

"She was wearing a blanket and her . . . uh . . . undergarments," the sheriff told him. "And a man's coat. I believe it was your coat."

"Yes, it was," David agreed. "Sheriff, do you remember if Miss Roarke had shoes on?"

"No, she did not."

"Do you know what happened to her clothes?" David asked.

"They're there." The sheriff pointed. "On the table next to the knife."

David walked to the table and picked up the sleeveless blue satin dress and held it up for the sheriff and the jury to see. The front of it, from the waist down, was caked with dried blood, and the bodice was marked with splotches. "Is this Miss Roarke's dress?"

"Yes," Sheriff Bradley said. "And those are her stockings. The deputy wrapped them up after she took 'em off and locked them in the safe."

David held up the black net stockings.

Tessa looked down at the table in front of her. She blushed at having her clothing displayed so openly.

David dropped the stockings on the table, then turned to the sheriff. "Did Miss Roarke have any other clothing?"

"No, sir. Except her . . . uh . . . you know . . ." The sheriff's weathered face turned a dark shade of red.

"Her underclothes. She kept those on."

"Sheriff Bradley, what was the weather like the night Miss Roarke was arrested?"

The sheriff smiled. "Just like it is today. Real cold."

"So your deputy brought Miss Roarke out of the Satin Slipper just as he found her?"

"Yeah. She didn't have shoes or a coat or a blanket or anything, until you brought them."

"No jewelry? Rings, bracelet, necklace, anything?"

"Nothing."

"Thank you, Sheriff." David walked over to the defendant's table, pulled his tablet out of his satchel and pretended to consult his notes. "Now, Sheriff, let's talk about Arnie Mason. Did you know him?"

"I knew who he was," Sheriff Bradley answered.

"Will you tell us how Mr. Mason was dressed when your deputies found him?" David paused. "Miss Brennan, the owner of the saloon, implied that he and Miss Roarke were lovers . . ."

The courtroom buzzed at the phrase.

David ignored it, continuing his line of questioning. "That Miss Roarke had invited Mr. Mason to her room. Was Mr. Mason found in a state of undress?"

"No, sir," the sheriff replied. "He was completely dressed. Down to his boots, spurs, and gun."

"Did your deputy find any personal belongings on Mr. Mason?"

"Yes, sir. They found a pocket watch, two cigars, a few matches, a train ticket stub from Chicago, some change, around forty dollars in cash in his wallet, and two pieces of paper folded up," the sheriff recited from memory. "Oh, and a piece of gold chain."

"Gold chain?"

"Yes, sir. The undertaker found it tangled around

a button on Arnie's right cuff when he was preparing the body. It's all there on the table." He pointed to the evidence table.

A woman in the crowded courtroom gasped aloud. David looked around, searching. He found the woman he sought. Her face was pale, but she was composed otherwise. He lifted a finger to his lips and kissed it in salute.

"Getting back to the folded pieces of paper," David said, turning his attention back to the sheriff. "Was there anything written on the papers?"

"There was a Chicago address on one."

Walking to the evidence table, David picked up a piece of paper and read it aloud. " 'Twenty-seven Lennox Street, Apartment four-B, Chicago.' "

Tessa came halfway out of her chair.

The judge pounded once with his gavel. "Be seated, Miss Roarke."

"Yes, sir." Tessa sat back down. Arnie Mason had known her address in Chicago. How?

David glanced at Tessa. He met her questioning gaze and nodded in silent confirmation. He returned the piece of paper to the table, then picked up the other and took it to the sheriff. "Will you read this aloud, please?"

Sheriff Bradley opened the note and read: " 'Arnie, meet me in my room when the saloon closes. It's important. Love, Tessa.' "

"Do you believe Miss Roarke wrote that note, Sheriff?"

"I did at the time we found it," the sheriff answered, "but now I don't."

"What changed your mind?" David asked out of curiosity.

"Well, sir, yesterday at lunch, Miss Roarke asked my wife for the recipe for that cake you liked. The missus wrote it out for her, but Miss Roarke asked her to tell her how to make it. She couldn't read. She never learned how."

"Thank you." David took the note from the sheriff and placed it beside the other one. "I have two more questions for you, Sheriff Bradley. Did you look at the wound on Mr. Mason's throat?"

"Yes, sir. I studied it real good."

"Can you tell from studying the mark how it was made?"

"Yes, sir, Mr. Alexander. You can tell from the angle whether a right-handed or a left-handed person made it."

David looked down at his boots, then back up at the sheriff. "I apologize, Sheriff. I said I only had two questions left, but now I feel I have to ask you one more."

"That's all right, Mr. Alexander." James Bradley chuckled. "Your job is asking questions."

"Absolutely," David agreed. "Now, in your expert opinion, did a right-handed person or a left-handed person make the cut on Mr. Mason's throat?"

"A right-handed person."

"Thank you, Sheriff Bradley. I have no more questions." David looked over at his opponent. "Mr. Cook?"

Jeremy Cook glared at David. "No questions. I think the sheriff has answered most of them."

David turned to the judge. "Your Honor, I'd like to ask for a show of hands of right-handed and left-handed people in the courtroom to demonstrate how many people could have killed Arnie Mason."

"This is unusual," the judge told him. "But I'll go along with it. How about you, Mr. Cook?"

"Fine with me, Your Honor." Jeremy chuckled. "I'm left-handed."

"All right-handed people in this courtroom, please raise your hands," Judge Emory instructed, raising his own right hand.

Other hands went up all over the courtroom.

"That includes our learned members of the newspaper profession," the judge announced when the reporters continued to scribble notes.

More hands went up.

David raised his right hand, then took a deep breath and turned around.

Tessa's hands remained folded together on the top of the table.

David released the breath he was holding. He searched the faces. Myra Brennan's hands were also down. Damn! He'd gambled on her being right-handed. Unless she was lying . . .

"All right, let's see a show of hands by all of the left-handed people," Judge Emory ordered.

Tessa raised her hand. So did Jeremy Cook and two members of the jury. David turned back around. Myra Brennan's hand was up too. Clever, he thought, very clever.

"Put your hands down," Judge Emory instructed.

"Thank you, Your Honor," David said.

"Call your next witness, Mr. Alexander," directed the judge.

"Your Honor, I'd like to call Coalie Donegal to the stand," David said.

"No." Tessa stood up.

"Be seated, Miss Roarke." Judge Emory gave her

a stern look. "This is your last warning. One more outburst and I'll have the bailiff remove you. Do you understand?"

"Yes, sir, Your Honor, but you see, Coalie's just a little boy. I don't think he should be here. I don't want him to see me here."

"Your objection is admirable, Miss Roarke." The judge was impressed. "But you're on trial for a very serious crime. If Mr. Alexander thinks this young boy should testify in your behalf, you should let him." He pinned his judicial gaze on Tessa. "Think of it as educational for the boy."

"Yes, sir, Your Honor." Tessa glared at David, then sat down.

"Where is he?" Judge Emory asked.

"At the sheriff's house, Your Honor," David answered, "playing with the Bradley children."

The judge turned to the bailiff. "Go get him." He pounded his gavel. "We'll recess for ten minutes."

"David"—Tessa faced him—"please."

"Tessa"—David looked down into her shining blue eyes—"I've waited for Lee as long as I can. Coalie can help you. He wants to help you."

"But—"

"He's proud, Tessa. As proud as you are. He knows you left Chicago to protect him, that you worked at the Satin Slipper to give him a home. Let him repay your kindness."

"He doesn't have to."

"Coalie knows that, Tessa," David said. "He asked me to let him tell the people about you."

"But I could lose him." Every instinct Tessa possessed urged her to protect Coalie at all costs.

"If he doesn't testify, he could lose you," David said

bluntly. I could lose you, he thought. "To prison." Or a hangman's noose. Forever.

Tessa couldn't speak around the lump in her throat. She nodded her assent.

"Thank you." David lifted one of her gloved hands and pressed it to his lips.

"Remember." She forced out the one word, reminding him of his promise not to let them take Coalie away from her.

"I will."

Ten minutes later Coalie entered the courtroom followed by the bailiff. David took him by the hand and led him to the witness chair. Coalie stood straight and proud as he placed his hand on the Bible and repeated the oath. Finished, he climbed into the chair. His feet dangled above the bottom rung. His hair was neatly combed and slicked back into place, his face red from exertion. Beads of perspiration formed on his brow and upper lip. Packed with bodies and heated by two huge stoves, the courtroom was overly warm. Coalie squirmed inside his jacket.

David smiled at the picture he presented of an all-American boy. "You may take off your jacket." David removed his own jacket to make Coalie feel more comfortable removing his.

Tessa watched the ripple of muscles through David's shirt and waistcoat, remembering the strength in his shoulders and how he looked without his clothes. Her face flushed; she lowered her gaze to the table and David's tablet. The pages were covered with his notes, but Tessa couldn't read them.

Coalie scrambled out of his wool jacket and handed it to David. David took the jacket to Tessa, then returned to Coalie. He pulled a chair up at an angle in front of Coalie and sat with his back to the gallery. "Now, Coalie, will you tell the court your name?"

"Coalie Donegal," Coalie announced loudly. Proudly.

Several people in the gallery chuckled. David glanced over his shoulder. The door at the back of the courtroom opened. Lee Kincaid walked in.

David stood up. He looked up at Judge Emory. "No more questions, Your Honor."

Coalie's expression clouded with disappointment.

The judge raised an eyebrow. "No? Well, I'd like to hear what the boy has to say." He smiled at Coalie. "I was looking forward to getting to know him. Would you like to ask the questions, Mr. Alexander, or shall I?"

David turned to Tessa.

The look in her eyes said, "Don't embarrass Coalie. Make him feel important."

"I'll ask the questions, Your Honor," David replied.

"Then, get on with it."

"Before we get started, Coalie, I'd like to know what you've been doing to work up such a sweat."

Coalie grinned. "Me and the sheriff's boys were building a snowman—a great big one, as tall as you."

"That's grand, Coalie," David told him. "And as soon as you answer a few questions, I'll let you get back to it. Okay?"

"Okay."

"Now, first of all, you told us your name is Coalie Donegal. Can you tell me your father's name or your mother's?"

Coalie shook his head. "I don't know 'em," he explained. "I'm whatcha call a orphan."

"Tessa Roarke isn't your mother?" David asked.

"She takes care of me," Coalie said.

David met Coalie's worried gaze. "Coalie, it's all right. You can tell us. Is Tessa your mother?"

"No." Coalie hesitated. "I wished she was, but she's not." He looked up at David, then whispered loudly. "But I'm not supposed to tell anybody that."

"Why not?"

" 'Cause Tessa's afraid somebody will take me away from her if they know." Coalie wiped his nose with the back of his hand.

David took a clean handkerchief from his trouser pocket and handed it to the boy. "You're doing fine." He patted Coalie on the shoulder. "Now, I'll ask an easy question. How old are you?"

He went through the story of Coalie's life.

"You delivered coal?"

"Yep. That's where my name come from. I had another one, but I don't remember it now. I'm Coalie 'cause I delivered coal and Donegal for Father Francis's home in Ireland." He swung his legs against the chair restlessly.

"Would you like to get down and walk around?" David asked Coalie, glancing at the judge for permission. Judge Emory indicated his assent with a quick nod.

Coalie scooted to the edge of the chair.

"How long did you deliver coal?" David inquired.

"Since I was big enough to carry the bucket. I'm stronger than I look." Coalie flexed an arm muscle to prove it. "I think I was four, maybe five, when I started. I carried coal 'cause I was too scared of the roofs to be a chimney sweep."

David wanted to cry just thinking about a child

of five carrying buckets of coal through apartment buildings in Chicago or climbing down into chimneys. "Father Francis sent you out to work when you were only four or five?" David couldn't hide the outrage in his voice.

"Not Father Francis. He was moved to another place," Coalie said, defending the priest. "The man who took over the orphans' home, he 'prenticed me to Mr. Clayburn, who owned a coal wagon."

"So you met Tessa when you delivered coal to her apartment?"

"Yes, sir." Coalie smiled. "She's the best friend I ever had. She lived over the bakery. She gave me pastries 'cause I was always hungry."

"Where was this bakery?"

"Twenty-seven Lennox Street," Coalie recited. "Tessa lived in four-B."

David smiled. "Did Tessa live alone in apartment four-B?"

Coalie's face clouded. "She had a brother until he got killed. Tessa was real sad when he died. I used to sneak back to her 'partment after I finished work, but I had to be careful not to get caught or Mr. Clayburn would beat me."

"Your employer hit you?"

Coalie shrugged his thin shoulders, then replied matter-of-factly, "Sure. All the time. Sometimes he took a strap to me, but mostly he hit with his fists." He leaned closer to David. "He drank a lot."

David turned to Coalie. "Why did you come to Peaceable?"

"We had to leave Chicago 'cause Tessa was afraid Mr. Clayburn was gonna beat me to death. She tried to buy me, but he cheated her. He took her money, then wouldn't let me go."

"Tessa Roarke tried to buy your work contract from Mr. Clayburn?" David said, paraphrasing Coalie's testimony.

"Yeah. He took almost all of Tessa's money, then wouldn't let me go." Coalie grinned. "But I sneaked out one night. We rode the train and came here."

"Is it correct to say Tessa Roarke took you away from Mr. Clayburn because she wanted to help you?"

"Yes, sir, 'cause Tessa loves me," Coalie said. "She didn't want me to be hurt anymore."

"Thank you, Coalie," David said. "Would you answer one last question for me?"

"Okay."

"Will you tell the court who hired me to defend Tessa Roarke?"

Coalie stood up. "I did," he announced. "I ran to your office. I woke you up when I saw the men taking Tessa away. I heard it was your job to help people. I got you to help Tessa."

David smiled down at Coalie. "Thank you, Coalie. I'm very proud of you." He turned to Jeremy Cook. "No more questions."

The prosecutor got to his feet, then walked over to Coalie. "I've got a few questions."

"Okay." Coalie climbed back into the chair.

"How much are you paying Mr. Alexander to defend Miss Roarke?" Jeremy asked.

"I ain't paid him anything yet," Coalie informed the prosecutor. "I'll pay him when the job's done. Not until." He stuck his hand in his trousers pockets. "But he pays me good wages." Coalie held out a silver dollar. "See."

David groaned.

"Mr. Alexander paid you to testify in court?" Jeremy asked.

"He pays me for fillin' the coal bin in his office and shining his boots. He says it's my wages," Coalie corrected. "I do chores and he pays me." He leaned over and whispered to the county attorney. "I didn't have any money when I hired him, but we made a deal. He pays me so I can pay him. We shook hands on it."

"Coalie, isn't it true that you would say anything Mr. Alexander asked you to say? Wouldn't you say anything to help Miss Roarke even if it wasn't the truth?"

Coalie thought about the question for a minute. He looked Jeremy Cook right in the eye. "I would have . . ."

The prosecutor glanced over at David. He was practically gloating until the boy completed his thought.

Coalie pointed toward Mary Alexander. "But Mary told me the only way I could help Tessa was by telling the truth"—he looked up at Judge Emory—"just like it says in the Bible."

"He can step down," Cook said to the judge. "I'm finished with him."

Coalie hopped down.

"Take him back to the sheriff's house," Judge Emory said to the bailiff. Then he turned to Coalie. "You did a fine job, young man."

Beaming with pride, Coalie practically skipped down the aisle. "Bye, Tessa." He waved at her.

"Good-bye." Tessa waved back.

"Do you have any more witnesses, Mr. Alexander?" the judge asked.

"One, Your Honor." David turned to the gallery. Myra Brennan stared at him. "The defense calls Liam Kincaid."

"What?" Mary and Tessa spoke simultaneously. Tessa clamped a hand over her mouth. Mary stared down at her shoes, too embarrassed to look at David.

Lee strolled up to the front of the courtroom. He placed his hand on the Bible and promised to tell the truth, then sat down in the chair Coalie had vacated.

David pulled the other chair out of the way. "Please state your name and occupation."

"Liam Kincaid. I'm currently employed as a bartender at the Satin Slipper Saloon."

"Is that your only occupation?" David asked.

"No," Lee replied. "I'm also employed by the Pinkerton Detective Agency."

A murmur of surprise rippled through the courtroom. Newsmen scribbled furiously on their notepads, and several artists hastily sketched pictures for their newspapers.

"Did you come to Peaceable on business or for pleasure, Detective Kincaid?"

"I'm here to investigate the death of Eamon Roarke," Lee stated, staring at Tessa. "He was the brother of the defendant, Tessa Roarke."

Tessa's head began to spin. She felt dizzy, lightheaded. She thought she might faint.

"How did Mr. Roarke die?"

"He was struck and killed by a wagon outside the Pinkerton offices in Chicago. We don't believe it was an accident. We believe he was murdered."

David paced the distance between the witness stand and the defense table once again. "Will you tell us why the renowned Pinkerton Detective Agency is investigating this man's death?"

"Eamon Roarke was also employed by the agency. He was working on a case centered in Peaceable when he died. I followed the man suspected of running Mr. Roarke down."

"Who was that man?"

"Arnie Mason." Lee looked out over the sea of faces until he found Myra Brennan's.

The crowd in the courtroom reacted, buzzing with excitement.

"How long have you been in Peaceable?" David asked.

"Five, almost six weeks."

"And how long have you worked at the Satin Slipper?"

"About a month," Lee replied. "I worked at two other saloons before I applied at the Satin Slipper."

"Was there any reason you chose Myra Brennan's establishment?"

Lee met David's gaze. "There were two reasons." He paused a moment, weighing his words, before he continued. "The first was that I knew Tessa Roarke had taken her brother's room at the saloon; Eamon was staying there before he died. I knew that because the agency had reimbursed him for expenses, including three months' rent at the Satin Slipper. The second reason was that the agency had reason to believe that a large-scale robbery and smuggling ring was operating out of the Satin Slipper. Eamon was investigating that operation. I was assigned to complete Eamon's case."

"You speak as if you knew Mr. Roarke well," David commented.

"Eamon and I were partners on several cases," Lee answered. "He was my friend."

"Did you know Miss Roarke too?"

"No, we'd never met."

"But you followed her to the Satin Slipper," David reminded him.

"I was with Eamon Roarke the day he died." Lee saw the shimmer of tears in Tessa's blue eyes. "I promised to watch over his sister."

David turned to face Lee. "Eamon Roarke asked you to look out for his sister?"

"Actually"—Lee's face reddened—"he asked me to marry his sister."

"What?" That revelation shocked David. He glared at his friend.

"I decided to look her over before I committed myself," Lee said. "When she left Chicago, I followed her."

"What happened next?"

"She walked into a vipers' den without realizing it," Lee explained. "Arnie Mason was managing a band of thieves. Running it out of the Satin Slipper. The gang was responsible for robbing trains and stagecoaches throughout Wyoming and Nebraska. They smuggled guns to renegade Indians, and they sold illegal and poisoned whiskey to the Indian reservations."

"All of that was going on in the quiet town of Peaceable? That seems incredible." David walked a short distance away from Lee, then turned back to face him. "How do you know all this?"

"I infiltrated the ring."

"Detective Kincaid, do you have any idea who murdered Arnie Mason?"

"The person who had the most to gain," Lee said.

"The leader. The brains behind the organization. Arnie controlled the gang, but he was getting too big for his britches, shooting his mouth off. He suspected Eamon of being a lawman from the start, and he traveled to Chicago to kill him. But he made a mistake. He acted without orders, and that made the boss very angry."

"You said Miss Roarke walked into a den of vipers," David reminded him. "Will you elaborate on that statement?"

"She upset the delicate balance," Lee said. "She walked in and announced that she was Eamon Roarke's sister and that she'd come to take his place. Miss Roarke meant that she would rent his vacant room, but Arnie didn't know that. He thought she meant she'd come to investigate his criminal activities." Lee paused in his narration. "The night Arnie Mason died, he went to Tessa Roarke's room to kill her, but someone killed him first."

"The boss?" David suggested.

"Yes."

David walked to the evidence table, picked up the note Tessa was supposed to have sent to Arnie, and handed it to Lee. "Do you recognize this note?"

"It looks like the piece of paper I saw Myra Brennan give to Arnie Mason the night he died."

"Do you recognize the handwriting?"

"Yep. It's Myra's. I've seen her sign invoices and papers dozens of times." Lee glanced over at Myra.

David reached into his waistcoat pocket and removed a length of gold chain. A tiny Celtic cross dangled from the end. "What about this? Have you seen it before?" David asked. "It matches the piece of gold chain found on Arnie Mason's body."

Lee grinned, a beautiful triumphant grin that illuminated his entire face. "I sure have."

"Do you know who it belongs to?"

"Yes," Lee answered. "Anybody who worked at the Satin Slipper can tell you that." He searched the faces in the crowd once again. "It belongs to Myra Brennan, the owner of the Satin Slipper. She wore it on her right wrist until the day after Arnie Mason's murder. The clasp was permanently fastened. She couldn't take it off." Lee couldn't contain his smug smile of satisfaction.

Myra Brennan leapt to her feet, pointing a finger at Tessa. "She stole the chain! You got it from her!"

David faced the judge. "Your Honor, I found this chain on the floor of Tessa Roarke's room the day after the murder. It was wedged in a crack in the floorboards under the washstand," he explained. "If you check Miss Brennan's right arm, you'll find the remains of the marks left on her wrist when Arnie Mason ripped the bracelet off while she held the knife to his throat."

Myra slipped from her place and headed for the front entrance of the courtroom.

"Bailiff, stop that woman!" the judge shouted, pounding his gavel on his desk as the room exploded in chaos.

"It's all right, Your Honor," David said to the judge. "We took some precautions; that's why Detective Kincaid arrived late." He watched with supreme satisfaction as Myra opened the door. "A federal marshal and several deputies are waiting to arrest Miss Brennan on a number of charges. Detective Kincaid concluded his investigation this morning." David turned to the prosecutor, Jeremy Cook. "I think this constitutes reasonable doubt."

Judge Emory banged his gavel again. "Case dismissed."

Tessa remained where she was, not quite comprehending what had happened. Newspapermen crowded around. Townspeople clapped her on the back offering their words of congratulations.

"Miss Roarke, you're free to go." The judge smiled at her. "And don't let me see you in my courtroom again," he admonished, "unless it's for jury duty." He motioned to David. "Mr. Alexander, I'll see you in my chambers immediately. We need to talk about Coalie's future."

The judge left his place on the bench and walked down the hall to his chambers. David followed him.

"Tessa?" Mary touched her shoulder. "Let's go. The trial's over. You're free."

Tessa looked up. She was free. This was what David wanted—her freedom and his own. Hadn't he said he wanted his apartment, his office, and his cat back? He wanted his life to be the way it was before Tessa and Coalie arrived. There wasn't any room for her or Coalie in it. David didn't love her, didn't want her to stay, and now there was no reason for him to take care of her. He'd won the case, and she'd lost him. Her dreams of making a home with him and Coalie were gone. The trial was over. It was time to go home.

If she only knew where home was.

CHAPTER 23

"Where will you go?" Mary asked when Tessa marched into the office and began packing her few belongings. Coalie sat on one corner of the bed watching her, Mary on another.

"I don't know," Tessa admitted, stuffing the green calico into a cardboard box. "The hotel, maybe. I can't stay here. I'm free." She turned to look at Mary. "I'm no longer in David's custody or his life."

"I think you should talk to my brother before you make your decision," Mary reasoned.

"I've already talked to David," Tessa said.

Mary got up from the bed and went to David's room. She opened the armoire, took out a leather suitcase, carried it back across the hall, and plunked it down at Tessa's feet. "If you're going to check into a hotel, at least do it with luggage," she said. "It looks better."

Tessa laughed. A sharp, high-pitched, bitter laugh. She'd just been acquitted on a charge of murder and Mary Alexander was concerned about her reputation.

That fact eloquently illustrated the differences between the well-to-do Alexander family and Tessa Roarke.

"You're becoming hysterical," Mary said. "I'm going to make you some nice hot tea." She left Tessa packing and went to put the kettle on.

A knock at the front door interrupted her. Mary opened it.

Lee Kincaid stood on the threshold. "I want to talk to Tessa," he announced.

He certainly hadn't wasted any time coming to propose, Mary thought. But maybe Detective Kincaid didn't see any reason to wait. He'd already told the whole town of Peaceable he was prepared to marry Tessa Roarke and fulfill her brother's dying wish. Maybe Kincaid felt justified in coming to claim his intended. But if he thought he could do it with Mary around he was sadly mistaken. David was in love with Tessa, and if he wasn't there to protect his interests, she'd do it for him.

Eyeing Lee Kincaid with the distaste she reserved for worms and spiders, Mary reached into the pocket of her skirt for the derringer.

Lee was faster, though. "Not this time." He grinned.

Mary glanced down. He held a Colt Peacemaker in his right hand.

"Take your hand out of your pocket. Very slowly," Lee instructed.

She followed his orders, withdrawing her hand from her skirt pocket, the little gun held firmly in her grasp. "Looks like we're at an impasse," Mary said.

"Yeah, it does. But you've only got two shots. I've got six." Lee winked at David's vixen of a sister. "And I'm faster."

"All right," Mary conceded gracefully. "You win. This time." She pocketed her gun and stepped back to let him enter.

"Atta girl," Lee said. "And, Mary . . ."

"What?"

"If you ever really need to use that gun, don't try to pull it out of your pocket," he advised. "Shoot through it. That way you won't waste valuable time."

"I'll remember that." She walked over to the sink and filled the kettle. "Tessa's in her bedroom, packing. First door to your left." She gestured toward the hall.

Lee holstered his Colt and followed Mary's directions.

Mary waited until Lee went down the hall, then moved closer to the door in case Tessa needed her. . . .

Lee Kincaid paused in the doorway of the bedroom. "Going somewhere?" he asked.

Tessa turned at the sound of his voice. "Anywhere."

"You're running away from your problems instead of facing them? That's getting to be a habit, isn't it?" Lee commented, moving into the room, seating himself on the bed.

"What are you doing here?" Tessa demanded. "What do you want?"

"I've come to fulfill my promise to your brother," Lee told her. "I've come to ask you to marry me."

Tessa couldn't have been more astounded if he'd walked up and pushed her. "You've got to be kidding."

"Had any better offers lately?"

"No," Tessa snapped. "I haven't had any offers at all."

Lee held out a handful of lingerie. Tessa quickly shoved it into the borrowed suitcase. "No?" He paused, considering. "I thought you'd have had at least one."

"Well, I haven't." She folded the canary-yellow wool dress and placed it in the suitcase.

"Don't forget this one." Lee took the green calico out of the box.

Tessa snatched it out of his hand.

"So what's the problem?" Lee wanted to know. "I'm asking you to marry me."

"That's the problem," Tessa told him. "You're asking me to marry you. What makes you think I'd even consider it?"

"I'm handsome, intelligent, trustworthy . . ."

"Modest?" Mary suggested from the other room. She mentally added: arrogant, conceited, and unbelievably appealing.

Lowering his voice, Lee spoke for Tessa's benefit, "I was your brother's closest friend." He sounded completely serious. "I'll make you a grand husband, Tessa." Lee reached out to touch a lock of her red hair. "Eamon would've wanted it. And I'll take Coalie."

That stopped her. "You'll take Coalie? And what? Turn him in for a reward?" She attacked him with words.

"Ouch!" Lee backed away, holding up a hand as if to ward her off. "That hurt." He tried to look wounded. "I'll take Coalie and raise him as my own." He ruffled Coalie's blond hair. "He's a fine boy. And I've got a real nice apartment in Chicago big enough for the three of us."

"Apartment?" Tessa glared at him. "You'll have to do better than that. I'm sick to death of apartments."

"Then you'll think about it?" Lee pressed her for an answer.

An idea occurred to Tessa. "Only if you agree to do something for me." She had no intention of marrying Lee, but she had no qualms about using his position as a Pinkerton detective to get the information she needed. For David. "Agreed?"

"That depends on what you want." Caution was second nature to Lee.

"Tessa?" Coalie spoke up.

"What is it?" Tessa asked.

"Could I go outside for a little while? I've been inside so long." Coalie managed a decent whine.

"As long as you stay close," Tessa told him. "And come when I call."

"Okay." Coalie jumped down from the bed.

"Don't forget," Tessa said.

"I won't," Coalie assured her. He waved good-bye and raced out of the room like a shot.

"Coalie, what happened?" Mary whispered, reaching out to grab hold of his shirt as he ran past.

"He asked Tessa to marry him," Coalie whispered back.

"He what?" She looked at Coalie. He looked at her. "We'd better find David."

Coalie flung open the front door. Mary slammed it behind them.

Tessa stopped packing and leaned on the bedpost. "I want you to find someone for me."

"Who?"

"A baby girl. Her name is Lily Catherine Alexander. Her mother was Caroline Millen."

"Christ!" Lee whistled. "Finding a needle in a haystack might be easier."

"I know," Tessa said, "but David doesn't want a needle in a haystack. He wants a family. He wants Lily Catherine."

"And you intend to give David what he wants."

"Exactly," Tessa confirmed. "It's my way of repaying him. A life for a life."

"David, David!" Coalie ran through the courthouse calling for him.

David opened the door to the judge's chambers and stepped into the hall. "Here I am."

Coalie panted, nearly out of breath. "You gotta come quick!"

David's heart raced as he remembered the first time he'd heard those words. The memory of Tessa being paraded down the street dressed in blue satin flashed through his mind. He'd spent the past hour talking to Judge Emory about the possibility and legality of buying Coalie's Chicago work contract. He'd managed to convince the judge that he planned to marry Tessa and give Coalie a loving home.

To his amazement, David found Judge Emory had a real soft spot for children. He'd also found himself telling the judge the truth about the Washington scandal, even asked Judge Emory to make inquiries about Lily Catherine on his behalf. All David wanted was to get home to Tessa. He had a romantic evening all planned. The diamond and sapphire ring he'd bought for Tessa at the jeweler's was burning a hole in his pocket. He couldn't let anything happen to her now.

Mary burst through the doors of the courthouse, gasping for air. "David, you'd better come quick!"

"Mary, what is it? Has something happened to Tessa?"

Mary nodded. *"He* happened to her," she managed. "I knew I should've shot him!"

"Lee?" There could be only one man Mary wished she'd shot.

"Yes," she panted.

"He asked Tessa to marry him!" Coalie announced. "And she's packin' her things. You better hurry!"

David looked to his sister for confirmation.

She nodded frantically in agreement with Coalie. "I'm afraid the silver-tongued scoundrel will talk her into it. That's why I came running."

"By dammit, I'll kill him!" David grabbed his suit coat.

"I hope you do," Mary fervently added. Liam Kincaid deserved to die. If he hadn't been set on proposing to Tessa, she would not have had to run to David for help. "And I hope I get there in time to see it." She gathered her skirts in one hand.

"Mary," David said, "take Coalie and go to the hotel for the night."

"I planned to stay at your apartment tonight. I thought I'd double with Tessa," Mary protested.

David fixed his gaze on his younger sister. "Mary . . ."

"All right." She recognized the look in his eyes and the tone of voice. "But I'll expect a full account of what goes on between you and Liam Kincaid!" she shouted as David sprinted for the door. "Punch him in the nose. Break it!" she advised. "It's too perfect. It makes him too handsome." She took Coalie by the hand. "Come on. We'd better go to the hotel and get a room with a good view of the street before they're all gone."

She could visualize the headlines: "Disgraced Attorney Wins Case and Fatally Wounds Surprise Witness."

* * *

"Where is he?" David demanded. He opened the front door with enough force to shatter the windowpanes.

"Liam?" Tessa hurried from her bedroom at the sound of David's voice.

"Yes, Liam. Who else?" David stalked into Tessa's bedroom and surveyed it with a jealous eye.

"He's gone." She spoke from behind him.

"Where?"

"How should I know?" Tessa snapped. "I'm not his keeper."

"Really? I heard you were about to become his wife."

"Who told you that?" Tessa wanted to know.

"Who didn't?" David countered, turning to face her. "By now the whole damn town must know."

Tessa thought of the newspaper headlines for the past two days. She couldn't read them, but she could see the big black letters. And she didn't have to be able to read to know the scandalous things they'd printed.

"Well, they'll know soon enough anyway," Tessa replied.

"You're not seriously considering marrying Lee." David ran his fingers through his hair. "Are you?" She didn't seem bothered by the idea that the whole town would soon know Lee Kincaid had proposed.

Tessa couldn't seem to control the urge to spur David on. "I could do worse." She stared pointedly at David. *Ask me, dammit, ask me.*

"Two days ago you hated the sight of him," David reminded her.

"I've changed my mind," Tessa replied. "Now I think he'll make a fine husband." For someone else. Not for her. She'd realized he hadn't meant his proposal any more than she meant to consider it.

"The hell he will!" David whirled around and stomped out of the room.

Tessa went back to her packing. She lifted Horace Greeley off the pile of clothes and hugged him. She hated to admit it, but she'd even miss David's ugly cat.

David. She snorted. He was angry now, but she was willing to bet that in ten minutes he'd be drinking with Lee and celebrating his lucky escape. He was free. He was rid of her. His life would return to normal. . . .

A small crowd had gathered outside David's office. He paid them no heed as he left to begin his search. He was too intent on finding Lee Kincaid.

He found him in the hotel bar, waiting.

"What the devil do you think you're doing?" David demanded, tapping Lee on the shoulder.

Lee read the furious expression on his friend's face and decided to push him a bit more. "I'm having a glass of Irish whiskey to celebrate my forthcoming nuptials." He held up his glass. "To Tessa Roarke. She'll make a lovely bride!"

David raised his fist.

Lee saw the punch coming a second before he felt it.

He rocked backward and fell off the barstool. "Damn it, David! I think you broke it!" Gingerly he touched his nose. His fingers came away with blood.

"Good!" David stood over him, feeling supremely satisfied. "Mary'll be happy!" But David's moment of glory was brief.

"What's she got to do with it? I thought we were fighting over Tessa." Lee came up swinging.

The punch to his midsection sent David reeling out the front door. He landed on the boardwalk. Lee bolted after him.

"We are!" David picked himself up, turned, and swung wildly.

Lee ducked. "Missed me!" he taunted.

David swung again and connected with Lee's jaw.

"Damn!" Lee swung back. "That hurt!"

David raised an arm, blocking the punch. "What the hell do you think you're doing, asking Tessa to marry you?" He swung a left.

"What's it matter to you?" Lee panted. He ducked again, but this time he rammed his head into David's stomach. "You never said you wanted to marry her." He grabbed David's jacket, pulling him back to head-butt him again. The coat pocket tore loose. David went sprawling backward into the muddy street.

Lee dove after him.

"Fight! Fight!" The cry broke out. The saloons and businesses along the main street emptied. Men, women, and children rushed outside to see the action. "The lawyer's fighting the Pinkerton man!"

Upstairs in the hotel, Mary and Coalie opened a window, stuck their heads out, and yelled encouragement. "Hit him again, David!"

"Well, I do want to marry her, dammit!" David rolled over, struggled to his knees, then came up lunging for Lee.

"I hate like hell to hurt you, old buddy, but you're so damned stubborn." Lee shoved David backward, then followed him. "Why didn't you say something?"

Lee swung. His right missed, but his left connected with David's ear.

David shook his head. The ringing in his ears continued loud and clear. "I was going to." He blocked another punch and landed one of his own. "Dammit, I can't hear a thing!"

"David!" Mary screamed. "Look out!"

Angrier now, he walked into Lee's fist.

"You won't be able to see anything, either." Lee managed a short laugh. He looked up and saw Mary and Coalie hanging out of the hotel window. "You bloodthirsty hellion, whose side are you on?" he shouted to Mary.

"Mine." David socked Lee in the eye. "And neither will you!"

Lee staggered back a few steps. "Hell, David, I don't want to marry Tessa. I'm only doing this for you." He cocked his fist.

"You proposed to my woman for my own good? I don't believe it!" David drew back his own fist.

"When did *you* plan to propose to her?" Lee demanded, going for broke. He let fly a punch.

David blocked. "This evening. I had it all planned, dammit!" He drew his fist back a bit farther. "I've got a sapphire the size of a bird's egg burning a hole in my pocket right now!" At that thought David froze. He unclenched his hands and used them to pat the pockets of his jacket. His left pocket flapped in the wind. "It's gone! I'm gonna kill you!" He glared at Lee.

"Wait!" Lee held up a hand. "Don't hit me! We've only got two good eyes between us." He stared at David's battered face through the slit of his own rapidly swelling eye. "I'll help you look for the ring."

"You bloody well will!" David got down on his hands and knees, searching the street. "And if we don't find it . . ."

Lee got down beside him, crawling around Main Street, combing the mud, looking for a sapphire ring the size of a bird's egg.

"David!" someone screamed.

Tessa ignored the noise coming from the street as she crammed the last dress into the suitcase and snapped it shut. She grabbed her hatbox, then lugged the suitcase off the bed and into the office. Steam poured from the spout of the teakettle. Mary was nowhere in sight. Tessa set the suitcase down and lifted the kettle off the stove. Where was everybody?

"David!" Tessa heard the scream echoing from the street. She plunked the kettle down in the dry sink, crossed the room, and opened the front door. She made her way down the street, but she couldn't see over the crowd of people standing in a large circle in the middle of the road.

"David!" Tessa heard the scream again. It sounded like Mary. Had something happened to him? Following the sound of Mary's voice, Tessa looked up.

"Why are you stopping?" Mary demanded of the men crawling around in the street. "What are you doing, David? Get up. Hit him again!"

"Shut up, Mary!" Lee yelled back.

It *was* Mary. She and Coalie were hanging halfway out of an open second-story window in the hotel.

Her heart pounded at the sight. "Coalie!" Tessa shouted. "Get down from there!"

"Aw, Tessa!" Coalie wailed.

"Don't 'aw, Tessa' me, young man," she shouted. "Get down and come over here. We're leaving!"

"Where we goin'?" Coalie yelled back.

"Anywhere away from Peaceable, Wyoming," Tessa answered. She went back down the street and inside the office to get her suitcase and hatbox.

"Christ!" Lee moved faster, scrambling to locate the missing ring.

"I found it!" David grabbed the ring, stood up, and held it out for Lee to see.

Upstairs in the window of the hotel, Coalie looked to Mary. "What do I do? I promised I'd come when she called."

"Coalie!" Tessa shouted.

"Go on," Mary told him. "But take your time. Slow her down before she gets to the depot."

"I'm comin'!" Coalie yelled to Tessa.

"Hurry!" Tessa urged. "We don't want to miss the train."

Coalie ducked out of the window, left the room, and inched his way slowly down the stairs.

Tessa stepped off the sidewalk to cross the street. Her progress was hampered by townspeople. "Excuse me." She bumped into someone's back. "Excuse me."

"We sure hate to lose you, Miss Roarke."

"Congratulations, Miss Roarke."

"Glad to see you got off, Miss Roarke."

"Hope you'll consider staying here in town, Miss Roarke."

All around her, citizens of Peaceable turned and spoke, offering their best wishes.

"That goes for me, too, Miss Tessa."

Tessa glanced up as Sheriff Bradley tipped his hat.

"Let me help you with your bag." He reached for the handle of her suitcase before she could protest. He picked it up and stepped forward.

The circle of people opened as if by magic.

"David! You'd better make your move before he does!" Mary shouted.

"I don't need your help," David yelled to her. "Or any more of yours." He glared at Lee.

"How about mine?" the sheriff asked as he carried Tessa's suitcase to the center of the street and dropped it at David's feet.

David turned around and saw Tessa standing next to the sheriff. He eyed the suitcase at his feet. "Yours, I assume."

"David!" Tessa ran forward and threw herself into his arms. "What happened to your face?"

Lee stepped up. "I happened to his face." His face was as battered as David's.

Tessa pulled away from David and rounded on Liam. "What did you think you were doing?"

"I thought I was marrying you," Lee said, smiling in spite of his split lip.

"I don't want to marry you," Tessa told him. "I don't want a rogue of an Irishman for a husband. I've spent my life with them. And you didn't mean that silly proposal. You only did it out of duty to my brother."

"Nope," Lee told her. "I did it for David."

"David?" Tessa didn't understand. "David doesn't need you to propose for him."

"That's what I've been trying to tell everyone." David turned to the crowd. "I can ask her to marry me without anybody's help. I plan to ask her to marry me, and I'm going to ask her to marry me." He moved closer to Tessa and took her hand. "Tessa, will you marry me and let me take care of you?"

"Take care of me?" Tessa threw the words back at him. "You want to take care of me?"

"Yes."

"Well, forget it!" Tessa shouted. Yanking her hand out of his grasp, she whirled around to reach for her suitcase.

David caught her arm and turned her back to face him. "Forget it?" he shouted back. "What do you mean forget it?"

"I mean forget it! I'm not interested in letting you take care of me! I can take care of myself!"

"But I thought you cared about me!"

"I don't care about you," Tessa yelled. "I love you!"

Frustrated beyond belief, David stared down at the woman. "It means the same thing!"

"Not to me, it doesn't," she informed him. "If you can't say you love me, then I don't want you taking care of me!" She stamped her foot in the street for emphasis.

"Fine. Take care of yourself. Take care of Coalie. Take care of me." David knelt at her feet and took her hand once again. "Take care of all the children we'll have, but marry me. Please."

Tessa glanced around at the crush of smiling people, at the artists sketching and the reporters filling their notebooks with words. "David, you're making a fool of yourself in front of the whole town."

"It's time I did."

"But you're causing a scandal!" She tugged on his hand, trying to pull him off his knees.

"I've caused them before." David grinned. One eye was swollen shut. His jaw was bruised. His injured shoulder throbbed with pain once again. He had a cut on his lip, and his stomach hurt like hell. But he'd never felt better. "So have you. I doubt this will be the last one."

"David . . ."

"I love you, Tessa Mary Catherine Roarke," he said finally, offering her the sapphire ring. "I love you with all my heart."

"Oh, David . . ." She bent down to hug him, but he lost his balance and sprawled in the dirt. "I love you, too!" Tessa knelt to kiss him.

David groaned. This wasn't the way he'd planned to deliver his proposal.

Tessa broke off the kiss. "I've loved you for the longest time. Ever since we—"

David kissed her again to keep her from incriminating herself. And him. He kissed her until they both needed to come up for air. "You *are* going to marry me," David said, "aren't you?"

"Of course." Tessa flung her arms around his neck. "I may need a good lawyer again someday."

David wiped the sapphire and diamond ring against the fabric of his trousers, then slipped it onto her hand.

Tessa looked down at her finger, admiring it. "It's beautiful!"

"It matches your eyes," David said. "That's why I bought it."

Then she whispered, "Was it awfully expensive?" She winced as she asked the question, afraid of his answer. At the rate he spent money, they'd never have a house.

"Awfully," he answered.

"Oh." She frowned, sounding disappointed.

"What's wrong?" He pressed a kiss against the worry lines on her brow. "Don't you like it?"

"I love it." She managed to smile at him. "But after we get married, I plan to save money for a house with a yard and some flowers"—she broke off when David hugged her to him—"and a small flock of sheep."

"No sheep," David said. He got to his feet and pulled Tessa up with him.

"Why not?" Tessa asked. "I like sheep. I thought maybe merinos."

"No sheep," David repeated. "They won't go too well with five hundred head of beef cattle." He draped an arm over her shoulder and picked up her suitcase with his other hand. She placed one arm around his waist. "Tessa, do you remember Coalie telling you about the ranch?"

Tessa raised a hand to her mouth. "Coalie." She glanced around. "Where is he?" She looked up at the hotel window. Mary was alone.

Sensing Tessa's concern, David glanced up at his sister. "Where's Coalie?" he shouted.

"There." Mary pointed to Coalie, who was dragging his feet down the street, following her instructions, taking his time. "Coalie," she yelled from the window. "You can run now. David asked her to marry him!"

"What did Tessa say?" Coalie looked up at Mary, cupping his hand around his mouth to make himself heard.

"She said yes," David and Tessa shouted in unison. "Yes!"

"Yippee!" Coalie's whoop of joy echoed through Peaceable.

David dropped the suitcase, knelt, and opened his free arm. Tessa went with him, opening her free arm, too. "Come on, son!" David encouraged as Coalie caught sight of them and raced forward. "Let's go home!"

Coalie ran into their arms.

Tessa pulled Coalie against her heart. David pulled Tessa to his.

Coalie hugged them both. The two people he loved most in all the world, David and Tessa. His family.

The people of Peaceable roared their approval.

"I told you something was going on between those two." Margaret Jeffers whispered to her employee as they stood in front of the mercantile watching the family scene.

Lorna Taylor sniffed into her handkerchief and wiped her eyes before she delivered a vicious elbow to Margaret's rib cage. "Shut up, Margaret. Stop being such a prig! Then maybe one day somebody will love you like that."

EPILOGUE

Peaceable, Wyoming Territory
Three days later

"I hope Coalie's all right," Tessa said. "I hated to leave him."

"He's fine," David told her. "He was having a great time when we left the ranch." They'd been married that morning in the church in Cheyenne, then gone to the Trail T ranch to celebrate with David's family. "I thought you said you wanted to honeymoon here in Peaceable."

"I do," Tessa replied. "I was just thinking about the wedding. It's a shame Lee couldn't stay a little longer after the ceremony." She snuggled into her husband's arms in the big bed where they'd spent the last few hours exploring the joys of marriage.

"Not for me." David kissed the corner of Tessa's mouth. He wasn't sure he was ready to forgive his friend.

"It was a nice wedding, wasn't it?" Tessa asked.

"The best," David agreed, "the absolute best I've ever attended." Her white satin wedding dress was draped across a chair. On top of it perched an enormous white satin hat decorated with artificial roses, orange blossoms, and a stuffed white dove, all of it covered with an Irish lace veil. The hat had been a wedding gift from David, who had shuddered every time he looked at it. But Tessa loved it, and that was what mattered. He kissed Tessa's shiny red hair, preferring it to any hat ever created.

Tessa raised herself on her elbow and leaned over him, bracing her hand against David's wide chest for balance. A thin gold band had joined the sapphire and diamond ring on the third finger of her left hand. Tessa never tired of looking at it. "I think Mary likes him."

"Who? Lee?" David laughed. "You've got to be kidding. She's the one who told me to break his nose."

"I'm glad you didn't."

"I tried." David smiled, planting a kiss on her nose. He lifted his swollen right hand for her to see.

Tessa wiggled against him, moving to kiss it. "Better?" she asked.

"Much better."

"I'll bet Mary's glad you didn't really break Lee's nose." Tessa continued her train of thought.

"Where'd he go in such a hurry?" David asked, humoring Tessa. She wouldn't drop the subject of Lee and Mary until she was ready, anyway.

"He had a train to catch," she told him. "To Chicago and then to Washington and Baltimore."

"How do you know that?" David wondered aloud. "Did Mary tell you?"

Tessa smiled at her lawyer husband. Now she had his interest. "No, Lee did. He read me a copy of his"—she searched for the word Lee had used— "itinerary."

David moved her aside, sat up, and looked at her. They'd been married almost five hours, and he wondered just what she was up to. "Why would he do that?"

"I asked him to keep me informed of his progress," Tessa answered.

"Progress? On what?"

"On finding my wedding gift to you."

"Which is . . . ?" David prompted. "I thought I got my gift when I got you and Coalie."

"I thought you might like a daughter to round out the family. A very special daughter."

David was almost afraid to ask. "Lily Catherine?"

Tessa nodded. "I've always wanted a big family, and I think it would be nice to have a head start with a boy and a girl before the others come along. Don't you?"

"I think it's a splendid idea." David hugged her close against his heart. For an articulate man, he found it difficult to speak. He couldn't find enough words to tell her how much he loved her. All he could do was show her. For the rest of his life.

"Sweetheart," he whispered, "do you remember when I talked about making a baby?"

"I'll never forget it." She wrapped her arms around his neck, pressing her body against him. She kissed him. "Do you remember?"

"As a matter of fact," David teased, "it's been so long, I think I may have forgotten how."

Tessa pushed him back against the pillows and climbed on top of him. "Then we need to refresh your memory."

Outside on the front door of the office of David Alexander, attorney-at-law, hung a freshly painted sign: Closed for Honeymoon. Will Reopen . . . Sometime.